NEW STORIES FROM THE MIDWEST

2021

NEW STORIES FROM THE MIDWEST 2021

MICHAEL MARTONE
Guest Editor

JASON LEE BROWN AND SHANIE LATHAM
Series Editors

newamericanpress
Milwaukee, Wis.

n e w a m e r i c a n p r e s s

www.NewAmericanPress.com

Printed in the United States of America
ISBN 978-1-941561-25-6

Book design by Shanie Latham
Cover photo by Arun Kuchibhotla on Unsplash

For ordering information, please contact:
Ingram Book Group
One Ingram Blvd.
La Vergne, TN 37086
(800) 937-8000
orders@ingrambook.com

All stories reprinted by permission of the individual authors and/or publishing companies. Grateful acknowledgment is made to the journals, magazines, and books where these stories previously appeared:

"Pinkie" © 2018 by Andrew Bales. First published in *Mississippi Review* Vol. 46, No. 1 & 2 (Summer 2018). Reprinted by permission of the author.

"Mr. Scary" © 2011 by Charles Baxter. Previously published in *Gryphon: New and Selected Stories*. Reprinted by permission of Pantheon Books, an imprint of the Knopf Doubleday Publishing Group, a division of Penguin Random House LLC. All rights reserved.

"Even Huck, Even Emmeline Grangerford" © 2018 by Lucy Biederman. First published in *Web Conjunctions* (2018). Reprinted by permission of the author.

"Selected Episodes from *Wartime Philippines* on Saturday Night" © 2019 by Anna Cabe. First published in *StoryQuarterly* Issue 52 (December 2019). Reprinted by permission of the author.

"Tell Yourself" © 2009 by Bonnie Jo Campbell. First published in the *Kenyon Review Online*, vol. 2, no. 4 (Fall 2009). Reprinted by permission of the author.

"The Scarecrow" by Wendy Chen. First published in *Mid-American Review*, Volume XXXIX, no. 2. Reprinted by permission of the author.

for Jay and Okla

CONTENTS

Editors' Note 13

Introduction 17

Bonnie Jo Campbell Tell Yourself 23
from *Kenyon Review Online*
and *New Stories from the Midwest 2011*

Christie Hodgen Bedtime Stories for the Middle-Aged 33
from *Cincinnati Review*
and *New Stories from the Midwest 2011*

Charles Baxter Mr. Scary 61
from *Ploughshares*
and *New Stories from the Midwest 2012*

Yelizaveta P. Renfro Splendid, Silent Sun 81
from *Glimmer Train*
and *New Stories from the Midwest 2012*

Justyn Harkin Rainbow Dogs 97
from *Annalemma*
and *New Stories from the Midwest 2014*

Alexander Weinstein   Heartland   109
from Pleiades
and *New Stories from the Midwest 2014*

Noley Reid   A Purposeful Violence   119
from Yemassee Journal
and *New Stories from the Midwest 2016*

Laura van den Berg   Lessons   139
from American Short Fiction
and *New Stories from the Midwest 2016*

Valerie Sayers   The Last Days of Peace and Love   157
from The Literary Review
and *New Stories from the Midwest 2018*

Rachel Yoder   The Woodcutter   171
from Southern Review
and *New Stories from the Midwest 2018*

Andrew Bales   Pinkie   189
from Mississippi Review

Lucy Biederman   Even Huck, Even Emmeline Grangerford   199
from Web Conjunctions

Anna Cabe   Selected Episodes from *Wartime Philippines* on Saturday Night   207
from StoryQuarterly

Wendy Chen   The Scarecrow   225
from Mid-American Review

Michael Czyzniejewski   With Nuts   231
from *Salamander*

Emily Greenberg   Houston, We've Had a Problem   239
from *Chicago Quarterly Review*

Susan Neville   Resurrection   249
from *Diagram*

Amber Sparks   The Language of the Stars   257
from *Split Lip Magazine*

Maggie Su   Tin   265
from *Diagram*

Valerie Vogrin   The Ophelia Project   271
from *Memorious: A Journal of
New Verse and Fiction*

EDITORS' NOTE

In the late 1990s, I read my first volume of Shannon Ravenel's *New Stories from the South* for the first time, while I was at former co-editor Jay Prefontaine's house. I liked everything about the anthology. I naively thought that if New Stories from the South existed then surely a *New Stories from the Midwest* series also existed. When I discovered it did not, I decided to create one. This was before I had worked as an assistant editor at a literary magazine or earned an MFA in creative writing. I knew I had no authority to edit a best-of anthology series. I could not answer my own question of why I should be the one to create the New Stories from the Midwest series, and I had no illusion that a press would either.

I continued constantly reading stories set in the Midwest or written by Midwesterners and continued asking myself why I had the authority to edit a Midwest anthology series. When I was near the end of graduate school, I found the answer. My passion for the project outweighed that of everyone else I knew who might be willing to put the time and effort into creating a New Stories from the Midwest series. Simply put, I cared more than anyone else.

My first attempt to co-edit a Midwest anthology—this one included poetry, fiction, and nonfiction—failed when the University of Nebraska Press accepted a complete manuscript from us that did not receive the necessary votes needed through the peer review process. That was the first of many times I wanted to give up on the project. Luckily, then-director of Ohio University Press David Sanders contacted me and asked if I'd be interested in editing an anthology focused exclusively on Midwest fiction. I again wrote a proposal, and Jay Prefontaine and I collected sample stories for a complete manuscript.

That same year, Jay was diagnosed with inoperable lung cancer, and he signed his copy of the publication contract for *New Stories from the Midwest 2010* on his deathbed. He died before the anthology went to press. After Jay's death but before the publication of the anthology, Ohio University Press wavered on publishing the anthology as a series. This time, instead of wanting to give up, I developed a callused determination to find the right press that would support this anthology series and help me make it into what I believed it could become.

The next breakthrough came when this volume's guest editor, Michael Martone, suggested I query the University of Indiana Press, which had recently begun a new Midwestern History and Culture series. Shanie Latham, who had been involved with the anthology project from the beginning, joined the anthology as co-editor. We decided to incorporate traits from other quality anthologies: focusing on a single region (*New Stories from the South*), a guest editor for each volume (*Best American Short Stories* and others), and soliciting nominations from editors (*Pushcart Prize*). We developed a robust solicitation campaign for literary journals and magazines that garnered hundreds of submissions from editors and writers. With John McNally as our first guest editor, we published what I believed to be a great best-of anthology.

However, after publishing *New Stories from the Midwest 2011*, the University of Indiana Press could not offer a publication contract that promised a consistent annual or biennial schedule for the series, and I again thought about letting the series fold and walking away. Around that time, *News Stories from the South* published its last volume, and I wondered what chance *New Stories from the Midwest* had if an established best-of anthology series like *News Stories from the South* could not make it. Then, I had a coffee luncheon with Okla Elliott.

Okla Elliott was a cofounder and editor at New American Press, and he was interested in publishing not only *New Stories from the Midwest* but also starting a regional poetry anthology, *New Poetry from the Midwest*, as a complement. After a three-hour meeting in which we agreed on virtually every aspect of our visions for the two series, it was clear I had found the right press to call home and the right people to support the series. We published two more volumes of *News Stories from the Midwest* (2013, guest edited by Rosellen Brown, and 2016, guest edited by Lee Martin), and the anthology established itself exactly as I had imagined it could. I was finally happy with not only the stories in the anthologies but also with the processes we developed for collecting, editing, and publishing them. I was even happier with the friendships we gained along the way.

Then in March 2017, Okla passed away unexpectedly, and I wondered if we would be able to put out another volume without him—but his co-founder at the press, David Bowen, and other editors carried on and kept the press running. In 2018 (or, technically, early 2019), we published our next volume of *New Stories from the Midwest*, this one guest edited by Antonya Nelson. I mention all this not to brag but to reiterate, as with any pursuit in life, achieving these goals of creating a respected anthology series was not possible without passion and relentlessness, but I also had to learn to balance that passion with whatever else life might deliver.

More than a decade after publishing the first volume, despite all the challenges faced both personally and professionally in 2020 and 2021 as a result of the COVID-19 pandemic, we are extremely pleased to present our latest *New Stories from the Midwest*, a ten-year anniversary edition. *New Stories from the Midwest 2021*, guest edited by Michael Martone, showcases ten stories from past volumes along with ten stories that are new to the series. We are happy that this anniversary afforded us the excuse to revisit stories the previous years' guest editors selected and to mix them in with new work and writers we hadn't read before.

I've learned many lessons during this decade-long journey and still can't stop wondering and worrying about the future of *New Stories from the Midwest*. Even if I lost the passion or capability for editing this anthology or unexpectedly passed away, I want a quality *New Stories from the Midwest* to continue to publish every other year. The stated goals of *New Stories from the Midwest* always has been to celebrate an American region that is often ignored in discussions about distinctive regional literature and to demonstrate how the quality of fiction from and about the Midwest (Illinois, Indiana, Iowa, Kansas, Michigan, Minnesota, Missouri, Nebraska, North Dakota, Ohio, South Dakota, and Wisconsin) rivals that of any other region. We wanted to bring more visibility to the flourishing crop of Midwestern writers who consistently produce work that is innovative, engaging, finely crafted, and strong in voice.

I believe *New Stories from the Midwest* has contributed to the exposure, expansion, and knowledge of Midwest literature, but the anthology also has a lot more work to do. One constant I've learned while editing this anthology has been that the love for Midwestern literature and its writers has never wavered. In fact, I believe the passion has become stronger in the past decade, and the anthology has reaffirmed what I always have known: the talent coming from Midwest literature is as quality and varied as any regional literature. I credit Stuart Dybek, MacArthur Fellow and author of *The Coast of Chicago*, for the best description of *New Stories from the Midwest* when he said, "As this fresh anthology proves, there's a mix of writers and sensibilities that inhabit the literary Midwest as to make the term unpredictable."

— **Jason Lee Brown**
  Founding Editor

INTRODUCTION

Michael Martone, guest editor

THE SOUTH BEGINS AT 38TH STREET

X MARKS THE SPOT
MIDWESTERN STORIES AT AND AS THE CROSSROADS

I.

"THE SOUTH BEGINS AT 38TH STREET IN INDIANAPOLIS," I USED TO KID, growing up in Indiana. My mother's side of the family, the Paynes, did come "up" into the state from Kentucky, Payne Holler, Meade County, near Fort Knox, a little west of Louisville. A classic story. Great Grandpa Shaker stepped out to buy some cigarettes and disappeared like smoke. Great Grandma, four kids in tow, went after him, tracked him, "up north," working for the Pennsy, living on McCarty Street, Indianapolis's south side with the other refugees from "down south" settled there. She *brung* him back to the Holler. That was the first of many migrations. He'd leave. She'd chase him with the kids. My grandfather, the eldest, finally just stayed in Indianapolis with his siblings, moved them further north to Fort Wayne where, 40 years later, I was born, a Midwesterner.

II.

Before I thought of myself as a Writer of "Place," of the Midwest specifically, I wanted to be a placer of Place. I thought I was, I thought I would be, a Geologist. A Geographer. A Cartographer. I had this urge to pin place down. Or, more exactly to ascertain the stasis of a place, its stability over time, its parochial nature of staying put. I liked the idea of putting places in their places for good. For good. Forever. I was soon disabused of the notion as I discovered that, over time of course, places literally move. Over time. Time being the one component we often overlook in a place, place-time being, well, glacial in nature. People, we migrate, but so does the ground beneath our feet. I love to visit the ox-bowed and cut-off floating islands of the Midwest, hunks of no man's lands once Indiana, now south of the Ohio, but not really the south, not really Kentucky. Or the other way around, the river channeled south. The actual meandering of places! Tectonic plates! Whole continents on the move, moving. Solid solid ground on the move, moving. We ride on places getting up and going, drifting on the surface of liquid fire.

III.

For the last quarter century I've lived in Alabama, below the Bug Line, writing about "up north." The Bug Line, a USDA distinction, a climate boundary, the demarcation of the zone in which it does not get cold enough over winter to kill insects. I am here right now writing about the Midwest, looking out at my garden where it is impossible to grow peonies, Indiana's State Flower, not because it is too hot but because it never gets cold enough to freeze the crowns of the plant. I dream of mulching those crowns with ice.

IV.

Grandfather remembers pasturing cattle on the grassy strip in downtown Fort Wayne where the US Highway now runs as Jefferson Boulevard. A place, that field, transmuting into a road, a street, a highway. A road is a "place." It remains still after all, but it is also a static depiction, even as it stays put, of an elsewhere, another place. Roads convey us through a place even as they knit together a static grid, the mesh of place. That road through downtown Fort Wayne is now reverting, maybe not all the way back to pasture, but to a "Business" route. One day, maybe, a pedestrian mall. There is a "Bypass" now that now bypasses nothing, and whatever the place named Fort Wayne is or was drifted to that periphery, a corridor of drive-ins, car dealerships and now dying malls. You know, that placeless place, a where that is in no way unique, a where that is everywhere.

V.

America and Americans have never experienced a diaspora. Or more exactly the American experience of diaspora was for it to be the place of landing, not launching, its people. Chicago, the largest Polish city outside of Poland. The Arab metropolis of southeastern Michigan. Little Mogadishu in the Cities. No, our emigrations are all internal immigrations. We take to the roads, to the Interstate to travel intrastate. One hundred years ago, The Great Migration of six million Black Americans commenced. The exodus was coupled with a universal abandonment of the countryside that reached its tipping point in 1920 when, for the first time, more people lived in cities than on the land. We recognize the earlier more visible westward bias and surge of unsettling and settling the frontier and its manifest destiny. But that is not what interests me here. The westward expansion was the tail end of the external immigration narrative, the scalloped exploration and exploitation, the extension of colonization. What interests me more is the churning of America once the country "settled down," those invisible drifts of place from place to place. How Oklahoma wound-up in Bakersfield. How Maine moved to Louisiana. How, until recently, there were no Indians in Indiana. How when people leave a place the place leaves with them. How the place that's left behind retains what has been taken away. The Midwest represents itself often as this pastoral and/or industrial ruin, this empty emptied place, flown over, overlooked. It is as if the Midwest is all road now, paved over, cleared out, clear-cut, this paradoxical place with lots of nothing to see, and, as the old joke goes, plenty of parking.

20

VI.

For a while there, I taught in an English Department that no longer privileged American and British literature. It had transformed into a Textual Studies Department, abandoning the coverage model, the canon of classic work because, well, what about the Canadians, the Indians, the Jamaicans, the Australians, etc., and the systemic blind-spotting of canon formation. Instead of great books and authors, we taught different ways of reading, reading any text. One semester there were no Shakespeare classes offered and then the next semester there were four Shakespeare classes at the same time, each featuring different lenses—Marxist, Feminist, Racial Theory, Queer Theory. Each focused on what was considered a "Site of Contestation"—class, gender, race, sexuality. I wasn't a literature teacher but a teacher of writing. I would suggest, meekly, at faculty meetings, a site of contestation that had to do with "Place." There is actual power invested in place through the vote, I suggested, that couples who you are to where you are. My colleagues argued endlessly, about which of these identity indicators was the primal one. But in the train of adjectival identity markers, could "Hoosier," could "Region," could "Place" even be the caboose?

VII.

The great drama in the narrative of America pits mobility verse stability. We know as Americans that the safe bet is on mobility to win, that Place will place. In our heart of hearts we may handicap the local (SHOP LOCAL!) but we know the race is run. The landmarked Morrill Act establishing land-granted schools to keep 'em down on the farm, of course, became efficient conveying machines, putting wheels on the feet of generations and making them move away. Move. Move out. Move up. I was born in Fort Wayne, Indiana, in 1955, the year the building of the Interstate Highway System commenced, the McDonald Drive-In franchise began to expand, and Disneyland opened. The dilemma storywriters confront is existential. The medium deployed is by nature lineal, one word follows the next, left to right in English, top to the bottom of the page. It must go somewhere. It has a beginning, middle, and end. A setting is never a story. It is a setting.

VIII.

As I write this Midwesterners are killing Midwesterners. One motive for the murders offered by the murderers is that the murdered trespassed in some way, that they, the murdered, didn't belong (literally to "be long" in time in a place) or took something that didn't "belong" to them. A young man, a Midwesterner from Illinois, equipped with a semi-automatic military assault-style weapon was driven by his mother to Kenosha to ostensibly protect property, that wasn't his, from "outsiders" who were local. I have no idea if the murdered or the murderer thought of themselves as Midwesterners or not. Nor do I know if they believed where he killed and they died was the Midwest. I doubt it. "America," maybe, but not the Midwest.

IX.

Most people believe that the great depression-era social realistic post office murals were installed as just make-work for unemployed artists of the time. But, no, Roosevelt was more calculating than that. He knew that his New Deal polices would fundamentally transform the citizen's relationship to the federal government. The PO was, up until the Great Depression, the single connection most Americans had with that government, so FDR built more POs and specifically called for a special kind of propagandistic art to be placed there. It was to contrast with the aesthetic of other nationalistic movements happening in Germany, Italy, Japan. There would be few or no eagles, flags, stars, slogans. There would be many celebrations of locality—its products and people, its stories and histories, its differentness, its uniqueness. The depictions affixed in place, depicting place. There they would be over the postmasters' doorways, those thresholds connecting "here" (via the mail) to the rest of the country. A delicate balance, then, this undertaking, to be pictured picturing both the local and the universal.

X.

"Who's from Fort Wayne?" There had been a knock at my door in Tuscaloosa. An African-American neighbor asked the question when I opened the door. My parents had driven down from Indiana to visit, parked in my driveway. Indiana, then, used a code on the car tags. The first number, 2, indicated Allen County, stood for Fort Wayne, the county seat. It was an insider's knowledge to be able to read the origin of that car so far away from home. I never knew my neighbor here in Alabama had, like me, grown up in Indiana, in Fort Wayne, his family gone "up" North at the time my family had. And now here he was, having moved South as the Great Migration reverses itself. He found himself, back "home" after leaving his home. It turned out my mother, a high school teacher, had taught my neighbor's siblings at Central High School in Fort Wayne, knew the extended family there. I asked him (the both of us only recently moved "down" South), "Do you still think of yourself as a Midwesterner?"

He said, "I guess I do." And then he asked me, his accent absent, "Do you?"

TELL YOURSELF

Bonnie Jo Campbell

"I'M NOT GOING TO BE HERE FOR DINNER, MOM," YOUR DAUGHTER says. You look up from sorting the day's junk mail to see Mary has emerged from her room wearing jeans that ride so low her pubic hair would be showing, if she had pubic hair. She swears all the middle-school girls shave down there, though surely your daughter could've had only a few baby-fine wisps to razor away. Under your gaze she tugs her jeans up and makes an effort to pull down her shirt, but the whole production leaves six inches of bare belly and hips. "I have to go to Amber's. Her dad's making us lasagna for dinner."

"You want a ride?" you offer. You wouldn't mind Amber's dad seeing you in your steel-toed boots and work uniform. You wouldn't mind reminding him that you are a formidable woman.

"It's only a half a mile, Mom."

"What on Earth do you do there all the time?"

You shouldn't question Mary this way about what goes on over there. If something unsavory happens between your daughter and Amber's young and curiously attentive father, Mary is probably not going to confide in you if you seem out of your mind. She would not tell you, for example, if Amber's father were wrestling with the girls on the braided rug and suddenly it was just he and Mary, if she relaxed beneath him and let her head fall back, if she let her narrow shoulders sink to the floor and looked up at him and parted her glossed lips, and he lowered himself onto her.

"We're doing a biology project. It's a poster about cells, and it's due tomorrow, but we haven't started it yet," your daughter says.

She likes science, and she didn't used to be a procrastinator. "Amber's dad is going to help us. Did you know there are thirty-seven trillion cells in the human body?"

Amber's father has never been convicted of diddling with minors or of any other sex crime (you've looked him up on the internet), and there is no reason for you to entertain the image of your daughter slipping down her low-rise stretch-denim jeans, or of Amber's father situating your daughter on his lap, under a blanket. There is no reason to associate Amber's father with your own pot-smoking neighbor whom you, as a fourteen-year-old, screwed while his wife was at work and while his young son napped in the bedroom adjacent. Both men have cowboy mustaches, but that's all.

"There's no reason to put off a project until the last minute," you tell her. And there is no reason for someone to design a midriff-revealing shirt like the one your daughter is wearing, with a pair of bigger-than-life-size cupcakes on the chest. You toss the whole pile of mail into the recycling. Calm yourself down, woman. Not all men will try to screw your daughter, however she dresses. There are men who will not even fantasize about touching her darling new breasts. Some men are distracted, for instance, or gay, while a few may actually prefer mature women.

You sit down in the wooden rocking chair you inherited last year from your grandmother, your mother's mother, may she rest in peace. At first you hadn't wanted the chair—what are you, an old lady?—but it's handmade, and you've found that rocking in it can take the edge off at the end of the day.

"Did you know that the mitochondria are the powerhouse of the cell?" Mary offers. She moves behind you and takes hold of the back of your chair and sends it rocking in her own annoying rhythm. Don't complain—at least if her hands are on your chair, they're off her cell phone for a change.

"You're working on a poster? Maybe I can help."

"So how come you broke up with Stanley Steemer?" Mary asks. "He's the only decent boyfriend you ever had."

"It's my own business," you say to your child, "who I date. Or don't date." This is the first time Mary has mentioned Stan.

"Then maybe what I do is my own business," Mary says and cracks her gum for an invisible audience. Then she stops the chair from rocking, so you are thrown forward a little. You get the idea she imagines her girlfriends are always with her, admiring her antics.

"It's not exactly your own business when I get called by the school principal about you flashing boys in the stairwell."

You stand up, cross your arms, and study the girl for whom you suffered thirteen hours of labor, the girl you've fed and clothed for thirteen years—though you don't recall buying any of the revealing items she currently wears.

"I told you, Mom. Amber dared me. We both did it. And there was another girl, too. But I was the one who got caught." She talks casually, but she's gripping the chair pretty hard.

"If Amber dared you to jump over a cliff, would you do it?"

"Yes," she says and lets go of the chair. She tries pulling up her pants again, though she's already working a camel toe.

"Amber is stupid in science, but she's smart about other things. She's street-smart."

There has to be a calm, reasonable way to express to your daughter why she should resist showing her body the way she has been doing, without seeming overprotective or crazy or even jealous. You can't deny how thrilled you were at the way your body got attention when you were her age. You would have bared your breasts for cute boys on a dare, no doubt.

"You know, I had to walk home from cheerleading practice today, three miles. Stanley Steemer drove right past me. He didn't even wave back."

"Stop calling him that," you say. "Anyway, you could've called me to pick you up."

The first time Stan gave your daughter a ride home, you thanked him, but you also recalled how your mother's boyfriend

Teddy used to drive alongside you sometimes when you were walking on the old road by the power company. He'd be hotboxing a Marlboro in the driver's seat, and he'd roll down the window and release a big cloud of smoke and tell you that you were looking fine. You thought it was flattering and funny, and you never told your mother. Not even when he molested you—at the time, it wasn't clear what happened in the back seat, but in retrospect it is painfully clear. You managed to not think about Teddy for years.

"That truck is embarrassing," your daughter says, referring to the Al's Appliances truck you drive for work. "You know, Nicole's mom got a stove from Al's, and it had a dead cockroach in it. And that guy you work with stinks like pee."

"Jimmy."

"He doesn't have any neck. And he's hairy like a Neanderthal." She laughs at this inside joke as though her friends are here with her. "Mr. Glover says we're all part Neanderthal, but some people are more than others."

When Stan showed up for dinner with your daughter for the fourth time, two days after the flashing incident in the stairwell, you couldn't get it out of your head that something was wrong. And then when you kissed Stan, his jacket smelled like Mary's fruity-candy perfume. You've known Stan for three years as your boys' Little League and Rocket Football coach, and you'd been dating him for three months, and he'd been coming to dinner a couple times a week, and you told yourself there was no reason to think he did anything other than pick Mary up and bring her straight home. It wasn't as though he'd had time to pull off into the old power company property—or that he would've even thought of such a thing. And after all, Stan really seemed to like you, admired your jaded view of the world, even laughed when you slipped into cursing. He'd had a rough go in his marriage, same as you, and you'd figured the two of you were kindred spirits.

That last time he brought Mary home, when Mary was doing her in-school suspension, all through dinner you kept telling yourself to calm down and not overreact. Afterward, Stan smiled at your expectant, anxious look as he sank back into the reclining chair to watch *Antiques Roadshow* with you. "Is something the matter?" he asked. "You seem on edge."

"Is something going on with you and Mary?" you asked.

Even now you can't believe it came out of your mouth, but once it did come out you didn't regret it. You hoped Stan would tell you, *Absolutely not, never in a million years,* or to laugh it off and say, *You have to be kidding.*

"What do you mean?" He tilted his head, squinted one eye. You'd seen him adopt this posture when a little knucklehead kid was explaining why he ran home from first base.

"Nothing. Not really. I was just asking." You told yourself he was nothing like your mother's old boyfriend or your pothead neighbor, and he'd never shown any interest in Mary beyond joking around and asking her about homework and cheerleading, but you just wanted to be absolutely one hundred percent sure your daughter was safe with him.

"Asking what? What are you asking?"

"I smell her perfume on you."

"She squirted me with that crap when I told her not to use it in my car," he said, and his speech slowed as he realized what you were suggesting. "You know what she's like."

"I know, but I wondered . . ."

You knew she'd sprayed perfume on her little brothers, too, even though it made them shriek. And of course she'd sprayed you.

"You wondered what? If I . . . if I had, what? . . . with Mary?" He seemed to wake up then. He looked hurt, then shocked. He fumbled at his pocket for a cigarette, got it into his fingers, and then forced it back into the pack, pushed the pack into his shirt pocket again. "You've known me a long time. Your kids have played with my kid for years."

"It just seems strange you're always giving her a ride without discussing it with me." Your calm voice defied the turmoil you were feeling.

"Did you see it was raining today? Should I have driven past her on the road? That would be something for a mother to complain about." He was getting mad.

"It's just that . . . And I know she can be a flirt." You hated the word as soon as you said it, though Mary *was* a flirt, same as you were at her age.

"Do you hear yourself?" He sat forward on the chair and looked hard at you. His eyes narrowed, and his lips, too. "Mary's a kid. I'm a coach. And an accusation like that could hurt me in so many ways, even beyond the personal, I can't even begin to . . . If you really believe I'm a predator—"

"I don't. I just need you to tell me."

"For Chrissakes, you act like you don't know me at all. And maybe I don't know you, either." When Stan saw your three kids appear in the hallway, his face went slack, and he got up, put on his jacket and stormed out. The screen door slammed shut as he muttered a final word about trust.

You weren't really accusing him, you told yourself. You hadn't meant to say anything, but you'd just asked.

"I guess you can give me a ride if you really want to," Mary says. "Oh, Mom, you should've seen what happened today in science. Nicole spit her gum into this girl's hair, and the girl didn't see it, and she kept touching her hair, and it got really stuck."

But really, what interest could a grown man have in a girl who chews gum the way your daughter chews her gum, noisily and with her mouth open? How could any man be interested in a girl who, whenever she isn't texting on her phone, prattles mindlessly about the other middle-school cheerleaders, tells what happened, play-by-play, in the last movie or TV show she watched? I mean, your daughter drives you and the rest of your family crazy with that mindless prattling, and you want to slap her at least once a day for the way she rolls her eyes at something you've said, even as you want to wrap your arms around her and hide her and protect her. Your shoulders are hunched up around your ears. Take a deep breath, woman!

"So the girl was going to cut the gum out of her hair, but then

Mr. Glover asked if anybody had a peanut butter sandwich in their lunch bag. He said gum is *hydrophobic* so it doesn't dissolve in water, so we had to take the gum out with another hydrophobic material. He wiped the peanut butter off the girl's bread and put it on the gum and worked it out. And then he let the girl go rinse her hair in the bathroom."

You hope her love of science will teach her cause and effect as it pertains to her body as well as to what goes on in a science lab. You hope it will allow her to succeed in ways you never dreamed of succeeding, but you don't know how she's going to make it safely through the next few years. You wish she could be a nerd girl in high-waisted pants. You wish she needed glasses, at least.

"Amber and Nicole didn't even know what *hydrophobic* meant," she says. "Can you believe it?"

"God damn it!" you shout at last. "Can't you see? I'm worried sick about you. I'm worried that all the motherfuckers in the world want to mess with you, and get their lousy hands on your body. Yes, I'm out of my mind with worry about what you do with boys at school in the stairwell. And worse, I'm afraid some man is going to sweet-talk you and lure you into his car and molest you, Mary. And I'm worried that you might like it. Or you might go along with it even if you don't."

Once you've said this, you can't believe you've said it. But you're not sorry you've said it. You don't know how you've gone so long without saying it. Mary looks stunned, but less so than you'd expect. Her arms hang limply at her sides, and her bare belly seems more pooched and unprotected than ever. Maybe she's been waiting for your outburst since the incident in the stairwell. You fall back into your chair in exhaustion.

"God, Mom. That's just gross," she says finally. "You know I don't like men that way. They're too hairy." She is trying to lighten the conversation, bless her. She tries again to pull up her pants, but even she realizes it is hopeless this time. "You know, I didn't tell you, Mom, but me and Amber were in Cooper Park after school on Friday, and this guy was staring at my boobs, and me and Amber threw our apples at him from lunch. We pretended we were calling the cops, and he took off on his bike."

"But what if he wasn't gross?" you ask. You wonder why she didn't tell you about this on Friday. "What if he was a good-looking high school boy? A handsome football player? What if he wasn't hairy at all? What if he shaved his whole perfect body and smelled like a flower?"

"Oh, Mom. The guy was gross. And you can trust me. I'm not stupid. And I'm not going to get pregnant, if that's what you're worried about."

"Did Stan ever try anything with you?" you ask and hold your breath. "Or say anything . . . weird?"

"Stanley Steemer?" Mary kicks at the rails of your chair and shakes her head. "You're crazy, Mom. You worry about the weirdest things."

Your daughter changes her shirt at your insistence, and as soon as her phone is charged, she heads out to Amber's house on foot, cracking her gum, shaking her head, rolling her eyes, and texting in a cloud of candy-flower perfume. You ask her to let you know when she gets there and then to be sure to call for a ride home. She mumbles an OK as the wooden screen door slaps against the frame.

You're busted up over Stan, more than you thought you would be, but with him gone from the house, you can be a little more certain Mary is safe. Of course, he is just one man among millions out there in the world, one of dozens of men who might take an interest in your daughter between this house and Amber's house. You close your eyes and tell yourself that not all men are like that neighbor who allowed you to skip school at his house and smoke bowl after bowl until you couldn't form a complete sentence. Not all teachers—even those who take a girl's hair in their hands—are like your tall, brown-eyed social-science teacher, whose attentions flattered you so much that you would never have said no. And girls are different now, too—look how your daughter says no to you all the time, as you would never have said no to your mother for fear of being slapped. Your daughter knows so much more than you did at her age, and she might even come to you with any problems she *does* have, if you don't work yourself into a state.

Stan hasn't contacted you since that night two weeks ago, and you haven't called him. You think about what it might take for you to be reassured that your daughter is safe. A definitive, *No*, every day, from Stan and from every man within driving distance. A definitive, *Yes, I understand*, from Mary every day to let you know she sees there is danger, that you're not crazy. That would be a start.

You heat the oven for fish sticks for the boys, something you give them when their sister isn't here, and you slice potatoes to bake alongside. You liked cooking for Stan, who was appreciative of a homemade meal of any kind, even fish sticks once when that was all you had. Sometimes when you were watching TV after dinner, Stan patted his thighs and invited you to sit on his big lap and relax. Sitting that way with his strong arms around you, with his belly pressing into the small of your back like a support cushion, made you forget about the day's appalling customers, the aches from negotiating washing machines into place, made you forget even about the way the passing years have thickened your body and lined your face. When you allowed your head to fall back against Stan's shoulder, the warmth and size of him made you feel small and pretty, like a girl again.

BEDTIME STORIES
FOR THE MIDDLE-AGED

Christie Hodgen

I.

ONCE THERE WAS A GIRL WHO WAS PRETTY BUT FAT. HER FATHER WAS a busy insurance salesman and her mother stayed home performing those duties necessary to the care and maintenance of the girl, whose name was Lisa. Lisa's mother was a beauty queen, a former Miss Kansas who kept a picture of herself, her crowning moment, propped on the mantelpiece. In the picture the mother wore a sparkling evening gown, a satiny sash, a bright red mouth. Her blonde hair tumbled over her shoulders and she smiled the smile of the genetically privileged. On her head was a twinkling crown. The mother's platform had been the cause of promoting physical fitness to America's youth. If someone had asked her then what she might do if she were ever faced with the challenge of raising a selfishly-fat child she would have said with perfect confidence, "Oh, *that* would never happen!"

It did not seem possible to Miss Kansas that fate could have matched her with such a daughter, pale and lumpy as gnocchi. And so she devoted the greater part of Lisa's childhood to fitness and weight reduction. She enrolled Lisa in tennis lessons, riding lessons, ballet, tap, tumbling. She sent Lisa to a dietician, a thyroid specialist, a hypnotist, a shrink. Every night she read Lisa fairy tales in which skinny, nimble children escaped the wrath of hungry wolves and witches, while their fatter, slower counterparts were eaten alive. "They were gobbled up," read the mother, "quite like dumplings!"

In desperation Miss Kansas mailed off for a series of cassette tapes which embedded subliminal anti-hunger messages deep within the melodies of popular country songs. Every afternoon she staged crowning ceremonies in which she forced Lisa to walk the length of the dining room table in a bathing suit, back and forth, while Hank Williams sang: *Hey, good lookin'! Whatcha got cookin'? Howsabout cooking something up with me?* At the end of the song, Miss Kansas placed a tiara on Lisa's head and told her how very, very close she was to being beautiful.

Because this was Kansas and 1975, Lisa was a Girl Scout. Every spring she was required to sell cookies—Thin Mints, Samoas, Jackie-O's—but was forbidden to eat them. She ate them anyway. One year she used her allowance money and bought herself three-dozen boxes, then stashed the boxes under her bed. When The Former Miss Kansas found the cookies, all hell broke loose. Lisa's mother chased her around the house taking pictures of her with her Polaroid Square Shooter, one after another after another, close-ups of her chin and ass, her thighs. When the pictures developed, Lisa and her mother stood regarding them.

"Is this who you want to be?" said the mother.

Lisa shrugged.

"If this is who you want to be," said her mother. "Fine! Be my guest!"

She was her mother's guest. She couldn't help it. Her father was a German who came from a long line of stocky peasants. In another time and place she would have been praised for her sturdy build, her ability to trudge up a mountainside while carrying two heavy pails dangling from a yoke. It wasn't her fault. This was, Lisa decided, who she was meant to be.

And so she carried on with life: fat honor roll, fat student council, fat church choir, fat pep club. She went to the state university, met and fell in love with an economics major named Jim Sherman, also fat. They graduated, married, moved to the greater Winston-Salem area, and had three fat babies. Jim worked and Lisa stayed home. For Lisa it was a full life, sunup to sundown, of feeding and changing, shopping, cleaning, laundry, play dates, church, haircuts and doctor and dentist appointments, maintenance to the home and vehicles, and of course children's television. Children's television was the soundtrack of her life. She knew every character by name, she could imitate their voices, sing their songs, dance their dances. For the most part she liked the characters and welcomed them into her home, though sometimes she had fantasies in which she stuffed them into blenders and killed them. Sometimes she sensed that the adults running the children's shows—the writers and producers and actors—had also been driven mad by the characters and were retaliating with obscene little pranks. On one of the shows Old McDonald decided to take a nap in the barn next to a sheep, and as they snuggled together Lisa wondered if it weren't perhaps some kind of joke.

In Lisa's free time she took pictures of the kids in funny costumes. She dressed them like businessmen, like Charlie Chaplin's tramp, like gangsters and priests, like pirates. For one picture she lined them up with their backs turned, naked but for wings: angels. Their thighs and buttocks were gloriously dimpled. She looked at them and growled, bit them playfully. Then she felt within her the urge to really bite them and worried it meant something.

Every week she emailed these pictures to her mother, and Miss Kansas wrote back more or less the same thing, something to the effect of: *The children are lovely!*, but what she really thought was that the children looked like they should thrown in a pan, dressed, and roasted. She imagined them laid out on their backs with their legs sticking up, paper socks on their feet.

In addition to photography, Lisa's major *creative outlet*, as she called it, was the Sherman family's annual Christmas letter. The first year she was married, she wrote the letter in early December, a week before mailing the cards, and she could hardly fill up a page. But in the following years she put more and more time into the letter— two weeks, a month, two months—until one year she had the idea of writing up each month as it went along. In January 1999, she wrote: *We had a lovely Christmas of '98 and rang in the new year by staying up late with videos and popcorn. Paul and Jake fell asleep before midnight but Billy made it all the way! The rest of the month was fairly quiet, as the weather was too cold to go outside and Jim was away on business with his secretary, Suzy, for almost two weeks! On January 23rd we were all saddened by the loss of our beloved goldfish, Curly, who turned blue and sat helpless at the bottom of the bowl for quite some time before passing away, God rest his soul. We miss you, Curly!!!!*

Lisa liked the way that the letters summed up her life and gave it a definitive shape, a sense of purpose. If her days, in and of themselves, were baggy and meaningless, somehow in their recapitulation they were transformed. As the years passed the letters grew longer and longer and eventually required multiple stamps. Eventually it seemed to Lisa that she wasn't really living her life in the moment, that everything she did, every little thing, had to be translated into Christmas-letter prose before she could understand and appreciate it. In the back of her mind, as she went about each day, she heard the voice of the letter, which was her own voice but slightly smarter, with a faint British accent: *On the morning of the 28th I woke up confused from the effects of a dream in which I was an eagle with the head of an elk,* she thought to herself. *Later that morning when I was driving the kids to school, I let another car pull in front of me and they didn't even wave! I don't know what's come over people these days but sometimes it can be very frustrating! I try to remind myself to rise above it and be a bigger person and set a good example for my children. After all, giving is the spirit of Christmas, and it should last throughout the year!*

More than anything else the letter was, to Lisa, an attempt to assure herself that the life she was living wasn't ridiculous, that it was in fact the same life that others lived in homes and neighborhoods and towns like hers the world over. When she went out to the store, or to church, or to book club, it was mostly for the purpose of meeting up with people who looked like her, who talked like her, who would act as a reflection in what she thought of as the pond of life. As she went about her days she looked at herself, then at others, to make sure that she was doing the same things they were doing. Mostly she looked at other women, other mothers. Like her they drove minivans, like her they were thirty or forty or fifty pounds overweight, like her they stopped at Starbucks twice a day and ordered skim hazelnut lattes, like her they spent their evenings watching soft-hitting news programs—Barbara Walters's interviews with celebrities, etc.—and then discussed these news programs with one another while waiting in line to order their lattes, like her they said to their kids, who were rising defiantly out of the seats of their strollers: *Sit down on your bottom! On your bottom! Sit down on your bottom right this instant or you're going to be in big trouble, Mister!* Like her they said, *Do you want a time out? Do you? I'm counting to three. One. Two. I'm counting, here! Do you want me to get to three? Do you? Two-and-a-half. Two-and-three-quarters! That's a boy. That's my little pumpkin muffin. Who's Mommy's little pumpkin muffin? Is it you? Is it?*

She wondered if other women went about the business of raising kids and keeping houses in the same way that she did, that is, in a way motivated solely by the fear of what others might say and think if she did otherwise. Sometimes she felt that motherhood was like the hearing tests administered at elementary schools, during which an entire class was herded into a room and commanded to wear headphones. Then the nurse said: *Raise your hand when you hear the tone,* and when the tone sounded everyone raised their hands. As a child Lisa had wondered to herself, *What if I didn't hear it? I could just raise my hand along with everyone else, and no one would know the difference! No one would know if I heard it or not!* Her life, the life of a mother, she wondered now, was she hearing it, was she really hearing it, or was she just raising her hand?

Sometimes at night she couldn't sleep and lay awake feeling vaguely dissatisfied, like a guest in a budget hotel, stranded there while her real home was under repair for water damage. She wanted something different to happen, something spectacular, as always did in the stories her mother used to read to her at bedtime—*Once there was a poor, fat, ugly girl who discovered one day, when her fairy Godmother appeared quite out of nowhere, that she was in fact a princess, that she was in fact beautiful, and with the flick of a wand she was quite transformed!*—but this, she supposed, was more than one could reasonably expect from life.

Then one January everything changed. First her father died, swiftly, of a heart attack, and then a month later her mother had a massive stroke, which paralyzed her and left her speechless, an aphasiac. The doctors tried to explain what this meant. In the simplest terms, they said, her mother was no longer able to process language. She could understand facial expressions and the tone of people's voices, be it plaintive or reassuring or commanding, but words themselves meant nothing to her. Basically she lived the life of a dog. She ate when she was fed and bathed when she was bathed. She went to the bathroom when someone took her to the bathroom. For the rest of her life she would have little choice but to tolerate the attention of upright people and endure their touch; occasionally she would be blamed for their farts.

Lisa didn't like the idea of her mother living in a nursing home, so she moved her to North Carolina, into the baby's room. The two younger children would just have to share a room. She tried to take care of her mother by herself, but the mother thrashed and moaned whenever Lisa tried to feed her, dress her, tried to help her onto the toilet, and so Lisa placed an ad in the paper. She wrote: *Attendant wanted for crippled woman. Basic companionship, plus some light cleaning and cooking.* The woman who answered was in her fifties or sixties, very small and finely-built. She was foreign in some way Lisa couldn't quite identify (Polynesian? Filipino? Aborigine? Mexican?) and spoke very little English. Lisa sat her down at the kitchen table and spoke to her loudly and slowly, motioning like a flight attendant. She did her best with what she could remember from high school language classes. She had taken Spanish and French and wasn't sure which was which anymore. "Mi mama," she said, pointing to her mother, who sat motionless in her wheelchair, "esta malade. La necessita una amiga."

The applicant, whose name was Patricia, looked at Lisa with a wet-eyed expression of pity.

"Est-ce que tu poder ayudarse?" Lisa knew that wasn't quite right, and she winced. Then it occurred to her that it didn't matter that Patricia didn't speak much English. Her mother didn't speak English anymore, either. All three of them would have to manage with smiles and nods, with the manic gestures of mimes.

Patricia turned and looked the mother in the eye. Since her stroke the Former Miss Kansas had an unsettling stare—one eye steady and hateful, the other unhinged and wandering—but this seemed to make no difference to Patricia. They regarded each other for a long moment. "OK," Patricia said, as if agreeing to something suggested by the mother. She picked up the mother's crippled hand and turned it over in her own, pulled straight the curled fingers, massaged the knuckles. The mother didn't scream as she would have done with Lisa. Instead the mother closed her eyes and seemed to relax.

"You're hired!" Lisa said.

The next week she jotted down a note for the Christmas letter: *We have a new member of our family! Her name is Patricia, and she is a Godsend! She takes excellent care of mother and the house. She cleans with rags and hot water and ammonia, not with paper towels and spray cleaners like everyone else. She spends half the day on her hands and knees—her hands and knees! She's like an angel! And her enchiladas are to die for!* The letter would be difficult this time around—it was going to be harder than ever to put a cheerful spin on the year's events—but Lisa felt compelled to do her best.

One day in April, the cruelest month, Lisa's fat husband told her he was leaving. He'd been unhappy, he said, for a long time, and that the arrival of the Former Miss Kansas had been the last straw. He said his soul yearned to breathe free, that he longed to make contact with the spirited boy of his youth. He said he was moving in with his secretary, Suzy. He said Lisa could keep the house.

Lisa said, "What?"

She looked at her husband. He looked tired and sad, very much like the week-old balloons that were still floating ghostlike around the house at knee-level, leftover from Jake's birthday party. She realized that she hadn't looked at him, really looked at him, in years.

Then he was gone, and surprisingly Lisa's life wasn't much different than it had been before. She still got up in the morning and got the boys ready for school, packed them in the minivan and drove them off to preschool, elementary school, and middle school, came home and turned on the television, picked up the house, cooked something and ate it, cooked something else and ate it, then put the leftovers in the fridge for dinner, went out and bought something or other, picked up the boys and drove them to their lessons, karate and music and dance (Dance! Jake danced! Was this a problem?), picked up the boys and took them home, fed them, supervised their homework, bathed them, sat them in front of the television, and then, her favorite part of the day: dessert. She and the boys sat eating pudding, ice cream, cupcakes, cookies, Ho-Hos, Malomars, Pecan Sandies. They ate chocolates, donuts, individual-sized glazed fruit pies. There was a small reward at the end of each day, just enough to keep her going, and indeed life wasn't much different from before.

When her mother had been there six months the boys started to complain. Whatever generosity they'd extended her as a result of her pathetic condition was long gone and they couldn't even muster a poor replica. "Nana," they said. "Smells funny. She gives us weird looks. We don't like her! We want to live," they said, "with Dad and Suzy!"

They went to live with their Dad and Suzy.

Once again the change was less drastic than Lisa had expected. Basically her life was the same as before except instead of having a husband and children she now had a job as a clerk at the Department of Motor Vehicles. There was very little difference, she found, between having a family and having a clerical job at the DMV. In both cases there were long lines of scornful people waiting around for her to help them with something they couldn't manage themselves, in both cases she carried out her duties with mindless, robotic devotion. They more or less amounted to the same thing.

Now in the house it was just Lisa and Patricia and the Former Miss Kansas, and so in the evenings Lisa took to giving her mother makeovers. "I know how you feel about your appearance," she said. "I know it's important for you to keep up your looks." Each night she combed and styled her mother's hair and applied a ghoulish amount of makeup to her mother's face. Then she settled a tiara on her mother's head, set her wheelchair in front of the television, and turned on Lawrence Welk.

Lisa told herself that she was doing the best she could by her mother. As she phrased it in the Christmas letter, *Mother is doing as well as could be expected under the circumstances, God bless her heart.* But one morning, after she had been staying with Lisa for about a year, Miss Kansas used all of her remaining strength to wheel herself out of the garage, down the steep driveway, and into oncoming traffic.

Now it seemed to Lisa that life had reached its absolute limit, the outermost edge of absurdity, and she started to wonder if she weren't perhaps a modern-day version of a Biblical character, someone who was doomed to walk the earth in devastated solitude for the rest of her days. Her parents were gone, her husband was gone, her children were gone. The friends she used to have—other housewives—weren't her friends anymore. And after her mother's funeral, even Patricia had left. All that remained in Lisa's life—the only human presence she had left in the world—were the individual meals that Patricia had cooked, packaged, and left in the freezer with notes attached to their lids. *Tortilla soup, Heat in the microwave five minutes and then decorate with corn chips. Enjoy!* Or, *Beef Enchiladas, heat at 375 for forty-five minutes, serve with salad.*

When Patricia's food ran out the only contact Lisa had with any living thing—besides the people at work, who couldn't really be said to represent living things—was with a cardinal who kept lighting himself on the flowerbox outside the living room window. This cardinal sat staring into the living room, staring at Lisa as she sat on the couch. It came every afternoon when she got home from work and sat there tilting its head from side to side. Sometimes it pecked on the glass as if trying to get a point across. It occurred to Lisa that the cardinal was the reincarnation of her mother. She began to think that the cardinal was staring at her just as her mother would, that is, staring at her with disappointment and disgust. One day she went outside to talk to it, to tell it to leave her in peace for once, and she realized that the cardinal was simply enamored with its own reflection, which convinced her more than ever that it was her mother. *Give me a goddamn break*, she said to it, *will you?* But the bird only continued to stare at itself and so she made a move for it, screaming, *Fuck off, why don't you, you fucking bitch!*, her voice rising up and out, high, hysterical, sounding through the neighborhood. In a rage she watched the bird fly off until she couldn't see it anymore. Then she burst into sobs.

That night she erased the year's Christmas letter (*We were all deeply saddened by the death of my loving mother*, it said) and started a new one in its place. Gone was the voice of the old Christmas letter, British and genteel, optimistic; in its place was a new voice, grating and snide, as subtle as Carol Channing's. *You turn forty*, she wrote, *and everything you thought was your life is gone and you're just standing in your front yard talking to a fucking bird!* She wanted to warn everyone what was coming. All around her people were going about their business as if life were fair, as if they were safe, and she wanted to warn them. *Go ahead and enjoy yourselves while you can*, she wrote. *Because the fact is there's no escape, the fact is that sooner or later you will all be gobbled up quite like dumplings!* When she finished the letter she realized it was the briefest and best she had ever written; when she finished the letter she realized she had no one, absolutely no one, to send it to.

II.

Once there was a boy whose father taught him everything he needed to know about life. By the age of five Kurt could recite all of *Aesop's Fables* and their attendant morals. By the age of thirteen he was a skilled woodsman, could track animals and pierce their hearts with an arrow, could skin, gut, clean, and cook them over a fire he built himself, could catch fish with a homemade rod, could make camp out of nothing but wet leaves and fallen branches. He could follow the stock market, could name the Dow's top hundred companies, could predict their rising and falling, could calculate the effect of hostile mergers and takeovers. In high school he was captain of the football, basketball, and baseball teams. He did well in his classes and dated the prom queen. He went to Yale, Wharton, and then to work on Wall Street. He bought and remodeled a condominium. He dated several beautiful women and in this way became familiar with a new restaurant every weekend. He had a penchant for exotic foul smothered in unusual sauces. He ordered partridge, ostrich, braised Alaskan pigeon. While his dates talked about their college years he savored his meals and tried to identify spices: Cocoa? Cinnamon? Cardamom? He was twenty-five, thirty, thirty-five, and all the while there were many pleasant, lingering tastes in his mouth, but he never once encountered anything that he would order again if given the choice between it and something new.

Every Sunday Kurt called his parents and spoke to them for five minutes apiece. More and more his father's conversation turned to matters of health maintenance. He had: shingles, neuromas, fungal infections, heart palpitations, tinitis, a persistent taste in his mouth reminiscent of aluminum foil. He named his medications, asked after the stock values of the companies who manufactured them. With his mother—a Junior Leaguer, a ladies' doubles seniors tennis champion—Kurt spoke more or less exclusively about vacations. She spent months planning them and then, after taking them, spent months discussing their merits and detractions. She liked Aruba better than Bermuda, Bermuda better than the Cayman Islands. On the advice of friends she went to Rome but didn't like it. "Too crowded," she said. At the end of every conversation she told him: *Go find yourself a nice girl and get married.*

This was the question plaguing him. He was going on forty now and had been dating for twenty years, and he had never even come close to marriage. To end up like his parents, who seemed to be spending their last years sitting next to each other waiting to die, what was the point? Also, there was the matter of a bizarre personal habit of Kurt's that was more precious to him than any relationship. There was something he did every day, without knowing why, that he felt he couldn't reveal to another human being, at least no one he had met so far, and until he found that person, there was no point even considering marriage.

Kurt's secret shame was that he wanted to be a country music star. When he was alone he closed all the blinds, shut off all the lights, turned on country music videos, and then acted them out as they played. He knew it was an absurd preoccupation—he was too old and had a terrible voice—but he wasn't ready to let it go. He sang along with the hit songs and the classics, performed the dance steps, looked pleadingly or threateningly into an imaginary camera as the case dictated. He stripped down to his boxers and strutted towards his reflection in the full-length mirror on the back of his bedroom door. *Hey, Good Lookin',* he sang. *Whatcha got cookin'?* He was living in a city, New York City, and there were thousands of exciting things to do, every minute of every day. But this was what he was doing with his free time.

Every day in the park and in the subway Kurt passed by people performing—playing their guitars, singing their hearts out, many of them without the slightest talent—and he wondered what it was that kept him from joining their ranks. He felt vaguely dissatisfied, vaguely yearning. There was something he was waiting for, something he felt would one day compel him to pursue his true passion, but he didn't know what that could possibly be. In the meantime, he waited. Often he felt like a guest in a fancy hotel, a guest who was staying only so long as his house, the place he really lived, was being painted.

One day at work Kurt picked up his phone and stated his name, Kurt Feldheimer, and from the other end he heard the voice of his mother saying, "This is Margaret Feldheimer." Since his mother had never once in her life called him at work, he knew immediately that his father was dead.

For several months after his father's death Kurt felt certain longings rising up within him. They demanded to be recognized and accommodated, but he didn't know what they were or what they wanted. Sometimes he was struck by an itch on his foot that no amount of scratching would satisfy. Sometimes he lay awake until four in the morning flipping through channels, looking for something he couldn't name and couldn't find. Sometimes he ordered something to eat, ate it, then ordered something and else and ate that, then ordered and ate a third thing and still wasn't satisfied. He gained twenty pounds. He stood naked in front of the mirror and said to himself: Get your fucking act together, Feldheimer. He slapped himself in the face. He leaned in close and stared at himself until his face no longer looked like anything he recognized.

He took to going for long walks in Central Park. He hardly took notice of his surroundings, except when he was hungry and was on the lookout for a pretzel or hot dog cart. But one day in the upper-west corner of the park his soul was stirred deeply by a performance artist named The Amazing Andrew. The Amazing Andrew was standing on a wooden platform dressed up as the Tin Man from the *Wizard of Oz*. His costume was impeccable, his face painted over entirely in silver—even his mouth, his neck, his ears! He held an axe mid-swing and stood frozen on the platform. At his feet was an upturned hat and when people put money into it they were allowed to grease Andrew's joints with an oil can, at which point he went through a series of tai-chi looking motions, swinging the axe around through a number of poses, then freezing again in mid chop. Kurt was mesmerized. He put money in the hat and oiled Andrew's joints. The can, which was filled with water, went: *glunk, glunk, glunk, glunk.* He paid five times, greased Andrew's elbows, his shoulders, his neck, his knees and ankles. It was the single most satisfying experience of his life.

Afterward he waited at a distance for Andrew to climb off of the platform, then followed him home to Brooklyn, three trains and a half-mile walk. The next day, a Sunday, Kurt rode to the tin man's building and waited outside for him to emerge from its depths. At first he wasn't sure that he was going to be able to recognize the Tin Man out of costume, but when Andrew finally appeared, around noon, Kurt knew him immediately. He was exquisitely built, tall and lean, with broad shoulders and long, muscular limbs. Looking at the Amazing Andrew, Kurt was overtaken with a desire akin to the desire he had felt as a child stalking deer in the deep woods, in a flash he saw himself tearing Andrew's limbs from his body, roasting them over an open flame, and sucking them to the bone. He followed the Amazing Andrew into a Starbucks and stood behind him in line, staring at his shoulders, his biceps, his forearms, at the slope of his neck and the veins that throbbed within it. He listened as the Amazing Andrew ordered a skim hazelnut latte. When it was his turn at the register he casually ordered the same. Andrew turned and looked at him, they looked at each other for a long moment, in Andrew's eyes was a look of faint searching, then recognition. "Hey, Man," Andrew said. They drank their lattes, walked down the street ducking into various shops—a record store, a second-hand clothing shop, a Chinese grocery—talking the whole while about Andrew, who, in addition to being a performance artist, was also a musician and an actor. At a Chinese grocery store Kurt bought Andrew a bag full of food, then walked him home. When they exchanged numbers Kurt's hand shook and he realized with horror that he was in love. He was in love!

At home Barbara Walters asked him questions and he answered them in front of the bathroom mirror. *I wouldn't say I was a homosexual, no*, he said. *I'd just say I'm in love with this one particular person who happens to be a male.* To indicate to viewers how difficult it was for him to put this all into words, he furrowed his brow. He was reluctant to open up, anyone could see, but Barbara Walters was persistent. *I think it took my father dying*, he said, *for me to be able to open up to new experiences and see myself for who I really am. My father was a very strong personality, a real traditional guy. He played football, he fished, he ran with the bulls once in Pamplona. It's like I couldn't even think about being gay so long as he was alive.*

The next time Kurt saw Andrew they went to bed together. They fucked on the living room floor, sofa, and ottoman, they fucked in the shower. They ventured out and fucked in a movie theater, in the bathroom of a bar. Kurt gave and received, fucked and was fucked. After they finished Andrew said, "That was a pretty good fuck," and Kurt thought, but never said, "If you're lovin' me like I'm lovin' you, baby we're really in love."

They saw each other all through the fall and into the winter. With his Christmas bonus he paid off Andrew's student loans. The vague dissatisfaction of Kurt's former life was replaced with a gnawing anxiety (When would he see Andrew again? Tonight? Tomorrow? How could he guarantee that Andrew would stay with him? Would Andrew leave? Was he going to leave suddenly, today, the way Kurt had left so many women before? Had he left already without even calling?) punctuated by brief moments of rapture and relief. When Barbara Walters asked him, he was forced to admit that he was happier before. More fulfilled and in control, better-adjusted. But it was also true that he wouldn't go back for all the money in the world. "All the money in the world," he told Barbara.

Then one spring day Andrew told Kurt that he needed more, he wanted to experience new things, see new people. He was, after all, only twenty-four.

Kurt said, "What?"

"It's not you," said Andrew.

"Why?" Kurt said. "I want to know why."

Andrew said, "Not to hurt your feelings, but the truth is there's not much to you. We never really talk. You don't have many interests. I couldn't really say there's anything unique or interesting about you. Not to hurt your feelings or anything."

Then Kurt almost died of grief. He felt running through him a pain so strong couldn't breathe. He called, emailed, showed up at Andrew's apartment. He waited for Andrew in the park and sat watching his routines. He went to all the places they used to go, the bars and clubs, but it was no use. Andrew was with someone else now—a short-haired, frail-looking woman after the fashion of Mia

Farrow—and made a big show of it, leaning down to kiss her, putting his hand in the back pocket of her jeans. One day in the park Kurt stood in front of The Amazing Andrew screaming. *I loved you*, he yelled, *and you left me!* It was quite a performance, but no one noticed. People walked by, assuming it was all rehearsed, some kind of amateur theater.

Kurt was sick and exhausted, he felt as though poison were coursing through his veins. He had trouble breathing and suffered from acute attacks of panic. He was disoriented and sluggish at work and one day was called in to see his boss, who fired him.

He walked home singing. Down the street, on the subway, down the street again, singing from the back of his throat, his voice trembling and breaking. *There's a tear in my beer!* he cried. And while some people laughed and most walked past without noticing, a few people stopped and regarded him with sympathy, and when you thought about it this was more than you could reasonably expect of people in Manhattan, this was a kind of communion. He knew then what it was that had always kept him from singing in public; he knew that in order to be a country star a man had to have loved—truly loved—and have been so broken by that love that he no longer cared what he looked like, how he sounded, who was watching.

At home he answered the probing questions of Barbara Walters. *I guess you'd call it the darkest time in my life. I don't have anyone to turn to, I have no one at all, in fact I'm so low and so lonely I think I might go home to my mother.*

He went home to his mother. He slept in his old room, in a twin bed with sailboats on its sheets. He slept on his stomach, face down. He drooled shamelessly onto the pillowcases, he fantasized about Andrew and jerked off onto the sheets. He stayed for a month, hardly getting out of bed. He relived every moment of his and Andrew's time together, which struck him as superficial and ridiculous, meaningless, absurd, yet still he longed for it, mourned it as though the loss of something extraordinary and innocent, a miracle.

Twice a week the maid (She had a name but he couldn't remember it. Pamela? Patricia?) came and he heard her vacuum running through the house, getting closer and louder. Finally the maid would knock on the door, ever so timidly, and he'd tell her to come in. She'd crouch down and pick up all of his crumpled tissues, she'd dust off all the artifacts of his former life—the trophies and framed newspaper clippings, the hanging ice skates, even the varsity jacket hanging from a hook, its vinyl sleeves, its gleaming gold pins—she'd vacuum, and then she'd motion for him to get out of bed so she could change the sheets. If the maid divined his sexual habits—and she must have, the sheets were like sandpaper—she was discreet enough not to say anything.

Whenever Patricia left (Pamela?) Kurt always felt a strange sense of calm and completeness. He'd lie in bed admiring the trappings of his boyhood, a museum of his former glory, and he'd remember the brilliant, heartless person he had once been. Then, slowly, thoughts of Andrew would overtake him and he'd fall back into despair. But each time Patricia came he felt a little better. After three weeks at his childhood home, and six visits from Patricia, he was well enough to pack his things and return to the city.

For a time, he was filled with resolve. He got a new job and performed adequately, then well, then very well. One day he was promoted and during his celebratory lunch he ran into an old girlfriend—someone who he had taken out to dinner and slept with a few times—and asked for her number. "I've been meaning to call you," he said. "But I lost your number! I'm so glad I ran into you!" He started seeing her again. She was almost forty and had gained twenty pounds or so in the time since he'd known her. She hadn't dated in over a year, she was desperate and bitter and broken. She was, in other words, exactly what Kurt wanted. He asked her to marry him and, having no better prospects, she agreed.

And so, Kurt married and resigned himself to a passionless, steady life. He sold his condo and moved to Connecticut. He stopped singing to himself in the mirror. He felt satisfied, in complete control of his innermost desires and demons, he supposed for a long time as though he would never fall prey to them again. Such was his faith in himself that he told his wife he wanted to raise a family. Eventually he had a son and taught him everything there was to know about life.

III.

Once there were two lovers, man and woman. Each was married to someone else, but this didn't seem to matter, at first this just seemed like an obstacle that required working around. The lovers met at a children's music class. Every Saturday the man's son and the woman's daughter met at the public library and spent thirty minutes singing and dancing with a woman named Miss Brenda. Miss Brenda was a failed country singer who accessorized herself something like a cowgirl, with boots and hats and fringed vests. When Miss Brenda danced she liked to imitate forces of nature—wind, rain, snow—and it was all that the woman could do, observing from the perimeter of the class, not to burst out laughing. It was during one of these dance sessions—Miss Brenda was spinning around the room in an approximation of a tornado—that the man and woman caught one another's eye. They shared a moment of mutual agony, of disdain for the sacrifices of parenting, they made faces suggesting torture and humiliation. After class ended they gathered up their kids and walked to their cars, matching Volvo wagons, and said what people say to each other in those situations.

"Nice car."

"Good taste you have, there."

"We're slaves to the same marketing campaigns, I guess."

"We've thrown away thousands of extra dollars to fulfill certain ideas of ourselves."

"We're smarter than other people."

"We're better."

"We're safer."

"We own the road."

"Everyone else is just a schmuck trying to get along."

"But we, we are the chosen people."

Here they leaned in their cars to buckle their children in their seats.

"We should reward ourselves," the man said, "for sitting through that. We should have a latte or something."

"Yes, let's," said the woman. She'd never before said, "Yes, let's," and wondered what was happening. He wasn't very attractive, this man—he was shortish and slight, with curly brown hair that was thinning on top, he wore thick glasses in thick black frames, and behind them his eyes were icy, shifty—and yet she'd changed her language for him, and surely this meant something. She got in her car and said to herself, "Yes? Let's?"

From there things proceeded as these things always do. On Saturdays, after class, the man and woman went to Starbucks for lattes (they favored the same kind: skim, hazelnut) and complained about their lives while their kids chased each other around and hid giggling under tables. The man and the woman had the same likes and dislikes, the same politics, the same pets. They had the same complaints about their peers—other parents—how idiotic and empty they were, how corporate, how robotic and stupid and pathetic. (Next to them two fat mothers discussed the Barbara Walters special they had seen the night before, how moving it was to watch a celebrity cry, how thrilling.) They complained about their careers—he was a Catholic school principal, she was a freelance copyeditor—which were beneath them, and which would have advanced much easier were they not confined to their present city and their respective marriages. Each had been educated at a fancy private school on the east coast and had gone straight into graduate school, each had married a lawyer and followed that lawyer reluctantly toward high-paying jobs in the Midwest. They were, essentially, the same person.

"Kansas," one said. "If you told me ten years ago I was going to be married with a kid and living in Kansas, I would have killed you just for saying it."

"I would have killed you," said the other, "and then killed your family."

"I would have said, 'You and your yellow brick road can go fuck yourselves, motherfucker.'"

"And your little dog, too."

 "I can't stay here much longer."

"Sometimes I don't think I can make it another day."

"Sometimes I wonder about picking up a crack habit just to amuse myself."

"Or meth. I hear the kids eat meth around here like candy."

"I know a guy."

"Me too."

"And if we get arrested I know a lawyer."

"Don't remind me."

Each felt clever and unappreciated, stifled and shortchanged, misunderstood, martyred, desperate, lonely, searching, bored, marooned. Each felt relieved by the other's discontent, each saw something of themselves in the other and in so doing felt affirmed. When they accidentally brushed up against each other, the man felt something like electricity go through him. When the man used an element of style uncommon to most speech (*And then everyone put on his jacket and went home,* he said. When, in speaking, he enclosed parenthetical phrases between pauses, as if commas—*My father, a staunch Republican, was horrified . . .*) the woman felt something like electricity go through her. She was a copyeditor, after all, someone in the habit of quoting Strunk & White's *Elements of Style* to herself, smugly, and these were the kinds of things that turned her on.

It should be noted here that in alternate cases the lovers weren't the spouses of lawyers but the lawyers themselves. Sometimes the lovers were the spouses of doctors or drug reps or real estate agents, or the doctors, drug reps, and real estate agents themselves. Sometimes instead of children they had dogs, or instead of dogs, cats. In many cases, the easiest ones, there were no children or diminutive life forms involved whatsoever and the man and woman met through work, at conferences, at weddings, at church. In the end it all comes out the same, in the end none of these details really matter.

Every week as they sat watching their children's music class the man and woman swapped books and magazines and CDs. They recommended restaurants and doctors to one another, veterinarians, babysitters, landscapers, maids, wines and cheeses. In their free time they prowled the internet looking for reference of one another and one another's spouses. After an acceptable amount of information had been exchanged they met at his office one evening under the pretense of looking for a book he wanted to loan her, and fucked standing up. He came in less than a minute and then the pulled up their pants, looked at each other, and slapped their foreheads like kids who had just accidentally knocked over a tower of blocks.

"Yeesh," one said.

"Shit," said the other.

"I can't believe we just did that."

"I've never done anything like that before."

"Me neither! You think *I* have?"

The fact was that the man had had several prior affairs, but this didn't seem reasonable or necessary to mention.

"Well . . ." said one.

"Well . . ." said the other.

"See you Saturday," I guess.

The man did a little dance, lilting and twirly, after the fashion of mist, and the woman laughed. The point of all this was, he made her laugh.

On the way home she thought to herself: *A name or a title in direct address is parenthetic: Well, Susan, this is a fine mess you are in.*

In addition to their public meetings, at music class and also at various festivals, birthday parties, and concerts related to the kids, the lovers kept meeting in private, first at his office and later at her home, on his lunch hour, while the kids were at preschool and her husband was at work. Everything was light, then, and fast, all that passed between them some kind of sly, quick joke. He came fast and she said, in a manner suggesting she was busy and eager to get to other things, "Thanks for coming." In this phase of the affair everything was thrilling. The world was bright and new and they felt satisfied with everything. They hardly ate or slept. It was fall and the air smelled wonderful, yellow leaves tumbled down from tall treetops, and they were happy.

But as the winter approached life became more difficult. The kids got sick and threw up, they ran fevers and suffered asthma attacks, they broke out in unidentifiable poxes, they entered phases of screaming discontentment and refused to go to sleep at night. All that season their spouses seemed to them like animals—brutish, filthy creatures whose every habit and gesture and accoutrement (the way they ate, the way they chewed their fingernails, dug at their ears, scratched themselves, the way they spoke and dressed, the smell of their perfume and cologne) disgusted them. The man came to resent his wife's habit of negotiating everything, every little thing, as if it were a contested contract. ("We could have dinner out and then make dessert at home," she said, when she called from the office. "Or we could eat at home and then go out for ice cream. It depends on traffic. I'll call from the car when I have a better ETA.") The woman, whose marriage lacked even so much as the closeness necessary for negotiation, suffered particularly. Every night when her husband came home from work he cleaned out the refrigerator—he often ate standing in front of it, shoving food in his mouth, bitching, bitching, bitching about his boss—*that bitch can go fuck herself, that fucking bitch*—then went to the bathroom and took a long, messy shit, took a shower, and passed out in bed. She sat for long hours in the living room, listening to him snore and wondering how it was that she could have possibly married such a person. He, in the first place, was terrible with grammar, a bad speller. In the beginning phases of their romance, when he had been inclined to leave her love notes, they said things like: *I know its love. Your so beautiful.* And how could she have ever thought, even for an instant, they were meant for each other?

In bed, the lovers complained to each other. Life could be easier, they said. Life could be better than this. The woman interpreted these complaints as interest on the man's part in leaving his wife. But the man said these things, and listened to them, and thought nothing more of them.

Then something bad happened. The woman's father died, and even though she hadn't been close to him—they talked once a month, at most—her grief was unbearable and she felt herself unraveling. Suddenly everything was difficult, leaden, veiled with dust, spotted with rust. "I'm like the tin man," the woman told her lover. "You know, from *The Wizard of Oz*? It's like I was going along fine, chopping wood and all that bullshit, and then a storm came and I rusted in place. It's like I can't move and it's like my heart is broken."

The man said, "Shit. Jesus. I'm sorry. Shit."

As was bound to happen, the woman came to see him as her only true friend, her lifeline, and she fell in love with him. After the man and woman made love the woman would cling to the man and talk of her father. He had been an editor, too, a lover of order and spare elegance, systems, regimens, rules on which to depend. He had always struck her as cold and distant, but now that he was dead she saw his flaws in a more sympathetic light. "One time my father picked me up early from school," she said, "for no reason, and we drove up to the beach and had ice cream cones and walked along the shore. It was October and we were the only ones there. At the time I thought he did it to surprise me but now I think he must have been troubled about something, he must have been sad. He didn't say a word the whole trip." The woman spoke at great length about what it felt like to lose a parent. Something happened to you when a parent died, she said, something went out of you and you felt abandoned, what was left in you of youth and playfulness—even if you hadn't known it was there to begin with—was suddenly gone, and in its place was drudgery, in its place was hardship and loss; worse, there was no one left to help you through it. It didn't matter what your parents had been like, whether they had been caring, loving people, or helpless, destructive drunks, it didn't matter, she said, you felt the loss. You felt death standing closer to you. You felt skinned, devoured, sucked clean of life, like a small pile of bones left on a plate at the end of a meal.

The man, whose parents were both alive and well and living in Florida, said, "Uh-huh."

"I miss him," the woman said. "This is awful. Life is awful."

"Do you think we should stop?" said the man. "We can stop. It might be too much for you right now."

"No!" she said. "God, no. Do you want to?"

"No, no!" he said. "Not at all."

"Good," she said. "Good. Because I think I love you."

The next Saturday the man's wife showed up to music class in the place of her husband, and the woman studied the wife with a pounding heart. There she was: the wife, the wife, the wife! The woman was sorry to see that the wife was beautiful—tall and elegant and well-dressed—far more beautiful than she appeared in pictures. More unsettling was that the wife appeared to be a superior mother than the woman was; the wife sat telling the other mothers about how she fed her child nothing but organic vegetables and whole grains, how she enrolled her child not only in dance lessons but also tai-kwan do and soccer, how she and her child were learning German together through a series of mail-order audio tapes. "Wirklich!" she said.

Already the woman was thinking of breaking it off when the worst happened. The wife said to another mother, "I'm so tired. You know how it is in the first trimester."

Pregnant! The wife was pregnant! The man was going to have another baby! With his wife! She was pregnant! The wife was pregnant! The woman's heart pounded. All the while the children sang, "Hey, good lookin'! Whatcha got cookin'?" and the woman thought her heart would burst.

When the woman broke it off the man was surprised at her emotion. "This was never, you know, *going* anywhere," he said. "This was always just for fun, we always said that."

She said, "Fuck you."

On the drive home, in an attempt to collect herself, she quoted Strunk & White: *Use a dash to set off an abrupt break or interruption and to announce a long appositive or summary.*

The man stopped showing up to Saturday dance class, and so the woman had to endure the company of the wife, plus the sight of her daughter and the man's son playing together. There they were, miniature versions of the man and woman, holding hands, delighting in each other's company. They chased each other around the room, squealing and laughing, they chased each other until one caught the other and they fell laughing to the floor. It was like something Hamlet might have staged to expose the sins of his elders. The woman almost couldn't endure it. After class she spent long hours crying and listening to country music, which she had always found to be a sloppy injustice to the English language, but which she suddenly felt was the only form of expression that came close to matching her condition of devastated, luckless despair. She sang—in the car, in the shower, in the laundry room—as if a spurned wife. "Your cheatin' heart," she sang, "will make you weep!"

Now and then she saw the man and his wife out in public, holding hands, the wife's stomach growing bigger, bigger, and the woman froze, broke out in a sweat. She had trouble breathing. During one of these seizures the husband asked her what was wrong and she said it was her father.

Here it should be noted that in some cases it wasn't a pregnant wife but something equally serious, like a cancer scare or a child falling ill, that changed things. In some cases, the woman herself— the adulteress—got pregnant and had an abortion and felt, afterwards, unable to carry on with things. In some cases, the spouses found out and that was the end of the affair. Or the woman met someone else, someone more tender and loving—a *second* affair on top of the first one—and dropped things with the first man due to scheduling difficulties. Sometimes the woman, or her husband, took a better job in a distant city, sometimes the man relapsed into alcoholism or suicidal depression and broke it off. In all cases, or at least in most of them, the man and woman returned home to their spouses and slowly forgot about the affair, slowly the thrill they had felt from that love, or obsession, diminished and then disappeared altogether, and they wondered what it was they could have possibly been thinking.

In this particular case the man watched his wife labor to birth their second child, he held her hand, he watched his son born and the experience wiped from his memory all of his previous mistakes. He became renewed in his devotion to his wife. Until he wasn't anymore and had another affair. But this was years down the line.

For the woman it was harder. The woman suffered particularly. It was a long time before she could look at her life, her own life, as anything of value. Her house was a mess, her work was dull, her marriage a ruin. For a while her husband left and moved in with another woman—he'd been having an affair this whole time, too, as she suspected—and even though it was a relief to be rid of him it was still sad, in its way. He'd ended it badly, with a note. *You're way too critical*, it said. *Not everyone is perfect you know. As far as I'm concerned you can take your little blue pencil and shove it up you're ass.*

Now she had no one. The only person she spoke to was her maid, Patricia, who didn't even speak English. Every Wednesday she followed Patricia around the house, cleaning alongside her, crying softly and telling her all that had happened, over and over again. "It's so good to have someone to talk to," she told Patricia, and Patricia looked at her with solemn, wet-eyed compassion, or perhaps pity, or perhaps barely concealed disdain; she didn't know and it didn't really matter, she just needed to talk. A question had formed in her mind that she felt compelled to ask. "I just don't know what happened," she said. "I fell in love, I got married, and then it all just disappeared, it just disappeared, and I can't figure it out. Then I fell in love again and it disappeared again. You're in love with someone, and then you're not, and where does it go? That's all I want to know. Where does love go?"

Then one day her husband returned, things having gone sour with his mistress, and they agreed to live together, for their daughter's sake, as if partners in the business of raising her. Life resumed as before. Most days the woman felt drained and hopeless, yearning. She felt tired and confused and wondered why she had ever married, why she had ever had a child. But then there were moments, glorious moments, in which her daughter did something charming—she'd say *heartbeep* instead of *heartbeat*, or *dollfish* instead of *dolphin*—and she felt it swell inside her, the exception that proved the rule, the thing she'd been missing: love. In these moments she felt that love was the world's single pardonable error, that its flaws were not only tolerable but necessary. Perhaps, the woman thought, the love she'd once felt for her husband hadn't died but only changed forms, like a frog into a prince. Perhaps it was true that she and her husband had emptied themselves of all the love they had for each other, but in its place was this, their daughter, who they would raise and set out into the world, carefully, carefully, as if a paper boat set adrift on a stream, and they would watch her go, off toward a love of her own, they would watch her go and know that she was the reason they had come together in the first place. Perhaps this was the most that could be expected of love, that it brought two people together long enough to reproduce itself. Perhaps, she supposed, this was more than enough, perhaps this was even a gift.

MR. SCARY

Charles Baxter

—for Richard Bausch

THERE WAS SOME SORT OF COMMOTION AT THE END OF THE checkout line. Words had been exchanged, and now two men, one tall and wide-shouldered, the other squat and beefy, were squaring off against each other and raising their voices. Their shoes squeaked on the linoleum. The short one, who had hair from his back sprouting up underneath his shirt collar, was saying a four-letter word. The other man, the tall one, shook his head angrily and raised his fist. An elderly security guard was rushing toward them. He didn't seem up to the task, Estelle thought. He was just a minimum-wage retiree they had hired for show.

"Good God," Estelle said to her grandson. "There's going to a fistfight."

The boy didn't glance up from his phone gadget. He held it in his palm and was rapidly clicking the letters. "They're just zombies," the boy said quietly and dismissively after a glance.

"Well, how do you know that?" the grandmother asked, trying for conversation. "I've never met a zombie." The men seemed to have calmed down a bit. They were just rumbling at each other now.

"Zombies *like* discount stores," the boy, whose name was Frederick, said patiently, as if he had to explain everything. He still wasn't looking at the two men. "They eat plastic when they can't get brains." The boy glanced up, showing his grandmother his bright blue eyes. "Just look around if you don't believe me," he said. "This junk? It's all *theirs*." The fight between the two men seemed to bore him, before the fact. Almost everything bored him.

Another security guard had arrived, a red-faced fellow with a crewcut. He would put a stop to things. Together with the older security guard, he herded the two men toward the service area. So: that had happened. Now it was over. Estelle handed the baseball bat she was buying for Frederick to the check-out clerk, who scanned it and who then held out her palm for money.

"You don't see *that* every day," Estelle said to the clerk, who was frowning.

"Ain't none of my business," the clerk said with shrug.

Estelle handed the bat to her grandson, who took hold of it in his left hand while keeping up his writing with his right.

"You're giving this to me because *why*?" the boy asked, glancing up.

Estelle sighed. She no longer waited for thanks for anything from him. Gratitude was simply beyond his abilities.

"For your baseball games," she said, over her shoulder.

"What baseball games? I don't play baseball."

"*Thank* you," the checkout clerk said behind her, belatedly, as if prompting Frederick. He followed his grandmother, his eyes downward again, oblivious to her, to the partly cloudy sky outside the automatic doors, to the untied shoe laces on his left foot, to his own waddling walk, to the folds of fat under his T-shirt, to the gift of the unthanked aluminum baseball bat. The poor child. He had been so beautiful once, years ago, with a smile to light up the world, and now . . . well, just look at him.

They drove across Minneapolis and stopped for a red light in front of the Basilica. At the corner traffic island stood a bearded panhandler with a cardboard sign that read, "HOMELeSS VetERaN. ANYThING WILL HeLP. GoD BLeSS." The man's face was wreathed in sunburned desolation, and she was reaching into her purse for a dollar when her grandson spoke up from the back seat.

"Grandma, don't give him anything."

"What? Why?" Estelle asked.

"He's a pod," the boy said.

"What?"

"*You* know. A *pod*. A replicant."

Estelle looked in the rearview mirror and saw the boy scowling malevolently at the homeless man.

"No, I don't know. Why do you say such things?"

"See, for starters, he's in the stare-at-you army," the boy said, with his eerie talent for metaphor. "They stare at you. That's the pod gameplan. I can always tell. I have *radar*. That guy is garbage." Frederick laughed to himself. "He's the lieutenant colonel of garbage."

"No human is garbage," his grandmother said defiantly, rolling down her window, "and I don't want to hear you talking like that."

"OK, fine," the boy said, "but I'm just saying? How come you *like* these creeps?"

But she had already reached through the car window and placed a dollar bill in the man's palm, and when he said "Thank you, and God bless you," Estelle felt a small feeling of satisfaction and pride. He might be a bum, but he knew how to be thankful.

"I suppose you think he's a zombie too," Estelle said, as she rolled the window back up.

"*No*," the boy replied. "He's a . . . *replicant*. Like I told you. He looks like a human being, but he isn't. Just like this car we're in now *seems* like a real car." Frederick smiled at his grandmother, a private smile, but the smile seemed to be poisoned somehow by the baby fat on his twelve-year-old face and by the boy's customary malice, a thin screen for his unhappiness. Often his face was unreadable: it was as if he had trained his facial expressions to be ungrammatical. The poor child: he even had a double chin, making him look like a preteen Rotarian. Curled into himself, having returned to his phone gadget, Frederick irradiated waves of unsociability and ill will. His being hummed with animosity toward the world for having staged the enactment of his various miseries. His revulsion at life had a kind of purity, Estelle thought.

Really, all she wanted to do was to take him into her arms and hold him. But he was too old for that now. What had worked once, all that love she had given him, no longer did.

"Mass times force equals velocity," the boy said, just before his grandmother dropped him off at Community Day Camp. "It's true. Did you know that?"

"No, I didn't. But actually, Freddie, that doesn't sound quite right."

"Well, it's true. *Absolutely.* I've been studying physics. And mass times force equals velocity. That's why a baseball travels faster if you hit it hard. You're forcing the ball to, like, accelerate." He waited for his words to sink in. "To escape inertia. You want to hear something else? This is even more amazing. *Gravity equals weight times voltage.* That's Yardley's Theorem."

"Yes. Well, OK. We're here," Estelle said, pulling to a stop in front of the Community Day Camp building, a grim yellow concrete-block affair with a flagpole hoisting a limp flag just inside the turning circle. During the winter, the building served as a community center. During the summer, they offered activities for kids from ages eight to twelve, with trips to spots of local interest. Last week the boys and girls had visited an institution for assisted living, giving each old person a gift of their own devising. Frederick had given his own old person an African violet. The day camp counselors also staged sports activities on the playground in back. Frederick hated all of it and performed his sullen silence with great majesty whenever Estelle picked him up.

"Do I have to go in there?" the boy asked, once she had stopped.

"Well, I *did* drive you over here. Kiddo, give it the old college try."

"I've done that all summer."

"So do it again."

"They all hate me," Frederick said. "They throw their lunch food at me."

"Throw it back."

"Yeah, *that'll* work. They throw sandwiches. Which *explode.*"

"Well, can't you—"

"—I got a cupcake in my hair yesterday."

"—Make an effort—"

"—All right, all *right*," he said

"—To go in there—"

"—I said *all right*."

There was a brief air-pocket of dead silence.

"See you in a few hours," Estelle muttered, as her grandson heaved himself out of the car. He was still writing something on his phone. He also had words penned on his arm.

"Don't bother coming back. Just call the coroner," the boy shouted, closing the car door and causing the baseball bat to roll again on the floor.

Her husband Randall, down on his knees in the garden, waved to Estelle absent-mindedly with his trowel as she pulled up on the driveway. "Not enough fertilizer for the pansies," he said to her once she was out of the car and behind him, leaning on him. Using his customary tone of comic despair, he said, "And I've been overwatering the snaps, damn it. Look at them." He stood up, shaking his head before turning and giving Estelle a quick kiss on the lips. When he did, the brim of his sun hat poked against her forehead. "Drop him off OK?" Randall asked.

"So I bought him a baseball bat," Estelle said, putting her hand on her husband's shoulder. "It was a hopeful gesture." She straightened her husband and dusted him off. "But he stayed grumpy. Oh, and this is interesting: There was a fight in the checkout line at the K-Mart."

Randall nodded, gazing at her carefully. "Sure. Of course there was," he said. As always, she was taken aback by his capacity for understanding her, for knowing her least little mood. "Stel," he said, "I've made some lemonade, and . . . Freddie's disposition isn't your fault, you know."

"I know," she said. "I know." She whistled to the dog, who regarded her with indifference from his shade under the crabapple tree. "I just wish sometimes that Freddie were, oh, I don't know, more . . . *normal*, and I hate myself for wanting that. Who wants normal?"

"You do," he said. "Well, let's have a softball game on the vacant lot when he gets home. Us and a few normal neighbors. With his new baseball bat."

"A softball game?"

"Yes. With Freddie. Or maybe we should just *let him be*." He gave her hand another squeeze and preceded her into the house, holding the door open behind him. How considerate! Randall had always been considerate: he was one of those easygoing persons—affable, graceful, thoughtful—on whom the sturdy world depended, and although her little secret was that she was fatigued with him and felt almost no passion for him, she still needed to have his calm presence around. He was like a preservative, and she would fight to keep him if she had to. He played poker once a week with his chums; he drank one beer per evening; he was semi-retired from his veterinarian practice; he never raised his voice. He was even a graceful and attentive lover. What a paragon of virtue Randall was! Nothing to excess, this husband. But he had never been wild, and Estelle couldn't help herself: she was bored by people like him. Secretly, men who started fistfights attracted her. They had sap. But it was boredom that had the staying power.

"Here," Randall said, handing her a lemonade in a Dixie Cup.

"Thank you," she said, leaning forward into him again. His skin had a kind of slippery silkiness, an odd texture for the exterior of a middle-aged man. Her first husband, the dreaded Matthew, whose nickname had been "Squirrel"—winsome womanizer, alcoholic, self-centered bum, gate-crasher, liar, charmer, deadbeat, and cheat—had felt like hair and sandpaper. Sex with him had always been burningly raw and fecund. Children came from it, three of them. Where was Squirrel Van Dusen now? Pittsburgh? Or was it Tucson he had recently called from, yes, somewhere in the Southwest, that sunny haven for bums, asking for a tide-over loan for his newest harebrained scheme? It was hard to keep track of him: Randall had taken the most recent call and kept her from whatever Squirrel had asked for. She still had a soft spot for the guy. The flame could not quite be extinguished. Human wreckage *had* always attracted her. "The Bad Samaritan," Randall had called her once, in that not-quite-teasing way of his.

"It's a stage he's going through," Randall said, sitting down at the dinette. "Frederick's going through a stage. All boys go through a stage. They have to practice at being bad before they become men."

"*You* were never bad."

"Well, OK. I guess I never was," Randall said thoughtfully, nodding his head once and turning away from her. "Not like that."

"You always got up at five o'clock. To pray. With the birds. Like Saint Francis. You were a boy scout," she said, knowing she was being petty. "You still are."

"That's unkind. And I never *prayed*, not like that. I prayed to someday meet someone like you. Actually, Estelle," he said, fixing her with a look, "what *are* we talking about? This isn't about me, is it? Or Frederick?'

"No, I don't suppose so."

"Well, my dear, what is it about?"

She looked at him. Behind her, she could hear the leaves of the ash tree stirring in the dry summer wind. She could even hear the electric clock in the stove, which gave off a dull but thoughtful hum, as if it were planning something.

"It's about the usual," she said. Of course he knew what it was about. He always knew.

They'd run off together as teenagers forty-five years ago, Estelle and Squirrel, and when their kids were still toddlers, they'd crisscrossed the country in the Haunted Buick. What fun it was, being young, rootless, those hours of driving when music would start up for no apparent reason underneath the car's dashboard and then stop a few minutes later. There was a short in the radio, but Squirrel liked to say that the Buick was haunted. An announcer would begin speaking in mid-sentence from that same place under the dashboard, and Squirrel would say, "Where did *he* come from?"

You couldn't switch the radio off: the dial didn't work. The Buick was beyond all that.

In those days, Estelle and Squirrel never stopped anywhere for longer than a few months. They would cross the border into yet another state they hadn't yet ravaged looking for opportunities, surefire moneymaking projects to *put them on the map*, as Squirrel liked to say. That was the expression he used after dark in bed with Estelle in one motel or another, whispering to her about what and where they would be, some day. They'd be settled; and happy; and rich. They'd be *on the map*. The children, the two boys and Isabel, the youngest, whom they called Izzy, slept in the other bedroom, a clutch of little snorers and bed wetters.

All the trouble had been manageable at first. In Maine, there had been midnight phone calls from a girlfriend Squirrel had acquired somewhere, and a day later they were treated to her sudden arrival on the doorstep of their rented duplex She'd been coarsely attractive, this girlfriend, furiously chewing bubble gum, and her waitress name-tag was still pinned to her blouse over (Estelle could not help noticing) her plump right breast. *Cheryl.* She was pregnant, this waitress, this Cheryl, said. She wanted satisfaction. *Satisfaction!* What a word. Or else. Or else what? She would be back, she said, with a court order. Estelle and Squirrel packed the car that night and were gone the next morning, the kids still asleep in the back seat by the time the sun came up. Estelle didn't speak to Squirrel, except about necessities, for a month after that.

In Montana, Squirrel's partner-in-business threatened them all—another midnight call!—with a court suit and, if that didn't work out, personal revenge Western style with a semiautomatic. By the time they had relocated in northern Minnesota, as temporary managers of the Trout Inn on Nine-Mile Lake, Estelle thought they were finally free of adventures. They'd come to the calm expository part of the movie, the part after the big opening attention-getting mayhem. Squirrel's mischief-making had been all used up, she thought, just flushed right out of him, and she was relieved.

And then one night Estelle had awakened to find that Squirrel had entered her while she'd been sleeping and was thrusting into her with a wild look on his face, with his hands around her neck as if he planned to strangle her, and she screamed at him and shook him off. She loaded the still-sleeping kids into the Buick, against Squirrel's pleading, and took off for Minneapolis. She remembered to take what money there was, and the credit cards, Squirrel pleading with her but not stopping her, and the children crying.

That was Part One of her life. Now she was in Part Two. There would never be a Part Three. Of that she was sure.

Mid-afternoon, Estelle pulled her car into the turning circle for Community Day Camp. Of course, Freddie was already there out in front, staring up into the sky as he were waiting for helicopter rescue. He lumbered toward the car, opened the front passenger-side door, and poured himself in. He aimed the air-conditioning vents toward his face.

"How was it today?" Estelle asked, too brightly.

Freddie sat silently as if the question were much too complicated to be answered. Finally, he said, "We're going to put on a play."

"Yes, I think you told me that," Estelle said. "What is it? What's the play?"

"We're all writing it. Or *they* are. The kids and the counselors." He gave her his best sour look. "It's called *Wonderful World*."

"And who do you play?" Estelle asked.

"Me? I play Mr. Scary."

"Mr. Scary? Who's that? And what do you do?"

"I stand up at the beginning of the play and I recite my fear monologue and scare everybody."

"Well, that's nice," Estelle said, trying to put the best face on things. "Do you have it? The monologue? Could you read it to me?"

"Yeah," Freddie said. "I got it right here with me." He heaved himself upward, trying to get his hand into his trouser pocket. After much poking, he pulled out a grimy sheet of paper. Her grandson unfolded the paper and began to read. His delivery sounded like a voice-over in a horror movie. "*Fear*," Freddie intoned. "What *is* fear? You and I live with it, interact with, fear. We know fear, but we *shun* it. But what if one were to *embrace* fear? Not to *live* with it, but to *be* it, to *become* fear. In our everyday lives we *divorce* ourselves from *fear*. We tell ourselves it is *distant*, it is *unreal*, it is *abstract*. But this is *not* so. Fear is *tangible*, more tangible than you or I. What if a man *became* fear? Where would fear *live*? He would dwell among us, *hidden* but not unseen. *Who* would fear be? For *what* would fear strive? What would be the *face of fear*? Ha ha ha ha."

"Very good, Freddie. But, well, that's a strange monologue to give to a twelve-year-old," Estelle said, after recovering herself. "The words are awfully big. What does it have to do with a wonderful world?"

"It's like what you have to get out of the way? *Before* the world is wonderful? And yeah, well, that's what they gave me," Freddie said, slumping down in the car. "The counselors wrote it. That's what Mr. Scary says. I've got to memorize it. Also we also made T-shirts today. I mean, we wrote words on tee-shirts. So they became ours."

"What did you write?"

Freddie held his shirt up. With laundry marker, he had written GOT HERPES? on his. "Well," Estelle said, "that's not very nice."

"It's supposed to be a public health warning," Freddie said. "A wake-up call."

"And the other kids, did they throw food at you?" Estelle asked.

"Not today," Freddie said. "Today was a good day. They liked how I did the Mr. Scary monologue."

"Freddie," Estelle asked, "do you really have to laugh at the end of that? It's a little corny."

"The ha ha ha ha part? I added that," her grandson told her. "That's my contribution." He took out his phone gadget and began tapping letters.

"Are you texting someone?"

"No," Freddie said. "I'm writing a story."

"Oh, good," Estelle said. "What's it about?"

"The underworld," he told her.

*

Sometimes, on certain days when Estelle had found herself sitting on the front stoop of the house, her coffee cup cooling between her palms, and the morning breeze riffling her hair, Freddie still eating his breakfast cereal inside, she would imagine that the way her grandson had turned out, with his sorrow and obesity and malice, had its own logic. But then at other times, particularly when the breeze stopped, time halted as well. And when that happened, Estelle was no longer sitting on the front stoop with her coffee but was back *there*, in time, in Part One, taking her daughter Isabel to a guidance counselor, and then to that killingly expensive, pill-dispensing psychiatrist in the circular building with curved interior walls that made Estelle think of a gigantic brain, and they, all of them, the brilliant professionals and Estelle herself, were trying to *talk* Izzy out of the sullen and then manic rages—shoplifting, a stolen car, drug-taking, car wrecks, god knows what kinds of sex, and with whom—that had overtaken her daughter and turned her into this oblivious bingeing adolescent force-of-nature who'd actually driven once into a parked fire truck. Well, at those moments nothing had its own logic, or it had the wrong kind of logic, because you couldn't *talk* anybody out of anything, could you? No. How many young women had managed to do what her daughter had accomplished? Had smashed a stolen car into a fire truck? An achievement. Her teenage accomplices had fled, but Isabel had stayed there, dazed behind the wheel but boldly confident that such an excellent accident gave her special monster status. Who else, among Estelle's acquaintances, had also hit, though not very hard, a pedestrian in a parking lot? Her daughter Isabel had, and had been unrepentant. *He shouldn't have been there*, she had said of her victim, a retired dentist. In her taste for mayhem, Isabel had truly been Squirrel's child. So there *was* a logic to her actions, of a sort.

Estelle thought that her own life had veered between long patches of drudgery, weeks and months filing claims in an insurance office during the day and then racing home to cook dinner for her children and to put them to bed, typical single-mom scheduling, and then, the next job, working in the front office at the veterinarian hospital where she'd met Randall, accompanied by a choral background of barking. Yes, all that domesticity. And classes taken at the community college including art history, her new passion. Then other stretches of time superimposed themselves on the dull ones, the moments of high drama, first the ones staged by Squirrel and then the ones staged by her daughter. Her two sons, Carl and Robert, seemed frightened by their little sister and had landed jobs after school at grocery and hardware stores; poor souls, solid citizens before their time, they almost didn't count, those boys.

But Isabel! Even on medications, she drank anything, she took anything, she went anywhere at night; she seemed to have no home place except the deep nothingness that she sought out. In Squirrel, those traits had been charming, for a while—they looked good on a boy—but with Isabel they were as charmless as her scowling face. There was really something demonic about her, almost bestial. Estelle imagined her as she saw her back then: twisted up with imagined injuries, avoiding eye-contact, the blond hair matted and unwashed, her jeans caked with dirt, her fierce young woman's sexuality attracting the worst of the boys who gleefully hovered around her waiting for her next bold move.

One night, one of many late nights, Isabel had come home at three in the morning. Estelle had awakened out of a shallow and dream-infected sleep and went into Isabel's room, where Isabel had thrown herself on the bed in the dark. She was muttering, and after Estelle had switched on the lamp, she noticed that the pillow where her daughter rested her head had turned gray at the indentation. Her daughter never showered anymore, and she smelled like a feral child.

"Where have you been?" Estelle asked her, trying not to yell.

"I've been inside and outside," Isabel said. "I've covered the world." She giggled. "Like that paint? That covers the world? I've done that."

"Jesus. What am I going to do with you?" Estelle said to herself, to the walls. "At least get undressed. At least get some sleep. And you're grounded," she said, automatically.

"Undressed?" Isabel asked. Every facial expression she gave her mother indicated that any and all requests were, at that moment, preposterous. "You want me undressed, Mom? Like those nine-to-five people who are undressed? Who go to sleep?"

"Yes," Isabel said. "Like those people."

Isabel glanced up at her mother. Picking herself up, she stood next to the bed, then lowered her jeans. "See?" she said. "I can do this." She swayed and laughed at herself. "Wanna see something?" She laughed again. "I'm a magician. I can do this amazing trick. Just watch. You've *never seen this before in your life*. I can make my panties stick to the ceiling."

"What?" Estelle said.

After stomping her blue jeans to the floor, Isabel lowered her underwear and clumsily stepped free. She bent down and picked up her underpants—pink, Estelle noticed, her heart breaking— and then threw them up at the ceiling. They fluttered back down to the floor.

Isabel gazed upward and said wonderingly, "I thought it would work. I had such a good time."

Estelle was staring, too. Her mind moved slowly. "What are you talking about?"

"Oh, poor Mom," Isabel said. "You're so sheltered. Can't you guess?"

"No."

"Well," Isabel said, putting her hand on her mother's shoulder to keep herself from swaying, "I was with a boy tonight. And we . . . you know. And Mommy, did you know, that after you do it, I mean when you do it with a boy, it drains out of you? Later? Onto what you're wearing? And it makes your clothes . . . sticky. And that's why I thought my underwear would be there up on the ceiling!" she concluded, triumphantly. "Except it isn't."

Of course Isabel would become pregnant. There was no such thing as safe sex with Isabel. Of course she would have a baby and give it to her mother to raise after naming the baby Frederick (who came out of his mother brown, so his father must have been African-American, or something), and of course she would disappear quickly afterwards, leaving no known address.

Poor crazy Isabel. Poor Freddie, her son. It wasn't about individuals anymore; it was about the generations, and what they handed down. The courtrooms, the hospitals, the doctor's offices, the classrooms, the jails where they had put Izzy overnight: sometimes, sitting on the back stoop with her coffee cup, Estelle felt all those places descending over her, as if another person had lived that part of her life and had *not* yet survived it but now was inhabiting her own body. Clouds would cross the sky, cumulus clouds puffy with their own complacency.

In the car, with Freddie explaining about his hero, Argo, and his descent into the underworld, Estelle turned toward Lake Calhoun. When she parked near the beach, Freddie sat up and said, "What're we doing here?"

"I thought it would be nice to go outside," Estelle said. "Just a stroll. It's summer, Freddie. We've got a little time before dinner."

"Of course it's summer. I mean, what are we *doing* here?"

"Well, look at the swimmers." Outside the car, she walked ahead of him in the mid-afternoon glare on a sidewalk that ran parallel to the beach. At some distance from them, young men and women were playing volleyball. Out on the lake she could see swimmers splashing each other, and, beyond them, hazed in the hot Impressionist light, the sailboats. The air smelled of suntan oil and lake vegetation. People were bicycling past on the bike paths, and everywhere men and women, children and dogs were enjoying themselves. Pop music floated on the air from some radio.

"I hate it here," Freddie said, from behind her. Estelle could hear the shuffling of his shoes on the sidewalk. "I need to practice my Mr. Scary monologue."

"We should have brought your swimming trunks."

"I can't swim."

"You could learn."

"Not if I don't want to, I can't," he said. "I'd rather sleep with the fishes."

"The fish. Not fishes. *Fish.* You shouldn't be so negative," Estelle told him.

"You mean I'm *supposed* to be happy?" He inflected the word with scorn. "Happiness sucks."

"Well, you could try," his grandmother said, feeling a wingfeather of hopelessness. Just to her right, a boy about Freddie's age, maybe a bit older, bronzed with the sun, a kid who obviously lived outdoors, was tossing a football to a friend. The wingfeather beat against Estelle as she watched him. Happiness only came to those who never asked for it.

"I'd rather be Mr. Scary," Freddie said. One of the boys close to them threw their football unsteadily, and it landed near the sidewalk. Freddie stared at it before kicking it out of the way. One of the boys said, "Throw it here!" while Freddie continued on.

Estelle raised her head, closed her eyes, and breathed in. "You could have thrown that ball." she asked. "Couldn't you?"

"No," Freddie said. "It's just a trick. They're trying to mess with us."

"Incidentally, I think," Estelle said, "that Randall is organizing a softball game for after dinner. We'll use your new bat!"

"Oh, that's great. That's just great."

"Don't you want to try it?"

He treated her to his silence.

Well, at least there was the Bakken Electrical Museum. After they had returned to the car, Estelle drove Freddie to his favorite place on the southwest side of the lake, the museum where they had a working Theremin installed. Freddie had been here half a dozen times, and each time he would push impatiently past the exhibits near the front door to the Theremin in the middle of the museum's stairwell. He'd turn on the old instrument and raise his hands in the air between the two antennae.

Here, he was in his element. His hands raised like a conductor, with his fingers out, Freddie would tap and poke the air in front of him, and from the old Theremin came pitched noises that sounded like music but really *weren't* music, Estelle thought, any more than screaming was like singing. According to the information on the explanatory wall plaque, other Theremins had been used for the Beach Boys' "Good Vibrations" and the movie scores for *Spellbound* and *The Day the Earth Stood Still*. Freddie, when he played this thing, had a beatific smile on his face, as if he were summoning his monsters from the deep. Once he had played "Jingle Bells" for her on it, and Estelle thought she would jump out of her skin with revulsion. He had learned through trial-and-error where to poke the air for certain pitches. Apparently he had a musical ear. He was getting good at it. Soon he would be playing "My Funny Valentine" on this thing and scaring away everybody.

But you couldn't take a kid down to the MacPhail School of Music for Theremin lessons, and you couldn't bring out your grandson in front of the guests to have him play his Theremin, causing the other grandmothers to applaud, because Freddie wasn't really *presentable*, and neither was this music, which sounded like the groans of the dying, oscillating at sixty cycles per second.

Still, she watched him, poking and prodding the air and producing the hellish glissandos, with something like admiration. Her own sons were not like that. There was no other boy like him.

"There's no one else like him," Estelle said to Randall, who was bending over the grill, the left side for the hot dogs, the right side for hamburgers. He had put on his chef's apron and was worrying the hamburger buns on the edge of the grill with a spatula. Freddie sat writing his story, sitting on a picnic bench, on the other side of the back deck. He was concentrating with fierce inward energy.

Late summer evening, and Estelle sat watching Randall cooking the hamburgers and Freddie working on his story. Somewhere in back, the cicadas, harbingers of autumn, were chirring away. Their neighbor, Jerry Harponyi, who played cello in the city orchestra, was watering his garden, and when he saw Estelle across his back fence, he raised his hand, still holding the garden hose, to wave. The water gubbled, airborne, in a snake-like line, before falling.

"No, there isn't," Randall said. "But let's not talk about this now. By the way, I've drafted about seven of the neighbors to play softball in the park in an hour. And Freddie said he'd join us."

"Freddie said that?"

"Yes. I used all my persuasive skills."

"What did you say?" Estelle asked.

"I said it'd be nice if he played."

"He didn't object?"

"I just said that it'd be a nice gesture." Well, Estelle thought, that was Randall, all right: the King of Nice Gestures. "After all, you bought him that baseball bat. And he loves you, you know."

"Who?"

"Freddie, your grandson."

"No, he—"

"—Of course he does, Stel. Please. You're the only thing in this world holding him on." He looked at her with a smile, his face disfigured momentarily by smoke from the grill. "I can't do it the way you can. You're his lifeline. Don't you know that? Can't you see it?"

Harponyi waved again. "Looking forward to the game!" he shouted, and the water from his hose flung itself out again in patterns in the air.

"Me?"

"Yes. My dear, you. You're a rock, an anchor. You're all he's got. I love you too, you know, but I'm not desperate. Anyway, you know what position you should play?"

"No," she said. "First base?" She always liked it when Randall told her he loved her.

"No," Randall said. "Outfield. You need a rest. You can just stand out there and wait for balls to fall into your glove. Like a nun. Like a little sister of mercy."

"I'd enjoy that, I think," Estelle said.

Standing in the outfield, with the sun setting below the park's trees to the west, Estelle felt the early evening breezes blowing across her forehead, the same breezes that blew Randall's hair backward on the pitcher's mound, so that he looked surprised, or like one of the Three Stooges, she couldn't remember which one. With grown children of his own, and his own sorrows—his wife had pitched herself through a window eight stories up two months after learning that she had inoperable cancer—Randall had every right to be moody, or grumpy at times. Or just sour. But, no: he was relentless in his cheerfulness. And tiresome, if you didn't share it. Somehow the tragedies he had lived through hadn't altered him. They had no relevance to him.. There he was. In the fading light, he still gleamed a little.

Randall had just struck out Harponyi, the cellist. The first baseman, a fifteen-year-old from across the street, whistled and cheered. His name was Tommy, already chunky with muscle, a real athlete who in a year or two would be playing high school football, and for a moment Estelle wondered whether it wasn't a bit unfair to have boys like that playing on their side. But it all balanced out: their second baseman was an office temp who lived down the block and who was, at this very moment, talking on her cellphone, and their shortstop was old Mr. Flannery, a retired social studies teacher who lived on the corner and who looked a bit like Morgan Freeman. He was old but wiry. Freddie, when he came to bat, wouldn't have a chance if the ball went toward Mr. Flannery.

These are my people, Estelle thought, and bless them all, here in Part Two. Strange how one's heart could lift sometimes for no particular reason. On the other side of the park, the sounds of the soccer players, their outcries, rose into the air and made their way toward her. A fly buzzed around her head, and she smelled the strangely green smell of the outfield grass. She pounded her fist into the baseball glove, a spare that Randall had found somewhere in the basement.

Freddie was up. He was practice-swinging the bat that Estelle had bought for him that morning. His swings were slow, and even without a ball anywhere near them, they seemed inaccurate, approximate.

Stepping up to the plate, Freddie took one hand off the bat to shade his eyes against the sun. When he saw his grandmother, he waved. Estelle waved back.

Randall's first pitch hit the ground a few feet in front of Freddie and rolled to the catcher, Tommy's brother, who threw it back to Randall. "Good eye," Estelle shouted, and people laughed.

The next pitch went into the strike zone, and Freddie swung at it and missed, by a considerable margin. His physical movements were like those of an underground creature rarely exposed to the light. The umpire, an insurance adjuster who lived with Harponyi, called the first strike.

Freddie took another practice swing.

When Randall threw the next pitch, Estelle could see that it would go into the strike zone and that Freddie would swing at it and connect with it, and when he did, the ball soared up, a high fly, slowly ascending, and as it rose into the air, Freddie headed toward first base, not really looking at where he was going but watching the ball instead and then glancing at his grandmother underneath it. For a brief moment they exchange glances, Estelle and Freddie, and he seemed to grin; and then the ball began its descent, as Freddie, watching it again, headed toward Tommy, the first baseman, a boy as solid as he, Freddie, was soft. Tommy had taken up a stance and had braced himself with his elbow out, and Estelle saw that when Freddie got there, he would slam into Tommy like an egg thrown into a wall. Estelle tried to shout to Freddie to look where he was going, but her shout caught in her throat out of fear or terror, just before the ball dropped in its leisurely way, with perfect justice, into her outstretched glove.

SPLENDID, SILENT SUN

Yelizaveta P. Renfro

11/6

Claudette—

You'll never believe where I am—or rather, you've already surmised from the picture on the reverse of this postcard. Yes, Nebraska. You know, that state in the middle somewhere, just another corn-filled patch in the quilt of indistinguishable states that make up the interior. You see that farmhouse and the gently rolling fields of corn in the picture? That's why I'm here. To find that. Not that particular house, per se, but what it stands for: that open and uncomplicated life that's vanished in LA. Nebraska. Just the sound of the word conjures up images of corn and wholesome tow-headed children and the 4th of July. It's more American than apple pie, right? Of course you've never thought about it. You've never been here. It's the coasts for you. Fine. But for me, this bland Midwestern Americana is the exotic. I'm here to see it all.

Brian

11/7

Claudette—

I went on a little stroll today around Dudley's neighborhood and had the scare of my life. I was maybe three blocks from Dudley's house, just walking along, looking up at all these grand old houses with big porches and porch swings, as Midwestern as you please. And then, out of nowhere, came this awful buzz like an air-raid siren—or at least what I imagine an air-raid siren to sound like. The noise was all around me, coming from every direction, and for a minute I thought: Holy Jesus, the Soviets have launched their nuclear weapons at last, and here I am stuck in Nebraska! Nonsense, of course—how long has the Cold War been over now? When did the Soviet Union fall? I guess it was some vestigial fear from childhood, when the commies were the bad guys. Who are the bad guys now? I couldn't remember, as I stood there paralyzed, listening to that awful wail, waiting for the big old planes swollen up with bombs in their bellies to come roaring overhead. Would they be painted with swastikas, Muslim moons?

B

11/8

Claudette—

I went back to Dudley's and waited for the sky to fall, but nothing happened. When he came home for lunch, I told him about the siren, and he just said, Yeah, it's the first Wednesday of the month. And I said, What's that supposed to mean? And he said, 10:15, they test the tornado sirens, that's all. So I had to let this sink in, and then I said, What if there's a tornado at 10:15 on the first Wednesday of the month, and everyone ignores the siren because they think it's just a drill? And Dudley just looked at me for a long time, and then he said, Man, you really need to chill, you never used to be wound so tight. Do I need to chill, Claudette? You tell me.

It's cold and gray here compared to back home. Compared to where you are. Compared to our LA-blue sky. That should be a Crayola color. The most beautiful blue in the box.

Brian

11/8 (#2 of 2)

Claudette—

Dudley lives in a neighborhood called the Near South. Go figure. He's bought this monstrous old drafty box of a house that he's fixing up. A prairie foursquare, he calls it. Built in 1922. The wood floors and the stairs are cold and creaky as hell. There's a giant porch on the front with the obligatory porch swing. He says in the summer months people sit out on their porches. He knows his neighbors and his neighbors' kids and his neighbors' dogs. It's all very Midwestern and homey. The porch is sagging and the steps are crooked. It's a very old house. You would hate it.

So I'm here for two weeks. Did I mention that? For better or for worse, I plan to spend precisely two weeks here so I'll have time for nothing else. You know why, babe.

Brian

11/9 (#1 of 3)
Claudette—

I rode the bus all over town today. It's funny because I'd never ride public transportation in LA. There was this old guy on the bus, wearing farmer overalls with no shirt underneath, hauling a giant bag of ancient jumper cables—there had to be thirty of them in there, all wound up like a nest of snakes, their connections all corroded. And he kept talking about the weather, to no one in particular. We'll have snow before Thanksgiving, he kept muttering, looking out at the sky, which was blue today—not LA blue, but a pale, tranquil blue. I couldn't gather whether snow before Thanksgiving was unusual here or not. I will have to ask Dudley. It was warmer and sunny—not a hint of impending winter weather. This city is full of parks which are full of kids. I don't remember the last time I saw so many kids out playing on the playgrounds. Maybe because it was a nice day. In LA every day is nice. No reason to go out and play. I kept waiting for someone to ask me where I'm from, but no one seems to notice me.

B

11/9 (#2 of 3)
Claudette—

Another thing happened today. The bus was going past this magnificent building, so I leaned over to the guy across the aisle and asked him what it was. He looked at me like I was crazy for a minute, then snorted and said, What? The penis of the plains? And then he laughed. And he was right, it is pretty phallic. See the picture on the reverse? And suddenly I pictured it rising up off the center of this nation, this great bold protuberance on a vast body, and it was like I could almost see where I was on the continent. Almost, but not quite. And it was like I could understand why, if you're stuck here in the middle of the plains, you'd want to build such a thing. And I know it's hard to see in the picture, but at the very top of the building, there's a statue of this "sower" who is sowing his seed all over the plains out of a great big pouch at crotch level. I am not kidding. You would have laughed your head off, C.

B

11/9 (#3 of 3)

Claudette—

I got off the bus at the next stop and walked to the building, which of course turned out to be the capitol. Duh. I wandered in and somehow got myself attached to a school tour with all these rowdy fourth graders. It was actually fun. I learned about this big blizzard they had here back in 1888 when a bunch of schoolchildren got lost. I learned that Nebraska is the only state with a unicameral legislature. Bet you didn't know that, babe. And they have a law that no one can build anything taller than the capitol. So it will always be the biggest cock on the block. There was this little Asian girl on the tour who kept wandering off and looking at things on her own. You could just tell she had her own agenda, wasn't interested in the "party line" being dished out by the tour guide. You could see she was a bright kid. Sometimes we ended up looking at the same things, me and her, like these mammoth marble columns. Just touching them with our hands. All these people live here, and they don't think about LA or people like me. Like you.

B

11/10

C—

What is near? Near to what? Near to whom? To some vague, unidentifiable, unknowable, inscrutable presence, some central beating heart or intelligence of this city? What does it mean to live in the Near South? Is there a far south? Is there a near north? The Near South is meaningless unless it's in relation to something else. I said these things to Dudley today.

And what about the Midwest? Can one ever be in the middle of the West? Isn't something west only in relation to something else? Why not the Middle East or even Middle North or Middle South? Why not just Middle, Mid for short? Aren't we practically smack dab in the middle? We could call this place anything. *This* is where the action should be, not on the coasts, the boundaries, the peripheries, the margins. I said these things to Dudley too.

Dudley said: Did you come out here just to make fun of people? And I said: Who am I making fun of? I have not made fun of a single person.

Have I mentioned that Dudley is a native?

B

11/10

C—

All I ever knew about Nebraska I learned from reading Willa Cather's *My Antonia* some dozen years or more ago in a class on "regional writers." Cather being representative of the entire amorphous middle "region," of course. And actually, I don't remember anything about the book. So, one can deduce, I know nothing about Nebraska. Except for one thing. There's that image in the book of a plow emblazoned across the red face of the setting sun, and I remember that my prof talked about it forever. Why it's significant I can't remember now—only that it symbolized absolutely everything in the book, and a few other things besides. It was so saturated with portent it positively dripped. A man could spend his life studying that plow-sun hieroglyph and still not get to the bottom of it. Oh, and I think Antonia was pretty hot, back before she had all those kids. You think she's around? Instead of sitting on an Italian beach with you, I am here. Maybe I should look for *my* Antonia. I doubt you've read the book, so this all means nothing to you.

B

11/11

C—

Yesterday Dudley and I went down to the Haymarket for what is known as "game day." You can see what the Haymarket looks like for yourself on the reverse—old downtown, shops, brick streets. Now imagine the streets swarming with bodies dressed in red. No, that does not do justice. I don't think anyone can really understand who didn't grow up in a football-crazy town. Everyone is together for the same reason, dressed in the same color. It's almost worth it to wear red just to be a part of that. Dudley and I sat on the dock at the main intersection, drinking lattes and just watching it all. Uncharacteristically, Dudley is not much of a football fan. He told me a story about someone who came through here on the train, stepped off onto the platform on a game day, saw all the lunatics in red shirts, and promptly got back on the train, believing he had stepped into the middle of some communist rally. He couldn't remember who it was. Happened years ago. I even saw a big group of fans from California with matching shirts. Traveled all the way here for the game. Amazing, all the stuff that goes on that you never knew about.

B

11/12

C—

My problem is that I cannot see the place I am from, the place I've lived my entire life. I can't see myself in that place. I am too big and too small. I am everything. My head is filled with myself. So I am not part of anything. I thought I would be able to see this place clearly, distinctly, because it was not part of me, but most days it's just another city. I see bits and pieces, faces, trees, buildings, patches of sky, but I cannot see the whole. Same problem.

I have this whole stack of postcards I've written you here. I haven't mailed a single one yet. Do you think I will? Ha, ha. Maybe I should give this series a title. Maybe "A Tourist in Nebraska." My seventh day here. And to quote an old song from our youth, I still haven't found what I'm looking for. Whatever that is. (You.)

B

11/12

C—

I want to tell you a secret: corn fields are terrifying. All dead and dry now, rustling, whispering. Dudley took me a ways out of town to a corn maze yesterday. A maize maze. Ha, ha. They were getting ready to shut down for the year and there wasn't anybody else there. Dudley and I went off in different directions, and as I started walking through that moving, shifting, dead corn, higher than my head, I can't tell you how scared shitless I became. I can't explain it. Just think of *Children of the Corn*. Think of those other movies with cornfields. Someone lost in the corn. Something coming out of the corn. Someone being chased by something through the corn. UFOs in the corn. Why? Why does this most wholesome thing terrify us? But no. High fructose corn syrup. That is not wholesome. Ethanol in our gasoline. Corn in our whiskey. Corn in our cows. Government crop subsidies. Not wholesome. There is too much corn. That is why we fear it.

B

11/13

C—

I went with Dudley to a reception for his boss tonight. He had won some local leadership award. So the boss gets up and makes a little speech. Talks about how he moved to Nebraska ten years ago to work for this start-up computer company. Says when he was offered a job in Nebraska, he had to pause a moment to figure out where the hell that was. From Boston originally. Says now he'll never leave. Says Nebraska's the best kept secret in America. Says he doesn't want the word getting out, or else everyone will move here, ruin the place. Says we're safe as long as we stay part of flyover country. Har, har. The crowd laughed at all his jokes, his put-downs. I didn't get it. How is it funny to put yourself down? I thought about it. And I think I understand. They only pretend to make fun of themselves, but actually they're showcasing, in their secret code, their superiority. Their Midwestern modesty is a type of smugness.

B

11/14

C—

Here is what Dudley said to me last night, almost verbatim: There is no such thing as a Nebraskan, OK? Not the way you're thinking of it, not as some unified honky white force, not as an identity that we all share, not as some secret society you can figure out, you with your LA sophistication, your cleverness. These are people. They live here. That's it.

We stayed up late on Dudley's porch, drinking Fat Tires. You never met Dudley. We were buddies at UCLA. My bud Dud. Both studied computer science. He went away to school, and then he moved back home. That was always his plan. And he's content. That's the thing that sickens me somehow. He's got his old house that he's fixing up. Family in town. An older married sister with kids. There are an awful lot of kids here, C.

B

11/14

C—

I just can't get to sleep tonight. There's a big fat moon hanging just outside my window. It's a bit drafty in here. Dudley says the windows don't seal properly. It's on his to-do list. We're a lot alike,

Dudley and I. It feels funny to say that. He's lived most of his life here, and I was born and bred in LA. As you know. We have similar jobs as database administrators at similar companies. But the sameness runs deeper than that. I can't explain it. You'd see it for yourself, if you ever met Dudley. Dude-ly, we sometimes called him. Or just Dud. We thought it was funny that we knew a guy from Nebraska named Dudley. Grew up milking cows, we used to joke, right off the farm. Truth is, Dudley's never milked a cow in his life.

When I scheduled these two weeks off six months ago, I never imagined I'd be here. In this place. Without you, babe.

B

11/15

C—

Gargantuan prehistoric elephants once roamed all over Nebraska. I've been going around, picturing it all day, ever since I saw the amazing skeletons at the natural history museum. You can't imagine how huge these things were. Their legs like giant cathedral arches. You could pass right under them. Stroll clear under an elephant and out the other side. Their tusks like twisted, curved tree trunks. Their skulls like bathtubs. All this life that clambered about here long before any of us. It makes me feel almost fine. Nebraska was a happenin' place if you happened to be a mastodon. So just to cheer myself up, from time to time I imagine this big-ass elephant lumbering down the middle of D Street, or peeking its head over the new movie theater downtown. Ten thousand years ago. That's when they all died. That's a long time. Three years seems like nothing. One, two, three, we're done. How does something like that just stall, give out? Can you explain this extinction in my head?

B

11/16

C—

While Dudley's at work I often find myself just wandering around his neighborhood, making bigger and bigger circles around his house as I become familiar with the streets. Today I passed by a tiny bookstore nestled into a residential block. Small blocky building with a tiny storefront window. You'd hardly know it was there. There were just three words stenciled on the window: *Rare Book Dealer*. I had a feeling for a second that I had found what I had come here looking for, but the place was dark, the door locked. And then the feeling was gone, and I walked on. And for some reason the goneness of that brief feeling made me start having crazy thoughts. Like maybe I'll stay here with Dudley indefinitely. Maybe I just won't go back to work at the end of my two weeks. I could sit on this porch for a long time. Just writing postcards to you. I could just sit here. For richer or for poorer. For poorer, with no job.

B

11/18

C—

Went to Dudley's parents' house yesterday for Pre-Thanksgiving. It was the only day the whole family could be together. Dudley's brother Mitchell was in town from Kansas City. They had the traditional T-Day spread. Dudley's sister's kids were into everything. How do you like Nebraska? people kept asking me. Oh, it's great, I'd say, grinning like an idiot. Because what do you say? And then Mitchell leaned over and said, It's nice to live here, but you wouldn't want to visit. And he grinned at me like we were sharing some secret joke that only outsiders can understand. So I grinned back, and we sat there grinning, clutching beers in our fists.

Maybe "Postcards from the Middle" would be a better title for this memoir-in-postcards or whatever the hell it's becoming. This is a substantial little stack I've accumulated. I ought to tie them all together with a shoestring or gather them up in a hobo pouch on a stick. I'll sling it over my shoulder as a I travel the country, the modern-day bum with literary pretensions and a short attention span.

Happy Pre-T-Day, babe.

11/18

C—

It's suddenly turned so cold. Dudley has lent me a coat. He says, Get your ass in off that porch. But I think best out here. He says, You don't see anyone else sitting out on the porch. So I say, How else are they going to know I'm not from around here? I've got to set myself apart. There is even snow in the forecast. I'm more excited than any Nebraska schoolboy. I've never had a snow day in my life. I holler in to Dudley: I'm waiting for it to snow! Not missing a beat, Dudley bellows back: I don't want any frozen corpses on my front porch! My fingers are too cold to write more. It's that cold.

Of course I never meant to mail these. I've left no room for an address or stamp. Just covered the entire backside of each one in my tiny print. Maybe I'll wrap them all up in silver paper with bells, my gift to you.

B

11/18

I can mark the day it was all over, even though I didn't know it at the time. Hindsight and all that jazz. April 18. Our apartment. Remember our "low key" celebration? A cheese platter, some wines, some fruit. We were both too busy at work to do more than that in the middle of the week. Three years. It was significant. But we still had time. Time to celebrate, time to do things right. You were wearing that mocha blouse with the ruffled front. Your eyes brown, your hair brown. Claudette brown. All browns are your browns— you own them all. A whole walk-in closet full. A sleek leather living room furniture suite full. Wall-fulls of modern art, selected for color, complementarity. Your cell phone kept going off. Work stuff, clients. You seemed distracted. Bored? Who the hell knows? You can read anything into a situation after the fact. The tiniest glance can portend the fall of civilization. A butterfly's wing can set off a hurricane. Something like that. A plow silhouetted against the sun can mean everything. In retrospect.

11/18

Ah, yes, in retrospect. And so I have caught the moment, trapped it in a jar, so it can never get away, even if it beats the hell out of its wings. And it was only this: You picked up off the counter the discarded wrapper from the extra-sharp cheddar. And you said, This cheese has been aged four years. And then you said, This cheese is older than our relationship. And that was it. And you know what, babe? People just don't say things like that unless the relationship is, in their minds, already over. What you meant was: this cheese will *always* be older than our relationship. This cheese is more substantial than our relationship. This cheese is just so much more than *us*. Our relationship is not worth a hunk of cheese. This cheese is older than our relationship. Indeed. That one comment—my plow against the sun.

11/19

My God, it's actually snowed! The jumper-cable farmer's predictions were right on! You'll never believe this stuff, so white, so clean. Crunch, crunch under your feet. Everyone out shoveling, hot breaths billowing out of their mouths. Clearing sidewalks and driveways, talking. This is Nebraska! This is America! And the hush, the incredible white hush all over everything. The quality of sound itself completely transformed, muted. I walked right down the middle of D Street, taking pictures of everyone out shoveling. The first pictures I've taken here. Yeah, I'm a tourist! I wanted to shout. And this is the greatest thing I've ever seen! But no one seemed to pay any attention to me.

And as to that question you posed six weeks ago on heavy card stock in that big periwinkle envelope: No, I will not attend your mid-winter wedding with a guy you've known for, what, three months. Sorry, babe. Now *that's* some young cheese.

11/20

My last day in Nebraska. How has it come to this? A day of slushy melting, of mud. The aftermath. There is always an aftermath. Maybe I will just stay here, in sickness and in health. In sickness. I've developed a cold. Probably caught it from all those toddlers at the Pre-T-Day feast.

I just couldn't get enough of the snow yesterday. I walked all over town, ended up in the Haymarket just after dark. This freezing, bitter wind came blowing in off the prairie, and I really realized for the first time that I was on the massive, dark, open Great Plains. With all that wind blowing right through Dudley's coat, chilling me to the core, I suddenly saw it all in my mind's eye. I had this grand, sweeping vision of the Plains, and the city, and the Haymarket, and all the people, and myself. There I was, part of something big, and for a moment I could hold it all in my head. My head was big enough, just for an instant. A flash.

11/20

This cheese is older than our relationship.

So are the shoes on my feet. So are my hands that touched you. So what.

This house is older than both of us put together.

This elephant is older than our nation. This tusk is older than Thomas Jefferson's bones.

This grief is older than our world.

This sun is older than our souls.

Eat your cheese, C. Eat a big honkin' hunk of stinky old cheese. Cram your mouth with it. At your wedding. Something old—why not make it cheese? I will be the something blue.

Is this too poetic for you, C? Never knew this side of me, did you?

I'll never ever mail this one, not in a million years.

11/20

Something strange just happened. Something I don't understand. I'm sitting here on Dudley's porch. It's close to midnight, and bitingly cold. The neighborhood was all quiet, and then suddenly someone ran out of the house across the street and started to yell.

I'm not having this goddamned baby! she yelled. And I could see she was just a girl, hardly a woman at all. And then this dark figure appeared in the doorway behind her. I thought at first it was a man. I thought he was going to calm her or contradict her or somehow squelch out her high-pitched late-night woman madness. I thought he was going to restrain her, reign her back in. So there was someone there to control the situation. That's what I thought. And then I got a better look at the other person and saw that it was a woman, and her pose was relaxed. She wasn't there to control anything.

11/20

I guess this just goes to show you that despite my best efforts, I'm a chauvinist. Because when I realized that there wasn't a man on the scene, for some reason I stood up and stepped down off the porch, as though I was going to fix everything.

I'm not having this goddamned baby! the girl/woman shouted again. Then the other woman came down off the porch.

That's right, the other woman said. Shout it to the wind, girl! she said.

Goddamn it! the girl/woman shouted, How did I ever get in this mess? And then she began to cry. And something started to pull at my legs so I was walking into the street.

Hey! I shouted, Do you need some help?

And then the friend of the girl/woman turned on me like some animal. This is none of your goddamned business! she screamed.

11/20

And it isn't. I see that now. Sitting here on this porch, I see that now. They've gone back inside. Their lives, gaping open to me for a moment like the private moist wink of a wound, have nothing to do with me. There was no reason for me to interfere. There was no reason for them to say one word to me. So I'll sit here and mind my own business in the cold. I'll just sit here and wait for the sun to rise. A fragment of something just came to me: the splendid silent sun. I was only an English minor. I can't remember where half the stuff I read is from. But I think that must be Cather. It must be about Nebraska. Those words could only be written about Nebraska. *The splendid, silent sun.* I will wait for it. A Nebraska red sun. It will come up, a red disk gliding up over the sharply pitched rooftops of the Near South, over the city, over the plains. And for a moment, I will hold it all, cupping it inside of myself like something splendid and fragile.

RAINBOW DOGS

Justyn Harkin

Steve

WE HAVE A NURSE TODAY WHOSE NAME IS STEVE. STEVE IS A NURSE but he is not a fag. Steve has sandy brown hair and it is short. Steve has a bristle brush mustache and it is serious. Steve wears dark blue trousers and a matching blue Dora the Explorer print scrub top. Steve has on a pair of Crocs. Steve is going gray about the temples. Steve keeps his emergency room ID on a North Park University Nursing Program lanyard. Steve writes left-handed. Steve looks like he could take care of himself in a scrap. The hair on Steve's forearms is darker than the hair on his head. Steve wants us to know that the doctors are coming. Steve sports a scar on his chin. Steve has muscles in his neck. Steve clamps a hemostat to his shirt. Steve calls my infant daughter "Princess" as he slides a needle up her arm.

Lumps

At a party at the in-laws, one of Karen's cousins, a nurse, noticed the baby had lumps under her jaw. "Those aren't supposed to be there," this cousin said. "You should take her to a doctor." We panicked. We cursed ourselves as unfit parents for not noticing the lumps on our own. We drove to the closest hospital and were seen at the emergency room as soon as we got there. The triage nurse weighed the baby, took her temperature, and escorted us to a private examination room reserved for children at the back of the ER. The little room featured teddy bear wallpaper, a wooden rocking chair, and an angry metal crib that looked like it was designed for monster truck babies. We sat in the room alone for a long while and joked about the décor. Then came Nurse Shelly, a big girl with blonde hair, thick wrists. Said she didn't want to draw my daughter's blood. She could stick little kids all day long, she said, but babies were different. She hated sticking babies. Karen got upset and left the room. Shelly motioned that she was ready, and I leaned forward to give the baby a kiss. I pressed my lips to her head and she screamed and balled her fist in my beard. Shelly filled one, two, three vials with blood. Said again she hated sticking babies, then wrung those chubby hands of hers.

Bovary Was a Country Doc

Well, folks, I gotta tell you that I'm gonna have to go to the books on this one. See, your daughter's neck masses—hi, cutie—your daughter's neck masses are presenting bilaterally, here and here, along her parotid glands. The parotids are salivary glands. Salivary glands make saliva, or spit. We have three salivary glands on each side of our faces: here, here, and here, and the parotids are the biggest. Now the parotids aren't connected to each other in any way—oh, I know, sweetie. Who's this strange man, huh? Who's this strange man, and why does he keep poking me? They're not connected, so if something happens to the parotid on the left side, then the parotid on the right side should be unaffected. Oh, you're a cute one, yes. Yes, you're a cutie. Now I'm thinking she might have the mumps, because of the classic inflammation of the glands here, but that would be unusual because she's so young—oh, you're still a big girl, sweetheart, I see you holding your head up by yourself—because she's so young, and well, because there hasn't been a major outbreak of mumps in this country in over 30 years. I mean we're just a community hospital here. We get heart attacks, trauma, broken bones, drunks. Still, this looks an awful lot like mumps—a lot like mumps—so I'm going to leave you for a moment while I do some research. I'll do some double-checking. Then I'll be back, OK? I'll be right back.

Rubberneckers

When the doctor left, Karen and I tried to soothe the baby, who was starting to fuss. She was naked, so we diapered her, put back on her clothes, warmed a bottle of breast milk in the sink, and fed her. When she finished, I turned off the lights and tried to rock her to sleep in a sturdy old rocker in the corner. Just as I was starting to fall asleep myself, two men rapped on the wall outside our open examining room door. They wanted to examine my daughter, and because they introduced themselves as doctors, I let them. "Dr. Murphy is a fine physician," the one doctor said as he tilted my daughter's head to expose her swollen lumps to his colleague. "He'll give you excellent care." "Wow, would you look at that," the other doctor said. "It is presenting bilaterally." "You two haven't been out of the country recently, right?" the one doctor asked. "And when did you first notice the swelling?" the other one followed. The doctors, swift in their examination, were polite. Not until after they left did I realize they hadn't come to offer their expertise.

Discharge

The ER doctor sends us home. Tells us he's sending the baby's blood to a lab in Indianapolis. The lab in the hospital can't test for mumps, he says. We should just sit tight. Keep the baby away from other babies, and see our regular doctor if anything pops up. Something does pop up. The baby looks awful, like someone stuffed a pair of chicken eggs beneath her ears. We call our regular doctor and ask what to do. The regular doctor tells us to take the baby to the emergency room at the children's hospital. Don't come to me, she says. Go to Children's. If it were my kid, that's what I'd do.

Menagerie

The emergency room is not a room but many rooms. At an adult's hospital, the rooms might be numbered. Because we are at a children's hospital, they are named. We wait in Bumblebee. Burn babies wait in Bunny. Smash babies wait in Frog. Cough babies wait in Horse. Rape babies wait in Newt. Sniffle babies and ankle sprain babies wait with TV outside. NICU babies never have to wait because NICU babies are born here.

Flight of the Bumblebee: How It All Went Down
Triage
Nurse
Resident
Nurse
Rubbernecker
Rubbernecker
Rubbernecker
Nurse
Technician
Nurse
Attending
Nurse
Pack your things
Orderly
Rubbernecker
Nurse

Dirt Baby
Dirt Baby lives in the room next to ours. We can't yet tell if Dirt Baby is a girl or a boy. Dirt Baby has white-blonde hair and a bright red Kool-Aid goatee round its lips. Dirt Baby has a load in its pants. Dirt Baby can walk, it sure can. Dirt Baby walks and walks and walks and squeals like crazy when it's happy, which it is. Is it Dirt Baby who's sick? We don't know. Dirt Baby has countless brothers and sisters. Maybe it's one of them. Dirt Baby wears a diaper and a pacifier only. Dirt Momma calls it a plug. Where's that baby's plug, is what she says when Dirt Baby cries.

Ultrasound: I Can See Right Through You
An ultrasound technician named Tammy helps some doctor find

out if our baby has cancer. If fluid fills the lumps on her neck, we should be OK. If they're solid, she's doomed. We get to watch. We accompany our thirteen-pound child, hold her hand, rub her chest. We sing to her. The room we're in is dark. We see what we see courtesy of the bluey white glow of Tammy's flickery blinking and blooping ultrasound monitor. The baby cries so hard she shakes. Tammy presses the probe against the baby's lumps, promising she's being as gentle as possible. Karen weeps. Sometimes she squeezes my hand. It's hard not to think the worst. If the baby has cancer and dies, what will happen to us? Can we survive? Will we be destroyed? How do people go on living after the death of a child? Do they try? Should we try? We won't make it, I decide. Karen will leave me. Maybe I will leave her. That'll be hard. I like our life. I like my in-laws. We'll leave each other. That's what we'll do. I'm pretty sure there won't be, but I'll have to check and see if there will be any money if the baby dies. I don't think so. How could there be money? Why would there be money? I'll be destroyed. Karen will leave me or I'll leave her. We'll sell the house. I'll get an apartment, a room or a loft. I'll live by myself, try to lose weight, try to look younger. Should I start drinking? Could I do that? How sexy, I wonder, is self-destruction? I mean, I'll be single. Karen will leave me. I'll leave her, both of us destroyed. I'll have nothing. A shell. I'll need something to remember. I should consider a monument to the baby. A tattoo. Many. Big ones. A full sleeve. I could cover my arm, my right arm, in tattoos for the baby. I'll hire an artist. I'm thinking maybe something in the traditional Japanese style. Something with a lot of color, a lot of flair. Something that tells the story. Something that honors her, the baby who died.

Rounds

OK, the meat is female, four months old. Initial complaint, irritability and swelling in the neck. Mom and Dad say they noticed lumps five days ago. Brought the meat to the ER at St. Anthony's in Crown Point, Indiana. Initial diagnosis, mumps. Labs requested and the meat sent home and told to see the meat's pediatrician after the weekend. Pediatrician refers the meat to the ER at Children's. On 21 April 2007, meat is admitted. Meat has no medical history. Mom delivered vaginally without complications. Vaccinations up to date. No known allergies. No international travel. The household includes Mom and Dad. No siblings. Mom in advertising. Dad a journalist. Meat has been exposed to cats. Meat has no other complaints. Meat appears agitated. The masses are firm with limited mobility, tender to the touch. Initial CBC shows a high WBC count and low RBC count. We're waiting for the cultures to grow, and the ultrasounds indicate cystic rather than solid masses. In summary, the meat is a four-month-old female meat with blood and guts and bone and gore and meat and meat and meat.

America's Dog

Because she breastfeeds, Karen gets meal vouchers for the hospital's cafeteria. Every time the baby takes the teat, she gets five bucks. It's very big of the hospital to do this, I think, to reimburse us for the cost of breast milk. We don't take advantage of the vouchers at first. The cafeteria is a cafeteria. It sells cafeteria food. We don't eat there. Instead we dine at Chipotle, America's Dog, Noodles in a Pot, The Pasta Bowl, and The Spicy Pickle. We go out to get food or someone brings food to us. We eat together, Karen and me. We eat in our room when the baby sleeps. We eat with our parents and we eat with our friends and we eat by ourselves, we two. We bicker about what to eat and when. We no longer want to see another America's Dog. We liked Chipotle better when we were picking it up last-minute on the way home from work. Nothing good is open late. What would we cook with if we walked to the grocery? Sandwiches again, I see. They made it too spicy. The lettuce is wilted. The noodles are cold. I don't want the cookie. How can you eat that? How can you eat? Not right now. Not when she's under. Not that it matters, but the next one is free. Whatever you want. You chose the last time. You decide. You're taking forever. Make up your mind. I don't care. I just don't care. Pick up whatever. It's chicken or fish. It's lunch until three. It's Wednesday. It's pasta on Wednesdays. Here, use a voucher.

America's Cat

Papagena is going to cost us a fortune. The vet called today, and we are going to pay through the nose for good old Papagena. Papagena is sick. She has a bum thyroid, and we're going to pay fifteen hundred bucks for radioiodine therapy. Fifteen hundred bucks at a time like this! And we'll pay, yes we will. Papagena is Karen's first baby. They are tight, those two. Thick as thieves. They have a history. They go back, way back. Papagena goes further back with Karen than I do. Karen loves Papagena more than me. Karen saved Papagena's life. She pulled her out of a storm drain when she was a kitten. She was tiny back then—a little furry can of Coke, a cuddly avocado, a fuzzy wuzzy cell phone. She was a button, a doll. She was so very, very precious. She has never outgrown her squeaky, chirpy meow. She's still very kittenish. Cute as can be. Papagena saved Karen, too. Karen was lonely back then. She was homesick all by herself. She was miserable. Karen became Papagena's mommy, and she loved that baby up. Papagena is rambunctious, more so now than ever. She's been getting into everything. She tears up furniture and cries out at night. Before Karen made me take her to the vet, I told the old girl that I'd put her ass on the street. I picked her up and kissed her and squeezed her and said, "I love you, Papa, but you're too much kitty. You're too much, Papa. You're too much. It's not fair for this family to keep you all to ourselves. We need to share you with America, Papa. You need to get out among the people! Walk along the fence-tops and chirp hello to the people you meet." The vet says now that Papagena is sick. She needs a shot, a radioactive shot, and it's going to cost us a fortune. Fifteen hundred bucks! We're going to pay, all right. We're going to pay and pay and pay because Papagena was Karen's baby first. It's so important. I should know. I had a first baby, too. My first baby burned up long ago. My first baby is gone, baby, gone. Through a six millimeter Karman-type cannula went my baby. Suck, suck, suck! A Synevac Vacuum Curettage System sucked my baby all up. Into the collection bottle went my baby. Into the incinerator. Into the atmosphere! It was tiny back then, my baby—a precious suprême of tangerine, an adorable little diet pill, a red and yellow slimy dime. Oh, I paid for that baby, my baby, my baby-first-baby. I paid for the hotel and paid for the gas. I drove my girlfriend to the free clinic in Indianapolis even though the one in Chicago was closer. I paid for that baby. I used my mother's credit card. I told her I had an interview at Eli Lilly. That's what I said. I paid for that baby. I paid for that baby and I pay and I pay and I pay and I pay.

America's Birds

I spoke with my boss today. I needed to touch base with my previous life. Karen did, too. She went in to work to talk to some people and to pick up some things. Today I got to go to the paper. I caught up with coworkers. I checked my email and I made a few phone calls. I spoke with my boss. I described for him the hospital and I did my best to explain the baby's condition. I brought him up to speed. Because he is a writer, my boss asked what I had been reading. Because he is an asshole, he gave a few suggestions. There are a couple sick baby stories that I should be thinking about. There's one in particular that maybe I should read when I get a chance. Oh, it's a little ray of sunshine, that story. I bought it at the bookstore and I read it on the train. I'm glad I read it. It's super. It's the greatest thing. I am happy I got to read this story and not Karen. Karen's far too sensitive, and now is not the time. I am a lot more tough than she. I can take it. Of course, maybe I should go ahead and have her read it after all. It'd be something we could share together, something we could talk about. I could give her this story and say, "I think you should read this, honey," and because she loves me, she will. I'd be sure to give her some space, though. She won't want me watching over her shoulder when she reads, and besides, she'll need some room to crumple. She'll need a place to sob. I could watch her then. Wouldn't I feel powerful? Wouldn't I feel great? Maybe that's what I'll do. Maybe I can be the monster who writes about that.

The Angels of Mercy

Lydia talks like a baby around the baby.
Olivia is the rectal temperature queen.
Meghan will pull a double nine times out of ten.
Mary commutes all the way from Milwaukee!
Ludwika loves America.
Tina B. is a stitch.
Rachel does it by the book.
Janice is going to have a word with Dr. Modi's attending.
Tina J. went to high school with this guy on the Cubs.
Cora doesn't want to get married.
Dale started a squirt-gun war in room 719.
Jill is the best of the best but always leaves trash in the crib.
Wendy, sweet Wendy, can't believe we're still here.

Rainbow Dogs

They've been advertising the Rainbow Dogs on the walls by the elevators on every floor since Wednesday. The fliers say, "Don't Miss Rainbow Dogs! This Sunday from 10:00 to 11:00 am in the Brown Family Life Center on the fifth floor. Come enjoy the therapy dogs visiting the hospital on Sunday. Play with them, watch them perform tricks, and get your picture taken with your furry friend!" Beneath the announcement is a clip art picture of a smiling boy in a baseball hat and another clip art picture of a big, happy dog that looks like it has stars and rainbows shooting out its ass. I see these little fliers all over the hospital all week long and I get excited. I start expecting a show. I mean, the kids in here are sick. They're bored. They need some excitement. I figure there's going to be like six or seven Rainbow Dogs. I figure they're going to walk on their hind legs. Jump through some hoops. Maybe form a pyramid. You're not even allowed to go to the Brown Family Life Center unless you're a patient or a family member of a patient, so I'm thinking these Rainbow Dogs must be pretty special. Those Rainbow Dogs are coming, and I just know that they have to be good.

Chart
CBC
Ultrasound
MRI
Labs
Ultrasound assisted fine-needle aspiration
Intravenous antibiotic therapy
Fever! Fever! Fever! Spike! Spike! Spike!
Emergency
Surgery
Penrose
Wait

Scar Tissue
At the conclusion of the baby's final surgery, we're summoned to the office of her surgeon, Dr. Modi, who explained that he was finishing his fellowship and would be moving to accept a faculty position at Cornell. Before he had to go, he'd like to take some pictures. Do we mind? This would be our last time seeing him, and he'd like to add the baby's case to his portfolio. We agreed. We liked Dr. Modi. He'd been good to us, and anyway he was nicer than his boss, an unctuous little weasel who always gave the same introduction and told the same jokes. We watched Modi unwind the dressings around the baby's neck. This seemed to make him happy. Pleased with his work, he explained that the matching sets of inch-long scallop-shaped railroad-track stitches would dissolve and the remaining scars would be inconspicuous. We wouldn't be able to see them from the front, and once the baby grew enough hair, we might not be able to see them from the side. As Modi took his snapshots, I tried to divert Karen's attention. I started talking, wanting her looking at me and not the fresh surgical wounds on our daughter's neck. I told Modi I hoped he enjoyed his time in Ithaca. I hear the country up there is lovely. Everybody raves about those gorges. Dr. Modi looked up from his camera and said, "Thank you." He paused a moment, confused, and added, "Dad." I worked

with this man every day for six weeks. He cut my baby open. He once consoled my wife by saying these things sometimes happen and you must understand that it's not your fault, and we are here to help you, and everything will be OK. Dr. Modi fussed with a button on his coat. He couldn't remember my name. We adults sat together in silence. Modi tapped his fingers along the edge of his desk. "Anyway," he murmured, "Cornell's hospital is in New York."

The Greatest Show on Earth

Sunday, Rainbow Dog Day, finally comes. We go down to the Brown Family Life Center, and when we get there, there's one dog. He's a big fellah—standard poodle—but still. It's just one dog. The Rainbow Dog's name is Bruno. He has an ID badge with his name and picture on it and everything. Bruno's trainer, Jill, has one just like it. Hers says, "Jill Witwiki, Child Life Volunteer." Bruno's badge says, "Bruno, Therapy Animal." Jill says that everybody that works for the hospital has to have a badge, including animals. They had to get Bruno to sit up in a chair in order for his face to show up in the badge maker's field of view. Bruno's not allowed to sit on furniture at home, so Jill was a little conflicted about permitting the shot. Dogs don't understand the concept of making exceptions to rules. Jill grew up with poodles. Loves the breed. She has another poodle at home, Dixie, who wasn't cut out to be a Rainbow Dog. She visits nursing homes instead. She does better with the elderly, Jill says. Little kids make her jumpy. Bruno is an angel, though. He is big and sweet and well tempered. Bruno wags his tail and the baby eats it up. She has never seen a dog before. She was born in January, and we couldn't take her outside much because of the cold. Anyway, the baby goes nuts. Karen helps put her tiny hands on Bruno's ringlet fur, and goes on and on about what a good boy Bruno is, and what a pretty boy Bruno is, and how Bruno can come and visit us any time, and when he does come and visit us, he can have a bone. Jill smiles and looks around the room for other kids. She excuses herself and walks over to the family center receptionist. I look to Karen and frown. "I thought there'd be more of them," I say. "I thought they'd form a pyramid." Karen laughs. "I'm sorry, baby." "The Rainbow Dogs are lame," I say. Karen gasps and covers her mouth. "Not in front of Bruno!" She kisses the top of the baby's head and says, "Daddy's going to hurt Bruno's feelings." "Bruno can take it," I say. Karen harrumphs and makes faces at the baby. Jill returns. She smiles at our little family and says, "Why don't you join us in the sun room? I found some other children, and we're going to get started." Jill pats the head of her big blonde dog and says, "Come on, dummy." Bruno jumps up and follows her to the other room. Karen hands me the baby while she gathers our things and places them into the stroller. "Come on," she says. "Let's get this show on the road." I smile and nod to let Karen know that I'll be right behind her. I kiss my baby. I whisper into her ear. "We both know that there is no show," I say. "There's no silly show here. No show." The baby tilts her head back into my chest and smiles at me because I am talking to her. She's old enough to smile now for real, and that's incredible. "Come on, kid," I say, standing up. "I'll show you some excitement, OK? We're going to get out of here, and when we do, I'll show you some excitement. We'll see a show then, huh? We'll have some fun. You just stick with me. I will blow your mind, OK? I will show you a show."

HEARTLAND

Alexander Weinstein

MY SON IS DOING FANTASTIC UNTIL THE ELIMINATION ROUND. THEN he gets to the quiz questions and I watch him fall apart. His little face goes tight, the way it does near a barking dog, and he starts haphazardly punching the buzzer—not even listening to the questions. For a moment I want to bury my face in my hands, almost do, but then I realize it'd be me and not one of the other usual schmucks on TV crying. So I sit up straight and keep my eyes on Sam, trying to look supportive as I watch him lose ten thousand bucks.

There are papers to sign and hands to shake when the show is over, and then we're driving home. Sam's strapped into his booster seat with the *Scaredy Cat: Home Version* game in his lap. By now it's dark. Only 6 p.m., but Indiana's late October light is long gone. I hold both hands on the steering wheel and stare out at the headlights of the opposite lanes and the blackness of the clay fields around us.

Sam was a beautiful baby, which is what helped us land him the diaper ads, but ever since he turned seven he's become a normal kid. *Scaredy Cat* was his one big shot. The winner of the show always lands a TV ad, sometimes even an appearance on KidMTV. That's how Mindy Sands got so big. But that's never going to happen to Sam. He doesn't even know how to play an instrument.

Sam's been quiet the whole ride. He can feel when I'm upset. Finally he speaks, his voice small from the backseat. "Daddy, are you angry?"

"No," I say.

"I thought I knew the answers."

"Yeah, I know," and before I can stop myself I add, "but you've got to listen to the questions."

"I know. I'm sorry."

"I mean, you weren't even listening to the questions. You were just hitting the buttons."

"I was trying to listen. . . . I mean, I was . . . well, I mean . . ."

Then there's just silence. I look in the rearview mirror to see Sam staring out his window, tears falling down his cheeks. "It's OK," I say. It's too late, though. The darkness of the backseat is broken only by the passing bands of light from the overhead streetlights. In those momentary flashes I can see he's still staring out the window, crying.

I let out a deep sigh. "It's OK, Sam," I say again. "You did the best you could." Then I put on my signal and head for the exit, where I'll find a place to pull over and give him a hug.

At home Cara hasn't started dinner yet. She's got Laurie in the crib, where she's gumming the corner of my old iPhone. Cara's at the computer, uploading photos of our furniture and Sam's older toys on e-auction. "Hey," she says, clicking the screen onto her feed when Sam runs into the room. "I saw you on TV, little man."

"Sorry," Sam says.

"Don't be sorry, you were great. Was it gross to eat worms?"

Sam smiles. "Kinda. Sorta like spaghetti that kept wiggling."

"Ew!" she says, scrunching her nose, and gives him a hug. Over his shoulder she mouths to me, *other room.*

"Come on, Sam, let's go make some funny home videos," I say, so Cara can finish uploading the photos.

"All right," Sam says.

We do a couple classic knock-down gags in his bedroom: Sam standing on his tippy toes, trying to hit the light switch and falling back onto his ass, Sam jumping on the bed and falling off the edge.

Decent stuff that probably won't make the cut. As a reward, I let him play VirtuCube.

Cara's still on the computer when I walk into the living room. "Dinner?" I ask.

"Laurie *just* stopped crying and I've been nursing for the past hour. Let's order in pizza."

I feel the familiar flush of irritation beneath my skin. "I was hoping you'd cook for us."

"Yeah, and I was hoping you'd prepped Sam better for the quiz questions."

"Thanks, you've got a real gift for compassion." I walk into the kitchen to get a beer. Cara's up from her chair, following me. I open the fridge and take a Corona.

"I thought you were quitting."

That was our deal. She would quit coffee; I'd quit drinking. I pop the bottle with a lighter and toss the cap into the garbage under the sink, where we keep our bucket of compost. A swarm of fruit flies is buzzing in the murky darkness of sponges and Brillo pads. "Can't you at least take out the compost?" I say.

Laurie starts crying from the other room. Cara looks at me. "It's your turn to take her."

"Fine, I'll take her *and* the compost out."

I put my beer on the counter and sweep Laurie from the crib. I turn her so she's facing me, then go into the kitchen and crouch to get the bucket. Laurie begins to cry again.

"Give me her," Cara says.

"I've got her."

"She's not happy with how you're holding her. Give her to me." Cara puts her hands around Laurie and pulls her away. I'm left with the bucket of compost and the fruit flies. I take the compost, step outside, and slam the door behind me.

What's left of our yard is a mess from yesterday's rain. Ever since we sold off the topsoil, the clay makes walking treacherous. It's the same for every yard in our neighborhood. I put on muck boots and climb down the makeshift steps that Heartland Gardens put in when they carted our soil away; then I slog through the slippery clay to the corner of our yard where we're trying to make dirt. Blackened banana peels, old coffee grounds, and moldy vegetables sit in the wired-off compost pile. At this rate we'll have usable soil in a decade.

I hear Laurie still wailing inside. She's been wailing since she came into the world. Laurie was born with a stray eye. Minor corrective surgery would've fixed it, except minor corrective surgery when you're not covered means no minor corrective surgery. Which meant no baby commercials for Laurie.

I crouch down next to the compost and look up at the sky, which is covered by gray clouds. Seems like it rains every day now. When I was a kid, we used to have these long beautiful Indiana summers. Now we just have a drawn-out rainy fall—all year long. With the soil gone, it turns our backyards into clay pits. The clay runs off onto the streets, where it hardens between rains until the city comes and sprays the sludge into the sewers. I look at the telephone and electric wires cutting across our patch of sky, feeling like the whole world is coming down around me.

Cara is nursing Laurie when I come back in. I lean over the chair and give her a kiss. "Sorry," I say. "I just don't know what we're going to do."

"I know," she says. Her skin smells like apricot, a familiar smell that I'd somehow forgotten, and for a moment I feel our closeness. "Did you remember to take out the recycling?" she says.

The moment is gone. I force myself not to say anything. I'll just be an asshole, she'll get angry, Sam will see us fighting, and we'll all be miserable. I can't go there. Not tonight. I take out my wallet and put a twenty by the computer.

"What's this for?"

"Pizza for you and Sam."

"Huh?" she says, and looks at me.

I go into the kitchen and finish what's left of my beer. Then I put the empty bottle in our recycling bin, overflowing with bottles of biodegradable dish soap and empty cans of beans. "I'm going out," I say.

"*Going out?* I've been taking care of Laurie all day."

"Sorry," I say. "I need some time alone." I tote the recycling past her, through the living room to the front door.

"What about me? You ever consider I need a break, too?"

I'm already out the door, closing it behind me. By the time I get to the curb, I imagine she's going to be in the doorway yelling at me for the entire neighborhood to hear. Not that it matters. Most of the houses have been empty for years. The only houses with signs of life are at the end of the cul-de-sac, where blue recycling bins have been set out in the mud. But Cara doesn't come out. Not by the time I've separated the cardboard from plastics, not by the time I've gotten to the car and unlocked it, not even when I pull out of our driveway and leave.

The Shovel is located down 37, just north of Martinsville. It's fashioned to look like the interior of a potting shed, a real note of irony for all us who no longer have our yards. The walls sport fake bags of potting soil, shovels, hoes, chicken wire, and dirt-stained terra-cotta pots. Jim's sitting at the bar, waiting for me with a pitcher of stout in front of him. He's my only friend left from the old job.

"Tough night, huh?" he says, filling a second pint and pushing it in front of me.

"Every time I think I'm going to quit drinking, the fighting starts up again. That's all we do now: fight, fuck, make up, then do it again."

"At least you're fucking," Jim says, and lifts his glass. "Here's to quitting."

We clink and I take a sip. There's the familiar tang of alcohol against the tongue, the molasses sweetness of the stout. *Dream Girls* is on the flat-screen over the bar. One of the frumpy wives has undergone reconstructive surgery to appear identical to her husband's favorite movie star.

"I just don't know what's wrong with us," I say. "We used to have it good together. Now it's like we're not even a couple. I come home, I want to be with her, and she just hands me the baby. She thinks I'm an asshole. Maybe I am. Tell me the truth: I sound like an asshole, right?"

"Nah," Jim says, and takes a sip of his beer. "You just need a job, that's all. And you've got to learn to swallow your pride."

Which is true. One of the things I like about Jim is that he's not sentimental. I overthink things. Jim watches shows like *Dream Girls* and doesn't give a shit. "How are things at work?" I ask. "Same crew?"

"More or less. The kid who got hired after you got canned yesterday. Larry caught him stealing topsoil. Had his trunk filled with it."

"What a stupid way to go," I say, and realize we're both thinking the same thing. "You know, I was just standing up for my family."

"Forget it," Jim says, looking down at his glass. "It's history."

"What would you have done? Just smile at him and take it?"

"Don't know what I'd have done, but I sure as hell wouldn't have hit the boss," Jim says. Then he turns his eyes back to the TV. On the screen, the husband is making out with his reconstructed wife.

Jim's answer is more or less the same one Cara gave me when I told her what had happened. There had been a car issue that day; Cara needed it, so she dropped me off at work. Sam and Laurie were in the backseat. Larry had been out front, straightening lawn displays, and had seen Laurie. On my way inside to clock in he'd joked, "I think your baby girl was giving me the stink eye."

"What did you say?" I asked, turning to face him across the small square of lawn.

"Hey now, don't you start looking at me cockeyed, too," he said. That's when I hit him. There was no conscious decision about it— just this surge of heat and a streak of green beneath me. Then he was flat on his back and I was on top of him, driving my fist into his face. Jim said I was lucky I only lost my job. Cara said I was a fucking idiot. Which I guess was true, because we were already behind on our second mortgage. Still, it was one of the few things

I can remember doing in the past couple years that I actually felt good about.

"You think there's any way I can get back delivering?" I ask.

"Not a fucking chance. You're blacklisted from Fort Wayne to Bedford."

"It's been over a year."

"People remember. Only way you're gonna get a job installing gardens is to move."

"How am I going to do that? I can't sell our house in this market. We're lucky we still have it. You've seen Downtown Indy—tent city."

"That's what I'm saying, *move*. Leave it all behind. Start fresh."

"Move where? Michigan? Illinois? They're all sheets of clay." Jim doesn't answer. "You know, I thought we were going to have a break today. Sam was on—"

"Yeah, Fran told me what happened," Jim says. "Real sorry to hear it. Here, let me fill you up." Jim pours the rest of the pitcher into my glass. "You know, there are still some jobs in Kentucky— they've got patches down there. South America's got some green, places in Brazil."

"Brazil's finished."

"So try something new, switch professions."

"And do what? Nobody's hiring. Do you know how long the list is to even get a job at *this place*?" I say tapping the bar.

Above us, *Dream Girls* is finished and the news has come on. It's day nine hundred of the oil spill. There's a picture of the Pacific Ocean, black as soil, followed by photos of obsidian waves crashing against the California coastline. Hawaii is on fire. A company spokesman is standing on a freighter, saying he believes they'll be able to cap the underwater well by July of next year.

"God," I say. "This is really the end, isn't it?"

"Nah," Jim says. "People have been saying the world's gonna end for years. It never does."

"Yeah, but look at that." I point to the screen with my glass. "The land's gone, the water's going. The Northeast doesn't even have decent drinking water anymore. We're done for."

"That's just how it feels 'cause you're in the dumps. Fran and I still got it good. Plenty of people still got it good."

"Yeah, well, we don't have it good," I say, looking into what's left of my pint. The alcohol is hitting me now, dragging me downward. My brain feels like it's full of dirt. "I think we're going to lose the house by Christmas." Above us are rolling photos of the earthquakes in Chile, followed by the recent floods in Japan. I take a long swallow of beer.

"Listen," Jim says, "Fran and I were in a rough spot last spring. Nothing too serious, but cell phone, Internet, cable, 24/7 GPS, online gambling, those kinda things add up. . . ." He takes a sip of his beer and lowers his voice. "You know, you've got a couple of good-looking kids. Really good-looking kids. You ever consider putting photos online?"

I grimace as though my drink's rancid.

"Don't give me that look," Jim says.

I empty my pint glass, put it down on the counter, and face Jim, looking him square in the eyes. "There's no fucking way I'm selling my kids' photos to porn."

"I'm not talking porn," Jim says, "just pictures of them in the bathtub, Cara changing her diaper. Mild stuff, practically family photos. No big deal. Look, it wasn't my first choice either, but I know a guy—completely confidential—you email him the attachments, he sends you a check. You don't have to have any contact with his clients. Two hundred full frontal for boys, three hundred for girls. You get a shot of them together, he'd probably pay six."

"I'm not putting naked photos of my kids out there."

"Who's it hurting? So a couple perverts are willing to pay good money to see them—so what? We're talking a lot of money for a few snapshots. Sure, it's not what anybody wants to do—I didn't want to do it—but it got us through a tough spot. Look, nobody's gonna see the photos except whoever he sells them to. And I'll tell you something, the market will be flooded before you know it. A year from now, those pictures will buried in the Internet. You need money—this is where the money is."

"I'm not interested," I say.

"Ok, so you're not interested now, but at least let me give you his email in case you change your mind." Jim writes the address down on a napkin and shoves it in my shirt pocket.

"I'm throwing it out," I tell him.

"Do what you need to do," Jim says. "As for me, I'm treating us to another pitcher." Which is kind of him, and though I ought to pay, I just nod my head and say thanks.

Really, I shouldn't be driving, and for this reason I take the long back road home, up old 67. Out here on the forgotten highway, I'm alone in the darkness watching my high beams cut across the land and the great pits. Twenty years ago it was all cornfields out here—Indiana soil so rich, you could put anything in the dirt and it would grow. Then the companies came for the soil, followed by the clay, and finally the bedrock. All that's left are these pits, abandoned and sinking. They talked for a while of filling the canyons with water, turning the place into a second series of great lakes—private ponds for the rich to float their sailboats on and their children to Jet Ski across. Then the rich moved on—away from this endless stretch of exposed rock and dead earth. Maybe years from now, when we're all gone, some new creature will step forth on these canyons and gaze out at the abyss, never knowing there were once cornfields here.

The rains have started again. The drops splatter against the windshield and make the roads muddy. At one point the mud gets so bad, the wipers can't cut it and I have to pull over to the side of the road. I park beside the tall chain-link fence that separates the state road from the pits. I pop the trunk and take the squeegee from the back. The rain feels good against my skin, sobering, and I take my time, running the rubber blade against the glass and flicking the mud onto the road. Across from the pits, all the foreclosed houses are abandoned. The empty sockets of front yards, yanked from the ground like teeth, are filled with rain. It's kind of beautiful in the darkness, as though the neighborhood is floating. Soon it will be dawn and everything will be ugly, but for now there's an eerie radiance to the world. Perhaps it will be OK, I think. The earth will recover; the world won't ever truly end. Perhaps it will be green again someday. I put the squeegee back in the trunk and start on the road toward home.

There's a story I would like to tell to my children. In this story a boy meets a girl and they fall in love. They both have good jobs and enough money to buy a nice house with acres of land. There are old trees on their land—apples and pears, cherries and plums, blueberry bushes and grapevines. In the late fall, the grass gets sticky with the pulp of fallen fruit, and bees buzz amid the fermenting cores. The family makes pies and the children's fingers get stained from the blueberries, a light purple hue that remains even after their baths that night. In this home the parents love one another. Sometimes the children see their parents kiss and they feel embarrassed. They are good children, healthy and happy. They ride bicycles with other kids; they grow up, fall in love, and have children of their own who they bring back to the land. And at night, when the moon rises full above their home, the family goes to sleep to the sound of crickets chirping in the high grass.

In this story there is no car pulling into the driveway at 4 a.m., there is no father stumbling to the door as he struggles to find his keys. In this story, when the father goes into his son's room to make sure he's sleeping, he kisses the small boy on his forehead and tucks the blankets up beneath his son's chin, never considering, not even for a moment, rolling the blankets down past the boy's small chest, which rises and falls with every breath, where deep inside there's a heart that loves his father and trusts he will protect him against the monsters of this world.

A PURPOSEFUL VIOLENCE

Noley Reid

Twilight on Koressel Street was shrouded in a sulfuric haze of other families' fountains, Roman candles, glow worms, and bangers held tree-level by clouds that refused to move beyond the Ohio River. It was Fourth of July, 1951, and Noemi had told the boys "No bottle rockets," so they pouted and whispered in the living room inside a fort of couch cushions. They had swiped a box of matches and Jack lit one and passed his palm over it. Leo lit his own only to blow it out and light another again and again. Leo was older by ten months, but Jack was in charge. In the kitchen, T.E. watched Noemi work at the stove. Peas and potatoes in the Revere, meatloaf in the oven. He was a lineman, so she had wanted electric burners, saying he'd be able to fix them if they ever faltered. She walked barefoot in the house, always had, and the *shoosh* of her tan nylons across the linoleum was at once a reminder of her body and her rules.

"Back me up on this, please, T.E.," she said, stacking four plates next to the stove. "You never know where they'll come down, and they shoot so fast up into the sky."

The timer dinged then Ludlow, Ohio, went dark.

"Tonight?" came her voice, but he had already shut off the gas line and was heading up the stairs.

He had no clothes other than uniform tans, so he needed only his lineman's belt and pole strap. Noemi had him keep these under the bed. She appeared in the doorway, hands pressed behind her back, elbows like a bird on a nest. "Be careful," she told him.

That was fine.

He fit the belt high to his waist, tight so the bulk of the flashlight and snips, rubber-insulated gloves and spools would stay up.

"I'll do sparklers with them," she said.

"Do the snakes."

"They make such a mess. Will you hose it down tomorrow if we do?"

He touched her waist, kissed her, and smiled. "Yes, dear."

"Don't joke like that. You know I don't like it."

"Yes, I'll hose down the driveway if you do the snakes," he told her.

"You're always joking like that." She was working her way to something but he was content to leave it in the house with her.

He went outside to wait for the truck, stood down by the sickly redbud tree that deer ate half the trunk of years ago. Truth was, he loved blackouts. In all that darkness, the trick was to find something live.

He had loved linework ever since he trained in the Army. He tested into gunnery but couldn't keep his equilibrium at altitude, so he'd gone on to electrical. Suspended midair from a helicopter's bonding platform, current buzzed every inch of him in the hot suit. He used a thirty-foot hot stick on the EHV lines that towered over the training classrooms. He hadn't been in a hot suit since he served in Tunisia, but sometimes while tying off a mule tape that bundled neutral and primary lines with others, he could feel a dull prickling of current through the rubber over his hands.

Now Will Newsome and he drove out to the river, where the boys' school sat on the other side of an old stand of serviceberry, bog birch, sweetgum, and spruce. The county had put in electric poles alongside the tree line to plan for new tract houses in a year or two, so anytime there was an outage, T.E. and Will covered that area looking for hanging limbs or downed trees creating a short circuit. They each took a direction and walked the line.

Pops of silvery light sputtered in the distance. Rockets whistled through the air and he wished they were the boys'. Ludlow didn't have its own Fourth of July parade or fireworks, so most of the families had driven up to Zanesville just over an hour away. T.E. shined his light up onto the wire, following its drape from pole to pole. Branches, he couldn't tell what kind they were by the light of his flashlight, were still as statues beneath and above the lines. The trees were supposed to be gone, and that they weren't meant he and Will would be out here working more and more and Noemi would be wishing she'd stuck with the gas range.

Slowly he walked south, deciphering the branches that posed potential trouble to the lines. He saw nothing. Another spray lit behind him and he could tell this was a pin oak tree. The pole came up only a third of its height. A shame to lose that one, but the homeowners would plant more trees: willows and elms that they would keep out of the wires.

The air off the river was thick. Stale air he was surprised could compete with the growing sulfur cloud. Here, the leaves beneath his boots were soft, winter's fall but gone to mold. He thought about each silken leaf, the way it must tear with his step. Tearing along the veins. Another burst in the sky lit the ground and he realized that was where he was looking, though he still trained the flashlight up on the power line. To the east, a gold constellation streamed from the sky, lighting up enough ground to see he was now behind the boys' school. The leaves shone wet with rot. The dimming flash of western tree trunks seemed people receding from sight.

Low sky absorbed the cloud of smoke. Bottle rockets shrieked in the night. He thought of the boys and then Noemi with sparklers, pictured her writing her name with his in the sky. Without cause at all, T.E. moved his light down to the earth. There was something there. Ahead of him. It was the body of an animal, something dead and undisturbed. Big like a dog or a deer. His light was meant to travel a tenth of a mile, was too bright. So even standing over the thing in the leaves, he wasn't sure.

He switched off the light, but the sky lit green and so was the little girl's face: sick green skin bruised and bloodied, her mouth a silent ocean of scream and dirt.

*

"What if we wear Dad's goggles," Jack said. "Then we can't lose an eye." He pressed his fingertip into one of the half-thawed peas Noemi had served thirty minutes after the lights went out. Not only didn't it squash but he lifted his finger and it stayed there, stuck to his skin for a moment.

"He only has one pair," said Noemi.

Leo got a pea to stick, too, one per finger. He held up his hand, appeared to conduct a symphony before shaking them off like mud from a dog.

"You'll pick those up and wash the floor before bed," she told him.

"He started it," said Leo.

"Then you'll *both* sit there till you're finished." Noemi took the candlestick from the table so they could no longer see just how much frost remained on their supper. She set it aside on the buffet then went in the kitchen to watch the sky, hear its distant crackling. T.E. stood outside the screen door. She could see his head and it was funny.

"I didn't hear the truck," she said. Through the door now, she saw him. He was naked. Not boots or belt. Nothing. "My land. What are you doing—come in!" She tried to push open the door but it knocked in to him. "Tandy," she said.

He did not move.

Noemi reached an arm through to help guide him around the swing of the door just to get him inside.

She stood before him in the middle of the kitchen but it didn't occur to her to touch him. This looked like a game. She could not touch him. When she looked, he was like a stubborn boy before a bath, hands at his sides, feet still. Her voice was tight and high. "You'll scare the boys," but they were away at the table until she would relent and dismiss them for bed.

He moved forward, went straight to his knees. Leo's and Jack's voices hushed. At first she stood over T.E. She did not know what to say or do. This sweaty, hairy man she'd loved enough for twelve years. His shoulders were wet, the muscles of his chest bright under the fluorescent. This man who swam the winter Ohio to save a favorite photograph of her. No matter that she'd thrown the picture in on purpose; no matter her tantrums. Now he knelt before her and so, chewing at half of her lower lip, she held him. A naked man. And the stench of his body was sweet like fire.

"Tandy," she said, and finally he looked up.

"There were all the firecrackers," he said. "Behind the school. I looked down and there was something."

He kissed her lips and she could feel a spark there, a bit of that lightning.

"I thought it was a dog."

His skin was not cold. She kept expecting it to grow cold. She touched his shoulder, his thigh, his cheek. No raised flesh, no chill. His cheeks were red like a burn failing to heal.

The boys weren't talking in the dining room. There was a naked man and maybe they could sense it. What a strange night this was.

"A dog?" she asked.

"A girl," he said. "A little baby. And she was dead."

It wasn't until two policemen came to the door later in the evening that he spoke again. Noemi went to get him clothing. She'd gotten Jack and Leo to bed finally and stood at their door wanting a do over because maybe if she'd let them have the bottle rockets, T.E. would have kept his eyes on the electrical lines, and Leo wouldn't be too afraid to cry. She took down trousers and a blue oxford, undershorts and socks.

One of the officers said, "It would sure help if you had seen anyone around the area."

"Why are their peas on the floor?" said T.E.

They sat at the dining room table. T.E. left the pile of fresh clothing in front of him, picked at the peas on the boys' forgotten plates. "She wasn't covered."

"Did you touch anything?" said the other. "Uncover her?"

"No," said T.E. He stopped eating. "Nothing."

"Right," said the first to Noemi. "We have to ask." And they left.

*

Once T.E. had told Noemi, he was sorry. He couldn't explain it, this sense that he'd been supposed to find the girl. Something like fate cleaning up the shit done by others, not that he could do anything that night or now, but he could think about that dead baby and respect her.

He stopped sleeping. He'd lie next to Noemi listening to how deep her breathing could go. How far in she could take herself away. He couldn't fault her for that. He didn't want to.

He stopped working. Went on a sort of disability from the union. Two stray albino cats appeared and he fed them. Tuna straight from his fingers because he liked the wet of their noses and the way they shook the hunks of meat to the backs of their throats. He went for walks. Long and longer walks. Through the neighborhood. Skirted the town, then past Crestview Trailer Park where the homes could blow away and a person could disappear completely leaving no trace. Then on past the rows and rows of new tract houses, Ludlow's own Levittown. One evening, when the boys were pirates in the tub and Leo refused to make his brother walk the plank, Noemi said, "T.E., you've made him go soft and the world will crush him." T.E. walked until Jefferson Memorial and dusk, and he was not surprised to arrive there.

He had not seen these woods in natural light since long before the Fourth of July. The ground dipped lower beyond the electric poles. Down he moved, down closer to the trees. He no longer watched the wire slung pole to pole. His eyes were in the leaves, the mounds and flat spaces.

Nearer and nearer until he saw there was a woman there at the edge of the trees. He stood back in the cool of this woodland watching her, listening to every breath as shallow as his. The woman wore an overcoat—in July heat she held it shut around her middle. Her hair was shoulder-length, black, a loop of bangs curled under like Noemi wore hers but this woman was not pretty like his wife. Disproportionately wide through the hips, her legs thick to her shoes, graceless in her movement. And when she turned and he saw her face, it was permanently and rawly ugly in a way he could not imagine as only recent. A pair of cardinals alit high in the woods, some color to this early evening's shade. The woman knelt down in the moss phlox at the base of one tree, one spruce where it looked as though a bleating doe had lain down to birth or to die. But that wasn't the tree. Not that one.

T.E. stepped forward into the light of clearing that was the spot. He knew who this woman was. There had been photographs: of the house the girl had been taken from, of the parents. He had no right to the girl or any grief going on here but he could not leave.

"You," said Kay when his feet came near enough the leaves.

He followed her onto the school's property, behind the playground and field where he knew Jack knew how to catch a football and run as fast as blood could push air through his lungs.

When they reached her black Nash, she sat inside it, filling the space of the cabin in a way Noemi never would let herself. Kay looked right at him and was not afraid. She drove. He didn't take his eyes from her as she made the turn away from the school. Past the trailers, past the streets of town and the lanes of Ludlow-proper where he lived, out beyond and up to Route 83. She pulled in to Ludlow Auto Lodge. She waited, stood at the first room's door while he paid $7.00 in the office for a key. Wrapped in her coat and her arms, fireflies lit and went out around her, she even shivered.

They lay on their backs atop the coverlet, arms at their sides and hips touching. He didn't kiss her. They didn't embrace. They still had their shoes on. They closed their eyes and neither one of them undressed—not even her coat—or made effort to push aside clothing, but it happened and when they were through fucking and lay again flatly beside each other, he heard her voice for just the second time. "What did she look like?" it said.

Eyes still closed, he could feel her rearrange the skirt of her dark blue dress. Her stockings were strangely woolen; they had chafed the crooks of his arms. He felt the burn there now, the sting of his sweat overtop panic. "Sleepy," he said. "Sleeping."

The mattress gave around him for she was sitting up and her heels touched the floorboards with a tap just like Noemi's whenever she slipped into them at the front door. Kay left the room, left the parking lot, who knows where she went, he didn't.

The next evening Noemi sent the boys up to their bedroom to bring T.E. down for supper.

"Daddy," said Jack and Leo, storming in on him where he sat at the end of the bed. There was a clothlike brown leaf next to T.E. but the boys didn't see it and when Leo jumped up to drive his favorite milk cart horse along the comb grooves of his father's Brylcreemed head, T.E. grabbed hold of both his upper arms and threw his son hard to the floor.

"What's wrong with you?" he said, standing himself. He had spent hours smoothing a crease from the veins of the leaf and now it showed again.

Leo nursed a knee scuffed by the floor, then ran his horse in place atop the pink scrape. He kept his eyes there, on the horse's hooves running the white line of skin rolled back from the curve of his knee.

T.E. handed the leaf to Jack to see what would happen. The mean was crawling all throughout him now. Yes, it was purposeful what he did, and when Leo's face worked hard to hold still, to not give sorrow its place, T.E. felt different. "You neither, Jack," he said and took the leaf away. "Go on down," he told them. "Go tell her I don't want a thing."

That evening, Kay's gray woolen stockings were oversewn with lumps of thread where a run might have started. Before shutting his eyes, T.E. saw these patches like scabs around her knees and ankles and all he could see behind his eyelids was the baby's blood and bruising.

Again, neither one of them took hold of the other, neither one seemed to manipulate clothing or flesh but, eyes shut, their bodies somehow came together in a fold of seeing and not seeing. "What did she look like?" Kay asked again, once they came apart. "Did you listen for breathing? Did you touch her? What color were her eyes— they can change depending."

"The leaves were last year's, from winter. They were what I was stepping on. I couldn't hear them—that's how soft they were." He placed his leaf upon her belly, death covering up where the life began. "They were in her hand. There were leaves in her hand. Just one hand."

Grief racked her body and he meant only to hold her then, but instead they fucked and when they were through with this new, purposeful violence, their breathing slowed and they finally slept.

It was days more before she asked him what the other hand held.

Days and nights more until the sheets cascaded to the floor and the bed's casters scuffed the boards beneath. "Her own mouth," he whispered then. "Full of dirt."

No one in Ludlow, Ohio, believed Tandy "T.E." Parsten was anything more than the poor sap who stumbled upon the body—not the cops, not the grocers or the little old ladies, not even the kids at school, but the *Courier*'s articles—"Mother of Baby Dinah Takes Comfort Where She Can" and "Affair to Shed New Light on Murder of Baby Dinah?"—months after, surely made them resent their sympathy. It was pure insinuation, nothing built on any of the reckless facts neither of them attempted to hide.

Noemi never told T.E. to move out. And they never spent a single whole night in any other bed. He seemed even to believe she understood. But a lump in his throat grew and it was cancer. After his surgery, Noemi sat in the waiting room. Kay came. She sat next to Noemi. She'd never seen T.E.'s wife, of course, but the paper had run the same sad photograph of Kay with Dinah blowing out last year's candles; Noemi certainly knew who she was, this frowsy sack of a woman.

"I'm sorry for your loss," Noemi said, looking right in to her eyes, as black as her hair.

Kay's lips parted as if she would speak but nothing came out, not even air. She tucked the ends of her scarf inside the lapels of her coat. September was trapped inside the hospital walls, and Noemi fanned herself with a *Family Circle*.

Noemi placed the magazine atop her lap, conscious of the pleats of her dress, conscious of the precision in the way her knees touched together. "You have a choice here," she whispered, studying the pointed triangle her skirt made in sitting. "One of us is going to take him home and nurse him. The other is going to leave and that will be the end of it. I have two boys by Tandy, but I suppose that's not what really matters." She touched Kay's hand. It looked like Leo's, with the ragged cuticles and chewed nails. "Tell me, please, do you love him?"

Kay was quiet. They watched the end of the hallway where doctors converged on the nurses' station. Two orderlies wheeled a gurney by their room, then left it and the patient atop, to speak with one of the nurses. It was hard to tell if the patient was alive or dead. He did not move. The sheet was up to his nose.

"I'm always so cold," said Kay. "Just always so cold." And she left.

Doctors performed a radical neck dissection on T.E., snaked and shimmied the lymph nodes right on out with forceps and a scalpel—that was how Jack thought of what his mother told him. She only talked to Jack. "Leo, well, he's so sensitive," she'd say. So now the boys' father was coming home like none of the other business happened at all. He would surely come walking through that door, scoop both of the boys over his shoulders, and holler at their mother that he never wanted to go out walking again. And maybe that could work just fine, since the *Courier* had finally stopped writing about the dead girl.

This morning, there was a tray with cereal bowls and a pitcher of milk on the floor by the bunk beds. Jack woke up to the clinking of Leo's spoon. They hadn't seen their mother at home—she'd leave early and be gone until late. Even when they vowed they'd stake out the window, they never made it. All week long she had been telling Jack what was going to happen, that Daddy's cancer was still bad in his throat and mouth, that no one knew why, but he'd be just fine. Jack carried that.

Leo didn't carry anything anymore, left his milk cart carriage horses lying around the house. Jack had stepped on one last night getting into bed and his heel still ached. He turned up his foot now and, sure enough, there was the pink welt. He nursed it, rubbed the pad of his heel. He called up to the top bunk, "She said he might die." It wasn't true, that she had said so, but Jack said it nonetheless.

Leo's face appeared over the side of the bed, a rug hung out to beat.

Jack slid a finger lengthwise down his throat and watched as his brother's Adam's apple moved down, up, down. So now Jack scaled his throat lengthwise and made like he was peeling back the sides, like curtains. He practically reached his entire hand inside his neck and felt around, started pinching bits of skin between his fingers. Leo went vomitous-pale. Jack's hand became what he sometimes dreamed, the doctors taking pieces of their father like souvenir shelling at Euclid Beach. He yanked at *Leo's* neck.

"Stop it!" Leo said, swatting at the fingers. "What *is* that?"

"Forceps," he said, letting go. "Tongs."

Leo shuddered. Spittle shook off his lips down onto Jack's quilt.

"Eee-ooo!" said Jack. And Leo, his face, still stricken, disappeared. "He won't," said Jack. There were ladder steps hooked over top the cheap maple frame. Jack kicked them to get his brother's attention. "He would have already."

Leo's curls made him look like a dog sometimes, the way they matted and snarled. That's what Jack saw when his brother looked at him wishing, wishing Jack wouldn't always try to push him off a ledge. But that was a big green monster under the bed and when the lights came on or early autumn sun filled the windows she wasn't there to draw curtains over, who could blame an eleven-year-old for feeling normal. Even so, Jack suspected there was a time before now and a time beyond now and they were entirely different places.

There they sat waiting on Leo's bunk. Jack rubbed his heel until it turned white. Leo poked a finger into the indentations from a horse ear. "Jesus, quit it!" said Jack. Leo laughed through his nose in and out like he wasn't himself. They settled in to the quiet, waited there until they heard the front door. Leo slipped his hand inside Jack's. They went extra slowly down the stairs.

Their mother looked taller through the spine, her arms longer and bowed out like a swallow flying. She stepped out of her pumps, click-clack, then gathered Jack and Leo to her sides. There was a stranger coming.

"Please don't stare," she told them. "Don't you break your Daddy's heart."

The boys nodded.

"There's one thing more," she said, whispering. She bent down, tugged a curl that hung down loose above her ear, and brushed it twice across her jaw line. Up she stood. "You should know, they took his whole tongue."

She spun back around to him so all they could see through the front door was the swing of her dress. "Let me, T.E.," and she reached for his elbow. She tried to help him in because something about lymph nodes made you weak when they were gone. Jack took one of his father's hands too, said, "Hello." Leo was right next to his brother, and they all looked at this sickly man to see what would he say.

Their father's entire face was twisted. Like if you took hold of the center of someone's face, the nose Jack supposed, and just started twisting all their skin: lips and cheeks clear out to the ears—one of his was practically sitting on his cheekbone now. Gauze encased the front and sides of his neck, and at their base an inch of putty-colored tube hung down. Alongside the bandage, his skin was gouged, pink and slick in jagged paths.

"Jack," said their mother. "You take these." So now Jack had a collection of paperwork and a crossword puzzle in his hand, her purse too, which he set down fast. She walked their father on down the hall to the living room and his couch and Leo and Jack followed to say it was them made it up for him.

Jack said, "Here," and handed him the papers and puzzle.

"Go on now. Daddy's tired," said their mother and she shut the door.

She stayed inside. Jack and Leo waited there in the hallway for her to come out. They wanted to know everything. They needed to be sure this was fine. That going in for cancer and coming out clean, that that meant everything else was healed, too. Just like he'd been a cable splicer with the 141st Signal Corps but come back whole.

Leo slipped to the floor and sat there. "You owe me a nickel."

"Huh?"

"Fair and square. You owe me a nickel."

"He came back," said Jack, disagreeing.

"Not all of him."

Jack stared at Leo. A kid in his class drowned and died at a birthday party. Jack and Leo had been eating orange sherbet. The boy's mother started crying on him and he coughed up all the water. After that, Leo pooped his pants the next time their mother served sherbet at home.

"Just go away, please," Jack said. He kicked at his brother's legs until Leo left.

Within the living room, Noemi positioned T.E.'s things on the coffee table—he was Tandy only when things were good and she was certain he wouldn't mind hearing his real name in her mouth.

"We'll start fresh," she said. She lifted his feet and stacked two pillows beneath them. She smoothed the sheet the boys had merely draped across the back of the couch, tucked its hem down behind the cushions. "I understand you," she said and meant to say more.

T.E. had been looking out the window since coming in the room. He hated this room. But he was weak, couldn't lift his left arm higher than his hips and his right not higher than his waist. Of course he had to live downstairs. Now dark was coming across the yard: the laurel and boxwoods, the berried hollies outside, all were in shadow. A lip of sunset held the clouds like blankets to a chin, but the sky would be thick any moment and the little china doll lamp's reflection would make it all disappear. He was glad for that. She would go away soon, too. There were the boys to think of.

"Just . . . ," she began, "don't ever talk."

She took away the pencil and folded newspaper Jack had carried. It was his puzzle but he didn't protest. He began to ease himself down to the couch, which was lower than the hospital bed. Noemi cupped his elbow and took on his weight to help him slowly down.

"We have you back now," she said. "Keep the rest to yourself." She dropped the paper and pencil into the wastebasket.

Now, Noemi stood in her kitchen all these months later wondering how she had got to here: fluffing his pillow, mopping the drool tangled at the edge of this grotesquery's mouth where it pooled and crusted. The discharge nurse had warned against letting it collect, said Vaseline would keep it from rashing in the night, but it must be tended to in the day. Daily, Noemi collected stray homework pencils and pens the boys forgot and snapped them in half for fear of her husband finding a way to speak.

He wasn't even going to die now.

As she filled fresh water in the white Corning bowl she had always mixed frosting in, and folded clean cloths—one dry, one in the water—she considered what she always considered, fantasies she would never commit: dirty rags, urine-filled water from those awful cats he made hang around the house, a dirty Kotex rinsed clean and pressed to his lips in the dark.

She called to the boys, "Take this to Daddy." She held out the dry cloth to Leo but he walked away, went back upstairs without a word.

The other boy came forward. "I'll do it," he said.

Jack pushed open the door to the living room. There sat T.E., lengthwise on the sofa, Ohioan Family Sweepstakes booklets across his lap. He tapped at the page of stamps Noemi had brought for him today.

There was nothing else now. And never would be.

A layer of fuzz encased his thinking, made dull and soft the pain in his neck and mouth. Noemi concocted gray puddings he ate with a special plunger spoon that shoved the food down his throat. The drains oozed putrid stink. But his tongue, his tongue moved through the vowels of each word they said around him. Until they stopped talking, which they always did, and then his phantom tongue slipped through numbers and alphabet cycles. If it ever stopped moving—when he lay in the dark on this couch at night listening to the boys whispering and Noemi's footsteps coming halfway down the stairs—then he felt its absence and what the absence of his tongue felt like was the same as gauze stuffed to capacity, was a gulp of water when he needed air, was a mouth full of screaming.

He gave himself—what there was left of him—over to this life. There was no alternative. In his hands, he held the sweepstakes booklet. It may as well be a winner, there was no meaning left anywhere in the world. He had to get all the blue stamps on the blue page, yellows on the yellow, like that. Jack held the bowl for him. That was one good thing, what change in Jack there'd been.

"Take it, Daddy." Jack gave him the fresh bowl and picked up the one on the carpeting. Barely a wisp of reflection in that one, he'd sucked the cloth dry. "Put it in your mouth." He looked away, out the window to nothing in particular.

His father took the dry cloth and held it to the side of his face, blotted the spit. Then he squeezed out enough water not to drip on the sweepstakes letter and envelope. He unfolded the cloth, tucked a corner between the edges of his mouth. Sometimes Jack wasn't sure where the pieces of his father's face would be when he looked; they seemed to move and never be where he expected them. The twist of his cheeks and nose and chin collapsed his lips inward so that they were nearly gone. Jack felt a duty to check because his father was sort of like having a puppy now. The lips were still there and Jack felt better, good enough to fill the booklet with stamps.

His father pointed at the blue, yellow, green stamps on the page, then at the empty pages in the sweepstakes booklet. He gave the page to Jack who began folding at the perforations.

Jack's mother came in. "You mustn't keep too much in your mouth at once," she nagged. "You know that, Tandy."

It could pool and sitting upright without a tongue, he'd have no way of swallowing it down. She'd warned Jack to keep watch of their father. She took the cloth's edge from his cauliflowered mouth, set it back in the bowl. "Every few minutes," she said, "or if you feel you're going to cough."

Just saying the word made a gagging terror creep up T.E.'s throat. He bit what lips he had left and shut his eyes until the cough passed. A sudden coolness on his chin reminded him to wipe the drying cloth there.

Jack held up the booklet and all the stamps were pasted in. Every page full. T.E. checked the letter again: *Simply purchase enough of the following products to fill the pages of this book. Every booklet is a winner. That's right, every booklet!* It was something.

Jack turned eleven that December and Leo tried to give him his milk cart horses. When February came, Leo turned twelve and enough time had passed that his mother made a sugar-dusted cake. She hid a fancy Wham-O slingshot beneath his father's couch's cushions. "Go find it," she said but Leo only stood in front of the couch blinking.

His father patted the cloth over his mouth, the skin of his hand so thin it looked like it had been cooked. Leo wanted to help his father, or crush him.

"Fine," said his mother, reaching behind the cushions and giving him the slingshot.

Leo never set it down. He stayed out of the house as much as he could, aiming mostly at basement windows already cracked by bigger neighborhood boys. Kids at school had forgotten their father, the girl, her mother, and the real man who took the baby. Leo hadn't. March came. His father began leaving the living room door open. April. He reclined on the patio chaise-longue, his bowl and cloths in his lap. May. The cats came back around, flicking their pointed white tails. Once Leo stood behind his father in the kitchen, startled to stillness at seeing him up and about, and watched as T.E. ransacked the drawers and, finding nothing, finally pressed his thumbnail to the paper to write what Leo later saw was TUNA.

On the last day of school in June, the boys came home to an empty house—his mother had taken a job at the town library after wages and IBEW Local 683 short-term disability ran out. They pushed through the front door and it was as though neither one of them had been aware it was summer again. That day, heat and sun made the world yellow. The cats nosed out of the bushes next door. Leo picked up a rock and aimed but it didn't hit either one. They walked Korressel to Lynch, Lynch to Prescott, Prescott to Dade. There was T.E., head on knees, sitting winded at the edge of somebody's yard.

"Dad," Jack called out and ran to him. Leo hung back.

T.E. looked up. He pointed to his chest, pointed to the road. His knot of a mouth nibbled at a gray cloth. He set it back down in the frosting bowl made luminous in afternoon sun. His breathing had calmed by now but he still didn't move. He seemed to be waiting for them to leave. Leo picked up a dusty piece of gravel broken away from the edge of the street. He fit it to the band of his slingshot and pulled the rubber taut.

"Jack," he said. "Watch this." And he aimed at a street-parked, brand new Buick LeSabre's hubcap and let go. The rock skidded beneath the car, and before picking up another, Leo turned back to look at his father, to be sure he was right: he could do anything.

T.E. swatted the air. He swatted and swatted, pointed to them and then the direction home. Go on, he wanted to scream. His chin dripped and the spit stung where he'd nicked himself trying to shave the deepest twist of skin beneath his lips. He held the dry cloth to his jaw. It was damp and sour smelling now because he'd been at this walk so long. The boys just stared at him. Jack's hands shrugged in his pockets. Leo had the look of a child wearing a grown man's shoes.

"*Unnnnnhhh,*" came out of T.E., the monstrous sound he never believed was his own. It didn't sound like a deaf person or a moron—what it sounded like were these impersonated by someone fully normal.

He waved both of his arms now and Jack and Leo both took off running. Adrenaline lifted and carried his body. He walked and walked, dabbed the cloth to his chin, looked away when cars passed to save them the horror.

*

The damage that had been cut through T.E.'s neck held his head nearly in place. His eyes strained to follow the black wire strung pole to pole. He used to drive this road in his bucket truck. Its electric lines often failed. Something about the narrowing of Dade Avenue out far enough to where the asphalt changed to red dirt and rock. The newer lines always needed something. He and Will would have had to open and close switches, replace fuses, locate the source of the current's sag. He walked the stand of scrub pines that edged the yards.

Babies were always crying and there were always babies—though none cried now—but when he stood square at the gravel drive of a small, moss-stained clapboard house, he was certain he'd long ago worked in her yard along with the dark of night and only candles within the houses. He was certain he had heard the girl, the baby, crying long before that night.

He arched his spine backward to look at the sky. No sycamores, no poplar trees here, no spruces either. June sun beat the shingles so black they looked soft, molten. A car passed by and somewhere beyond a backyard, a screen door tapped shut in its frame three times. He knocked at the door.

Kay appeared, looking around his body to the other yards more than at him. She took his wrist, then the bowl and drying cloth, which he'd held with both hands.

You still wear sweaters, he wanted to say.

"I cannot help you." But she was drawing him in to the house.

She pushed aside a cheap empty dish meant maybe for candy, set down the bowl on the hall table, turned back to him and studied his face. She had never seen him like this. T.E. dabbed the drying cloth to his chin to catch the drool and cover the worst.

It's like a mouth full of dirt, he needed to say, like I have a mouthful of dirt.

"Please don't show me that again," she said.

It didn't matter that this was a mistake, a colossal mistake now; he was doing it. His head floated above them from the effort of his walk and her words. He seemed to watch his free hand pull her body to his, his free hand unzip his trousers, his free hand lift the heavy folds of her winter skirt and penetrate the shadows beneath the hang of her abdomen. Against the hall table, his bowl sloshing the inch of water that remained, Kay's eyes were shut.

Open them, please. Please open your eyes, he could not say.

So he pushed her, fell with her to the floor, one claw-foot of the table catching her button earring and tearing it free. He never knew her ears were pierced. He'd never seen that. Her ear bled and his prick went soft but he kept thrusting at her, until all it was was pelvic bone to pelvic bone and the abrasions of force.

She did not stop him. She did not try. She only cried, and that was a voice he knew, too: sorrow turned rage turned back to desperate grief. How many times had he been sick thinking about how long she'd lain there wanting to breathe right.

He'd walked in the house three minutes prior and now what he hoped was that their brief and last noise would bring someone. A neighbor, an aunt. The husband with a gun to shoot him, shoot him please. Another child with all her teeth unbroken.

But evening fell around them with moon and owls hooting. Kay still lay partially beneath him, though free enough she could move if she tried. T.E.'s penis hung out of his pants, no longer wet from Kay's body, just cold and obscene.

He sent his mind back up to the ceiling, to the sky now. Told it to travel Dade to Prescott, Prescott to Lynch, Lynch to Koressel. To leave the frosting bowl and Noemi's rags here. To slip back inside the house, his house, that kitchen. Let the drool pour from the twist of his face, let Leo turn bad with it, let Jack be the one soft now as dough. Let Noemi follow him upstairs and let him tell every single second of this past year to her through the pressing of his unclean skin to hers. Filth would be his words, the soil and leaf mold would be his tongue. And she, Noemi, would learn every word of its scream.

LESSONS

Laura van den Berg

1.

THERE ARE FOUR OF THEM.

Dana, Jackie, Pinky, and Cora are cousins. Pinky is also Dana's little brother. They call themselves the Gorillas because all gangs need a name—see Hole-in-the-Wall Gang, Stopwatch Gang, Winter Hill Gang—and also because they wear gorilla masks during their hold-ups. They are criminals, but they still have rules: no hostages, small scores, never stay in one town for more than a week. It's late summer and they're roving through the Midwest, from motel to motel, making just enough to keep going. Dana watches the impossibly flat landscapes of Lafayette and Oneida pass through the car window and wonders how they all ended up here. Why didn't they go to school and get regular jobs and get married and live in houses? The short answer: they are a group of people committed to making life as hard as possible.

Cora says they need to think bigger. No more knocking over delis and drugstores and dinky banks. They need to do a real heist. There are millions to be made, if they could just grow some balls. Jackie has simpler desires. She wants a boyfriend and a set of acrylic nails. Pinky is thirteen and wants to build a robot. Dana is more about what she doesn't want, as in: she doesn't want anyone to go to jail or die.

In L.A., a gang of female bank robbers have been making headlines. They wear Snow White masks and carry semi-automatics. Witnesses have reported them doing tricks with their guns during heists. They're rumored to be retired Romanian acrobats. Naturally the press loves them. They've been nicknamed the Go-Go Girls.

"Why aren't we ever on TV?" Cora complains one night. They're in a motel in Galesburg. They have plans for the Farmers & Mechanics Bank on Main Street. Dana lies on one of the musty twin beds; her cousins are curled up on the other. Cora is green-eyed and lean with cropped auburn hair, like Mia Farrow in *Rosemary's Baby*. Jackie is shaped like a lemon drop. Her dark, wide-set eyes remind Dana of a well-meaning cow. Pinky is working on his robot in the bathroom. He's been collecting materials from gas station and motel dumpsters: pins, wires, batteries, little black wheels. Earlier Dana stood in the doorway and watched him screw two metal panels together. He sat cross-legged on the floor, his lips puckered with concentration. The overhead light flickered and buzzed. The spaces between the shower tiles were dark. She'd never seen him work so hard on anything before.

"Those are the kind of people who end up in shootouts with the police," Dana tells Cora. The Go-Go Girls have just stolen two million in diamonds from a bank in Beverly Hills. Dana picks up the remote and changes the channel to a cooking show. A woman is finishing a dessert with a blowtorch. Dana closes her eyes and listens to Pinky rattle around in the bathroom. Did they want a shootout with the police? She considers the Dalton Gang and John Dillinger. Is that what they want, to bleed to death on the street? The room is hot. The smell of burning rubber wafts through the bathroom door. No, she decides. No it is not.

There is a river in Elijah, Missouri, that always appears in her dreams. They all grew up in Elijah. In this river they learned to float. Dana would stare up at the clouds and imagine they were spaceships or trains. In this river they would dive and search the bottom for smooth, flat stones. In real life it's a slender, slow-moving river, but in her dreams it's as wide as the Mississippi and silver, as though it's made of melted-down coins. From the shore she sees a raft with no one on it. She wants to get on the raft, but doesn't know how.

That night she wakes sweaty and breathless. She sits up. Pinky is next to her, asleep on top of the covers. He's rangy and sharp-elbowed. His arms are folded under his head. His mouth is pink and sticky from chewing Red Hots. She touches his pale hair—tow-headed, her father used to say—and feels heat rising from his scalp. Outside she hears rain falling. She lies back down. She tells herself to go to sleep. She tells herself to stop dreaming.

In the morning, they case the Farmers & Mechanics Bank. They drive around the block twice in their Impala and then park at the pizza place across the street. To their left is a small roundabout with a patch of green and two withered trees in the center. It's called Central Park, which makes Dana think of the real Central Park in New York City, a place she will probably never see. A truck rattles past. The exhaust pops and Dana twitches in her seat. Cora is driving. Dana is sitting next to her. Jackie and Pinky are in the back and of course her brother is trying to wind two wires together. Dana imagines that when the Go-Go Girls case their new targets, it's all high tech, with thermal imaging binoculars and fancy cameras. They just have their eyes.

They watch people come and go from the bank. They consider the flow of traffic on the street. They send Pinky in to pretend he's filling out a deposit slip. In Central Park, an American flag snaps in the breeze. A church bell calls out the hour. The bank is unassuming, just a brick building with tinted windows. When Pinky returns to the car, he gives a report on the interior layout, the number of tellers, and the points of exit and entry. According to him, there are only two tellers and they're both fat and slow. Dana watches a young woman emerge from the bank; a white envelope is tucked under her arm and she's holding a little boy by the hand. It startles Dana to think that the course of your life could depend on when you decide to cash a check or buy a roll of quarters.

"This one is going to be a breeze," she says.

"Where's the fun in easy?" Cora replies. She turns on the radio and surfs until she finds the news. Tornados are in the forecast. Last night one of the Go-Go Girls was spotted at a nightclub in Malibu. There was a big chase with the police. Naturally she escaped.

"A nightclub!" Cora slaps the steering wheel. "She was probably sitting in some guy's lap. She was probably drinking champagne."

"Champagne gives me a headache," Jackie says from the back.

"That's because you've never had the good stuff," Cora tells her.

"How would you know what the good stuff is?" Jackie replies.

At the motel, they clean their guns. Except for Pinky, who locks himself in the bathroom. They can hear him banging around in there. It sounds like he's acquired a hammer and a drill. Dana doesn't know where he could have gotten those things.

"He really wants to finish that robot before we leave town," she says.

"What if someone has to pee? Or take a shower?" Cora asks. "What then?"

"Your brother is so weird," Jackie says.

Their guns are old Smith & Wesson revolvers. They wipe them down with the white face towels they found in the motel room. Afterward they take out their gorilla masks and line them up on a bed. Black synthetic fur surrounds the rubber faces. The mouths are open, showing off plump pink tongues and fangs. They put the masks on. They pick up their guns and point them at each other. They aren't loaded, so they pull the triggers and listen to the hollow click. *Bang*, Dana whispers into the sweet-smelling rubber. She can see a bullet flying from the chamber and pinging her right in the forehead. She can see it burrowing into her brain. When people get shot in the movies, they flail and scream and stagger. Sometimes they even pretend to be dead and then come back to life. But that's not what it would be like at all, Dana thinks. She imagines it's just like turning out a light.

2.

In Elijah, they lived on a farm. The property held two gray houses, a chicken coop, and a dilapidated barn. The metal skeletons of cars rusted in the front yard. The barn was filled with dust and moldy straw. On the edge of the property, a small cross made from sticks had been pushed into the ground. It was a grave, but Dana never knew who it belonged to.

The mothers—hers and Pinky's, Cora and Jackie's—were both the same: long-faced women scrubbed free of dissent and desire. Dana never heard either of them make a joke or sing. One of her earliest prayers was asking God to not let her end up like them. Cora and Jackie's father was gone. Years ago he had driven away in the middle of the night. Dana remembered him being like lightning cracking in the sky, quick and mean. Her own father was stern but quiet, the kind who didn't need to raise his voice to incite fear. Once, during a homeschooling lesson, she learned ninety-five percent of the ocean was unexplored and thought her father must be like that, too: filled with dark, unseen caverns. Sometimes she longed for a father that popped and exploded like Cora and Jackie's had. At least then you knew what they were capable of.

Little was actually farmed on the farm. Her father didn't believe in working for pay. That was the government's system, he said. They were sovereign citizens. They ate homemade bread, snap beans that grew on vines, peppers, collards, and venison; they drank water that came from a well. They had chickens and a milk cow and a white goat. By the time the girls were seven, they knew how to handle a gun. They could hit the center of a bulls-eye. They could shatter the clay pigeons Dana's father tossed into the air. Every Sunday they had target practice because that was God's day and He would want them to be prepared. Cora always had great aim. Pinky never liked the shooting. He got his nickname from the way he flushed whenever he fired. He didn't like the weight of a gun in his hands. He didn't like the noise. He knew better than to say these things in front of his father, of course, but he told Dana when they were alone. She would lick her index finger and wipe dirt from his face and tell him that he would get used to it in time.

Once, when Dana was thirteen and Pinky was eight, their father took them turkey hunting. They were instructed to climb a tree and stay put until he called. From the branches of a chestnut oak, they watched him crouch in the tall grass and lure the turkey with a whistle. The bird moved slowly through the woods. Fall leaves crunched under its scaly gray feet. When it appeared, its tail feathers were spread into a beautiful rust-colored fan. Dana thought he looked big and regal, and for the first time the gap between what she knew and what the animal knew seemed cruel. It only took one bullet for the turkey to fall, heavy and silent as a sack of grain. Pinky put his hands over his eyes. Dana rubbed his back. When their father called, she hesitated. She pretended they were invisible in the tree. He kept calling, but his voice never sparked with anger. It wasn't patience, though. Dana understood that it was something else. When they finally went to him, he rolled the turkey over and showed where the bullet had gone in. He made them kneel beside the bird and touch the hole. It was gummy and warm. He told them fear of death was their greatest human weakness. He pulled a brown feather, the end tipped with white, from the turkey's tail and stuck it in Dana's hair.

The winter the girls turned eighteen, everything changed. A notice came in the mail. No one had paid taxes on the farm in decades and now the government was saying they owned the land. Her father tore up the first notice because he didn't believe in taxes, but they kept coming. Dana saw the envelopes stamped with *URGENT* that he brought home from the P.O. Soon they had just sixty days to pay. That was when their training became serious. They had target practice daily. They had drills where they would run along the perimeter of the property, rifles in hand. Even Pinky had to come. He always lagged behind the girls. Dana worried about him slipping on the ice and shooting himself in the foot. They would go out bundled in parkas and leather gloves and hunting caps, their breath making white ghosts in the air. After the first hour her arms would burn from the weight of the gun, but she would keep going. They were given a pair of binoculars and told to look out for strangers. Every night their father waited up in the kitchen for something to happen, for someone to come. Every night they recited a prayer that was meant for the eve of battle: *His days are as a shadow that passeth away/touch the mountains, and they shall smoke/Cast forth lightning, and scatter them.* During a snowstorm, Dana said she didn't see how anyone from the government could find them in this weather, and her father pointed out that snowfall could give the enemy perfect cover. That night, he asked her to wait up with him. He kept opening the front door and looking outside. Snow gusted into the house and padded the hallway with white. Flecks of ice got stuck in his dark eyebrows and hair. He showed her a pamphlet newspaper called *The Embassy of Heaven*, which had a Bible quote on the cover: "Do not suppose that I have come to bring peace to the earth." He said he had been writing to the newspaper and asking for help.

"Help with what?" They were sitting at the kitchen table. A rifle lay across his lap. Last week he'd torn out the landline and now a bundle of red and green wires dangled from the kitchen wall. They had a radio that got two stations, local news and gospel music; in the background she could hear the drone of an organ. She kept telling herself that the tax notices and her father's new habits would all pass eventually, like a hunting season.

"With the soul of this land," he told her. "With the soul of this family."

They'd turned the generator off for the night and the kitchen was cold. Dana had wrapped herself in a wool blanket. The room was lit by an oil lamp. In the half-dark, she could see how much her father's face had changed. The crescents under his eyes had hollowed out; his pupils looked darker, his cheekbones and chin sharper. His skin carried the sheen of a light sweat, even though it was freezing outside. The surface was falling away. She was finally seeing what lay beneath.

No one from the bank or the government ever came to Elijah. The snow kept falling. The river stayed frozen. By February the notices had stopped appearing in the mail. It seemed they had been forgotten. Still things did not go back to the way they were before. Dana's father thought it was a trick. He started working on a secret project in the barn. His face kept changing. At night she could hear her parents arguing and sometimes Dana would find her mother crying as she collected eggs from the chicken coop or squeezed milk from the cow. Both the mothers seemed exhausted by the vigilance they'd been required to keep. They lost the energy for homeschooling. When they gave the children their schoolbooks and sent them away, Dana's father didn't notice.

Of course the children weren't really children anymore. There was only so much time they could spend shooting skeet and patrolling the property and flipping through musty textbooks. The idle time sparked a curiosity they had never felt before; it was as though they had each swallowed an ember and now it sat simmering in their stomachs. One afternoon Cora had this idea to wait on the road for a car to pass. They had some sense of what the outside world was like. They had accompanied Dana's father on trips to the farm store and the P.O. in West Plains. Once a month they went with the mothers to Fairfield's Discount Grocery, just a few miles down the road in Caulfield. Every fall they drove to visit Dana's grandparents, who had a computer and a TV, in Arkansas. But they had never done anything on their own, just the four of them.

After an hour of waiting, a truck rolled by and they hitched a ride to Miller's One Stop in Tecumseh. They wandered the dusty gas station aisles. Under the glare of florescent lights, Dana stared at the rows of cokes and the freezer full of ice cream sandwiches. Before they hitched a ride back, Cora pocketed a tube of chapstick and a plastic comb. At home, they mashed the chapstick into Pinky's hair and then combed it so it stood upright.

On another outing, they discovered that, five miles beyond the gas station, there was a town with a movie theater and a liquor store. The theater had an old-fashioned marquee and two screens. One of the films was always R-rated. The girls started talking the liquor store owner into selling them cigarettes; Pinky was the lookout. They would smoke behind the store and then toss the butts into a field. Once they let Pinky smoke. He coughed and dropped the cigarette and Cora flicked his ear. They were always back well before dark. Their parents didn't seem to know they'd been gone, or catch the strange smells they brought home. The farm was over two hundred acres and Dana figured they thought their children were out on the land, like they'd always been. But their children were learning quickly. They were learning the outside world and the pleasures it held weren't so bad. They were learning that they had never really believed in God; they had only ever believed in fear.

After they stole a map of American highways from the gas station, they spent hours sitting on the floor of Pinky and Dana's room, tracing the lines out to California and Oregon and Florida.

"Here." Cora lay on her side and pointed at San Louis. She had been eating sugar cubes from a cardboard box and her fingertip glistened. "That's where we should go."

Jackie was interested in traveling south, to New Orleans or Fort Lauderdale, but Cora said those places were too hot. Dana was intrigued by the small patchwork of northern states. They had studied geography during homeschooling, but now they were looking at the map in an entirely new light, as being full of places they might one day go.

"Too cold," Cora said when Dana touched the hook of land extending out of Massachusetts.

"Do you promise to take me with you?" Pinky asked. He didn't look his age, thirteen. He could have passed for ten or eleven. He reminded Dana of a rabbit; he had the same nervous nature and quick-beating heart. He never requested any particular place. He just wanted to make sure he wasn't left behind.

"We'll see." Cora ran her finger along the edge of California.

"Of course we'll take you," Dana said. He wasn't cut out for life in Elijah. It was too rugged, with the target practice and the long winters and the dead animals. She didn't yet know that he would be even more ill-prepared for the life she and her cousins would choose.

One night, in the early spring, they packed a single suitcase, hitched a ride to West Plains, and kept going. That was six months ago. Their parents never came looking for them, or if they did, they must not have looked very hard. Maybe they thought their children had fallen in with the government or the devil and were beyond hope. Or maybe they just didn't know how to search.

At first Dana thought leaving Elijah meant getting away from how things were on the farm, but now she thinks the past is like the hand of God, or what she imagines the hand of God would be like if God were real: it can turn you in directions you don't want to be turned in. They are still in a battle with the laws of the land. The laws that say they shouldn't steal or point guns at people. And she feels the same resistance to these laws that her father must have felt toward paying taxes. Why not do these things? she found herself thinking. Who is going to stop us?

Their first robbery was at a feed and grain store. They wanted money to buy a used car. It was so simple. They had stolen a shotgun from the bed of a truck they'd hitched in. All they had to do was walk inside. Dana told the teenage boy behind the counter to empty his register because that was a line she'd heard in one of those R-rated movies. She called him a cocksucker, too, since criminals seemed to say that all the time and she wanted him to know that she was to be taken seriously.

The boy gave them everything he had. Feed and grain stores aren't used to being robbed.

3.

The night before they hit the bank, Pinky tests his robot in the parking lot. Dana is the only one interested enough to watch. The floodlights are on; tiny bugs hover around the glow. The robot is covered in a pillowcase. It stands on the black asphalt like a ghost. Dana is smoking one of Jackie's cigarettes. She doesn't smoke much anymore, but it's the night before a job and that always makes her nervous. Once the thing is started, there's no sense in worrying because it's done, it's over. You can't rewind. But being on the edge, that's the hardest part. It's like standing in front of a burning building and knowing that it won't be long before you have to walk inside.

She sits on the ground and watches her brother peel away the pillowcase. The robot looks like a kid's science project. It has a round silver head and black buttons for eyes, an economy-sized tomato soup can for a body, and large plastic suction cups for feet. It doesn't have any arms. Dana realizes that, for some reason, whenever she thinks of a robot, the first thing that comes into her mind are its arms.

"What do you think?" Pinky says.

"Nice work." Dana flicks the cigarette into the lot.

He tweaks some wires and the robot starts lurching in Dana's direction. It squeaks and sighs. A suction cup slips forward. It's working! She can't believe it. She stands up and begins to applaud. She feels proud of her brother for building something. For finding a way to escape his circumstances.

The robot takes one full step before toppling to the ground. The eyes pop off and slide under a car. The head gets dented. Pinky rights it and adjusts the wires, but he can't bring it back to life. Dana stops clapping. She sits down on the sidewalk.

He carries the robot over to her. "Do you want to hold it?"

"Sure." She holds it away from herself. It's surprisingly light.

"On TV people build robots that can talk." Pinky licks his lips.

"It probably takes a lot of practice," she says.

An old woman with flame-red hair shuffles past and disappears into a motel room. Above them Dana hears slamming doors.

"I don't want to leave," Pinky says. "I want to stay here and keep practicing."

"You want to stay in Galesburg?"

Pinky tells her that whenever they leave a place, he worries they won't make it to the next town. He worries the car will break down and no one will give them a ride and they'll starve to death or get heatstroke or something equally horrible. He's breathless. His eyes are glassy. She pictures his rabbit heart pulsing under his ribs. Probably leaving him in Galesburg would be the best thing for him, though she knows she could never do such a thing. She was the one who took him away from the farm and now she has to live with the consequences.

She gives the robot back to him. She doesn't tell him that if they die, it won't be from starving to death in their car. Instead she says everything is going to be fine, just like she used to in Elijah. No one is going to die. Soon he'll have all the time in the world to build a new robot.

"Does this one have a name?" she asks.

"Donald." He squeezes the robot's metal stomach and asks Dana what she thought their father was building in the barn.

Dana shrugs. She's never given much thought to what he was doing. She just remembers looking out her window and seeing him trudge into the mouth of the barn at dawn and not emerging until after dark. His skin would be caked in dust, straw caught in his hair. But mainly she had been preoccupied with figuring out how to live her own life, with how to spend her time. Dana wonders if her father is still working on his project in the barn, whatever it was. She imagines going back to Elijah one day and finding him a shrunken old man and feels an ache shoot through her chest.

"I snuck in there once and watched him." Pinky describes pliers and cords and strips of metal. He talks about smelling smoke and seeing tiny silver sparks. "I think he was building a robot. I think that's what he wanted to do."

Dana looks at her brother and feels woozy. She never should have taken him along. It was a game at first, but now it's something much more serious and he is becoming an attachment she doesn't need.

"You know what they say in the movies?" she asks him.

"What?"

"They say you have to be cool." She can see a man in a ponytail delivering the line, but can't remember which movie it's from.

"OK." He's staring at the ground. She can tell she's not getting through.

"Say it to me."

He keeps hugging the robot. In his arms it looks like a heap of trash. It's only recently occurred to Dana that some people might call what she did—taking her brother away from their parents—kidnapping.

"Be cool," he tells her without looking up.

"You got it," she says.

4.

Dana was questioned by the police only once. It didn't have anything to do with the Gorillas. Rather she was a witness to a hit-and-run. This was two months ago in Jefferson City. She had just walked out of a bank the Gorillas were casing and was waiting to cross the street. A car ran a red light and struck a girl on a bicycle. The girl was dead by the time the ambulance came. Dana could remember the twisted handlebars and the crushed bell. She could remember the peculiar angle of the girl's torso and her open eyes. Her lips were parted. Her teeth were straight and white. She was still wearing her helmet. She looked like a life-sized doll someone had left in the street. Pedestrians gathered. The police were called. Dana tried to slip away, but someone identified her as a witness and she was taken down to the station. She got to ride up front with the officer. She wondered what Cora or Jackie would think if they saw her, if they would think she had turned on them.

At the station, the officer brought her a cup of coffee. He was handsome, with his broad shoulders and gelled hair. So this is the lair of the enemy, Dana thought as they settled into an interrogation room. She held the warm Styrofoam cup with both hands. If only this officer knew what she had done, what she was going to do, she would not be answering questions over coffee. There would be handcuffs and threats. She figured that one day he would see her face on the news and feel like a dolt.

He asked her the usual questions: what she'd seen, if the light had been red, if she'd gotten a look at the driver, if she remembered the license plate. She answered honestly. She hadn't seen anything but the collision itself, hadn't taken in anything but the shock of the crash. She didn't mention that she hadn't been paying closer attention because she'd been busy imprinting the interior of the bank onto her brain.

"Do you need someone to identify the body?" Dana asked. She surprised herself with the question.

"You knew her?" The office frowned. He pulled in his chin and a little roll of fat appeared.

He had mentioned the girl was a college student. Dana muttered something about being classmates and seeing her around campus. She didn't know what had come over her. She had never seen a dead body before and up until then, that was A-OK. But she had been gripped by an urge she could not recognize or understand, only follow.

"Her parents are coming in from Chicago," the officer said. "We could save them the grief."

Dana sighed. Didn't he know there was no saving anyone any grief?

They took an elevator down to the morgue and passed through a cool, shadowed hallway. They stopped in front of a dark window. Dana could hear music coming through the glass. It was faint. A Michael Jackson song. For a moment, she imagined the medical examiner moonwalking around the autopsy room. The officer asked if she was ready. She nodded. A light came on.

The girl was lying on a coroner's table. She was naked, which alarmed Dana. It didn't seem right for her to be uncovered; someone had been careless. Her breasts were small and her knees seemed too big for her body. Her eyes were closed. Her hair looked wet and sleek. The blood had been cleaned away. Dana wondered where her bicycle helmet was. She couldn't believe this was the same girl she'd seen sprawled out on the street. It looked like her body had been replaced by a fake. How could these parents from Chicago identify their daughter with any kind of certainty? Maybe that was what happened when you died, Dana thought. Your real body went once place and a replica was provided for the rituals. And if that were true, where did the real bodies go? Someplace nice? Probably not.

"So is it her?" the officer said.

"What?" Dana turned from the window.

"Is she your classmate? Do you know her name?"

"It's not her," Dana said.

"What do you mean it's not her?" The officer frowned again. He was getting less attractive by the minute.

"I made a mistake," she said.

"Who makes that kind of mistake?" For the first time she noticed the gun holstered to his hip.

Dana wasn't afraid to just tell the officer the truth. After all she hadn't broken any laws, that he knew of.

"Look, I wanted to see a body. I wanted to know what it would be like." She thought of that turkey in Elijah strolling through the woods one minute and still the next.

The officer said she could show herself out.

5.

At first everything goes perfectly at the Farmers & Mechanics Bank. They are all in their gorilla masks. Cora is pointing her gun at the tellers. Dana is aiming hers at the handful of customers who had the misfortune of being in the bank. They are crossed-legged on the floor; they have been ordered to sit on their hands, like elementary schoolers who can't stop hitting each other. Dana tries to ignore the little girl with braided hair. Pinky is guarding the door. Jackie, the getaway driver, is idling around the corner. Dana watches one teller load bricks of money into a bag. He has red hair and a moustache. The other teller is a woman. She's used so much hairspray, her hair doesn't budge when she whips her head left then right. Her lips are slick with pink, her lashes clumped with mascara. There's no sign of the fat, sluggish tellers Pinky described, but it looks like these two will do just fine.

It's the woman who fucks everything up. They see her hand slide under the counter and know she's going for the alarm. Cora shouts at her—*hands in the air*—but the woman doesn't listen. Pinky is pacing by the door and pawing his rubber face. Dana takes small, quick breaths behind her gorilla mask. *Be cool*, she whispers, but it sounds artificial and weak. Stronger words are needed. She just doesn't know what they are.

The gunshot stops everyone. The mustached teller stops putting money in the bag. Pinky stops pacing. The customers stop squirming. The female teller is clutching her left eye. Blood seeps between her fingers. Cora's gun is still raised. It takes Dana more time than it should to understand that one of the Gorillas has just shot a bank teller in the face.

Her hands are numb. She concentrates on not dropping her gun. She opens her mouth, but nothing comes out. She thinks she's going to suffocate behind the mask.

"Give us our money." Now Cora is aiming at the other teller. His shirtsleeves are drenched in sweat. He goes back to heaving cash into the bag.

A woman in cowboy boots raises her hand. Her mouth is open, but she's not saying anything. She's pointing at something by the door. Dana turns and there's Pinky, slumped against the wall. He's kneading his gorilla mask in his hands. The customers and the tellers and the security cameras are all taking in his face. They are memorizing it. They are branding it onto their brains like Dana did with the interior of that bank in Jackson City.

"He is in such deep shit." Cora is waving her gun. She swivels toward Dana. "Can't you do something?"

But Dana can't. If she were a Go-Go Girl, then maybe she could, but she is just herself. The female teller is hunched over the counter and whimpering. She sounds like the wild dog Dana's father once had to shoot in Elijah. He kept coming onto their property, frothy and snarling, but once he had a bullet in him, he was docile as a lamb. Blood is still squirting through her fingers, as though her hand is a dam that's about to give. She's blinded at best. In the distance, Dana hears a siren. She looks at Cora and her cousin nods. They run for the exit. She pauses only to yank Pinky up by his shirt collar. He drops his gorilla mask on the sidewalk, but right then it doesn't matter. All that matters is diving into the waiting Impala. Of course Jackie wants to know what happened and where's the money and why isn't Pinky wearing his mask. Cora tells her to shut up and drive. They blast out of Galesburg. It's nearly dusk. The sun looks like it's setting the sky on fire.

They drive through the night. Pinky is up front, next to Jackie. Dana and Cora are in the back. The window is cracked and Jackie is chain-smoking. They are heading to a little town called Wapello. They think it will be a good place to lay low, but soon Pinky's face will be all over the news and there will be no laying low from that.

"He can't stay with us anymore," Cora hisses in the backseat.

Dana just shakes her head. He could get plastic surgery, she thinks. A crazy idea. She gazes at her brother's profile. They are on a dark, straight highway. A little slicing, a little rearranging. She thinks of how handsome he could be.

On the radio, they hear that one of the Go-Go Girls has been shot in the stomach. She fell behind during a get away. The officer who shot her said that he meant to hit her shoulder. Turns out that she wasn't an acrobat or Romanian. Just a girl from Minnesota.

"This is the problem with being famous," Dana announces to the car. "It makes everyone want to kill you."

No one says anything. Not even Cora. Dana leans her head against the window. As they're passing signs for Kirkwood, she thinks of the girl at the morgue and her parents in Chicago. She wonders if the cop ever tells her story, about the woman who conned him into checking out a dead body. If anyone ever tells her story.

Tornados are still in the forecast. A few times Dana thinks she sees a big black funnel moving toward them in the night. She thinks she hears that locomotive sound and feels the ground shake. She imagines being swept away. But there is nothing coming for them. Not yet. There is only this highway and this car and this darkness. She leans forward and squeezes her brother's elbow. He doesn't move, doesn't look at her. The remaining Gorilla masks are piled in his lap. He knows he's in a world of trouble.

They stop for gas and Dana makes Jackie hand her the car keys. When she says she wants to be sure no one gets left behind, Cora gives her a look. Pinky needs to use the bathroom. Dana stands outside and jingles the keys. She can see her parents hearing about Pinky on the radio. She can see them turning up the volume and leaning in close. Maybe they are being kept company by a robot made of soup cans and chicken wire, or maybe they are alone.

Through the bathroom door, she hears the toilet flush. Her brother takes his time washing his hands.

When they're all back in the car, Cora passes her a note written on a paper napkin. *We are leaving him at the next fucking gas station!* it says in jagged black letters. Dana crumples the note and drops it on the floor. She slumps back and something crunches under her sneaker. She peers between her knees. It's the robot. Pinky got one of the eyes glued back on. If she tilts her head the right away, the metal gleams and she can tell herself it's their treasure, their loot. She thinks about rescuing the robot from the floor and giving it to her brother. She thinks about doing him that kindness. Instead she nudges the robot under the driver's seat and then feels sad about it. Poor Donald. She has to remind herself that robots don't have feelings. All these little choices that push her closer to something she's not sure she wants.

They pass a billboard with the slogan: WANT A BETTER WORLD? It's too dark for Dana to see what's being advertised, but she guesses it's something religious. Of course she wants a better world. Who wouldn't want that? A world where everyone was like Pinky, pure and soft and full of dreams. Or she could just do things differently when it came to those small choices. She could give her brother the robot. She could throw her gun in a river. These could be her lessons. It's right there for her, that better world. She barely has to go looking.

Dana knows this, just as she knows that this is not the day she will find it.

THE LAST DAYS OF PEACE AND LOVE

Valerie Sayers

THE FIRST TIME I SAW THIS CHICK IN A SKIN-TIGHT MICRO-MINI, I knew her. She was everything my mother had spent a lifetime warning me not to be: fishnet stockings, skirt barely covering her crotch, so much dark eyeshadow she looked like her boyfriend had popped her in one eye and then the other. The other typists wouldn't have dreamed of showing that much flesh—they wanted to get home on the subway without getting groped—but maybe this one hadn't heard that the Sixties were over. She was on her way to the ladies' room, thrusting her pelvis out in a kind of runway walk crossed with a keep on truckin' slouch. When she spotted me, she gave a little wave, as if she'd figured out who I was too.

I was an actor—I guess in those days I said actress—so I knew how to look like I hadn't been staring. This was only a three-week gig, at a structural engineering firm: I was the receptionist at the front desk, answering the phone in my best Judy Holiday voice. The typists were hidden away in back, and once I saw her, I knew why.

The Seventies were just the Sixties dribbling away: the war was finally over, but Jean-Paul and I were still nostalgic for demonstrations and street theatre. We spent so much time in acting class, or posing for glossy eight-by-tens, that we hardly knew who we were in real life. Married? What was that? Our apartment was so small we had to wedge ourselves into the single bed Jean-Paul brought from his parents' place.

So the next morning, when the Sixties chick stopped at the

front desk on her way in, my nerves tingled all over again. She took her sweet time and leaned over my phone console in such a seductive slouch that I wasn't even surprised when she batted her eyelashes at me. "Didn't you used to go to the Fillmore?"

"Sure," I said, "sometimes." She was certainly alarming. Now she was wearing a floral scarf in a gauzy material tied tight to form a halter. Jeez: nobody wore a halter to work in an office like this, much less a scarf pretending to be a halter. Where'd she think she was, Altamont?

"I think maybe I danced with you one time."

I gave her a noncommittal smile. Her nipples were tight little corkscrews poking through her gauzy top.

"Wanna go to lunch later?"

I couldn't afford to go to lunch—I always brought a yogurt and passed myself off as a starving artist—and I didn't know where to look when I looked at her. "Sure." I was mesmerized and besides, she was as sweet as a puppy. Her name was Lorraine Straveski. Sweet Lorraine.

When we walked out on Broad Street that noontime, Sweet Lorraine Straveski linked her arm through mine so that all the men ogling her perky breasts, bouncing along under her yellow daisy scarf, had to glance at me too. I thought I was playing a grown-up— I had on a thrift-store Christian Dior jacket—but next to her I probably looked like a nun. Her crazy ringlets were streaked with gaudy yellow, and my mother would have pointed to her dark roots as the definitive evidence: she was a slut, all right.

Somehow Sweet Lorraine picked up the mother-vibes right away. At lunch the first thing she said was, "What's the worst way your mother ever humiliated you?" and I was so freaked by her mind-reading that I drew a blank. I wasn't a big confider, the kind of instant-girlfriend who could tell the story of my life to someone I'd just met. She had mossy green eyes, lined with brilliant blue, and teeth that protruded ever so slightly. When she took out her aviator glasses to read the menu, I could see her at forty, ruling the typing roost in a peekaboo blouse. If I really wanted to tell her the worst thing my mother did, I'd tell how she wouldn't let me visit when my father was diagnosed with lung cancer because I was living in sin.

"Let's see. She used to come tearing down the driveway when my boyfriends brought me home late." I heard myself giggle.

"Ha," she said, just like that: ha. "Mine took my favorite bikini and shredded it with her toenail scissors. Her toenail scissors."

I liked her. My family tensed at touch—my brother was ten years older and tried not to touch me at all—but when Lorraine came up behind me to knead my shoulders, I felt us both melt away. "I've got tits," she said the first time we hugged, "but you've got boobs."

When the job was over and I scored a bit part in a domestic comedy working itself out at the Playwrights Workshop, Lorraine made sure we got together on Mondays, when the theatres were dark. We went to happy hour at one Wall Street bar or the other. My girlfriends had drifted away since college—well, maybe even before then, maybe since I got married—and I liked hearing Lorraine chatter, liked the sample bottles of perfume she got from who-knows-where, liked sitting under the gaze of so many eyes, even if they were gazing at her and not at me.

She told me she didn't speak to her mother in Dayton anymore, not at all, and maybe I liked the sound of that too. Once Jean-Paul married me, my mother forgave me, but now my father was dead and I was nineteen-and-married and I wasn't so sure I forgave her. Lorraine said Oscar, her shrink, advised her to cut her mother off cold. What kind of shrink would advise such a thing? She said Oscar was SAI, for Self-Actualizing Interpersonalist, and all her roommates were too. They all lived in single-sex apartments and slept with each other as often and variously as possible so they didn't get "y'know, all hung up on somebody." We were in a smoky bar when she told me about sleeping with as many guys as possible and then blew Marlboro rings, wondering whether she'd shocked me.

I put on my Jeanne Moreau face and aimed for unshockable. "SAI guys?"

"Mostly. Once I had, like, three dates in one night? And I put in my spare diaphragm by accident? I mean, on top of the other one. Six months later I go to the E.R. and they tell me it's like a petri dish in there."

"Oh man." I probably blanched. OK, so I was no Jeanne Moreau. No matter how much sex talk you heard back then, somebody was always upping the ante: I mean, the whole concept of a Sexual Revolution was still pretty new to me. I'd slept with a few too many boys before Jean-Paul, but how many guys could you fit in by nineteen? This talk of back-to-back men was like news from an exotic country I'd never get the chance to visit now.

"So what do you think?"

I thought this SAI thing was like Amway or Scientology, and Lorraine needed to find new members. I smiled mysteriously. I had about twenty-five smiles in my repertoire: this one was my Jeanne Moreau special.

After a while, Lorraine started slipping complaints about the Self-Actualizing Interpersonalists into our Monday nights. They made her feel like shit for skipping out on college. They were always telling her how much she didn't know. They picked on her at their weekly critiques. She made life among the SAIs sound like Vietnamese re-education camp.

One night, she lowered her voice as if there might be self-actualizing spies all around us. "I have to get out of that apartment. It's just, like, where do I go?" She looked as miserable as I'd ever seen her. Jean-Paul and I had just rented one of those huge apartments off West End Avenue and the only way we could afford it was to get roommates, but I hadn't mentioned the move to Lorraine—I could imagine doing all kinds of things with Lorraine, but living with her wasn't one of them.

She drummed her fingers on the table hard enough to make my ice clink. "Oscar says yeah, move out, but that's only cause he wants to get his hands on me."

How did a typist pay for a shrink, anyway? And how about Oscar getting his hands on her? Was that literal? It was enough to bring out my own maternal side, and the Kahlúa—Lorraine's drink—brought out my bad judgment. I told her about our apartment after all.

"Yeah?" She did her best not to look too eager. "A commune? Is it gonna be, like, political?"

"I guess we're mostly looking for company." It finally occurred to me—I can be a little slow in the insight department—that I hadn't mentioned it before because of course Jean-Paul would look at her the way every other man did.

"I can't believe it! It's like the answer to my prayers."

Somehow I couldn't imagine Lorraine praying among her interpersonalists, and I had a bad feeling. How could Jean-Paul help looking at her the way every other man did?

I hadn't lied to Lorraine: Our ersatz commune wasn't political in the least. We had a freelance (meaning unemployed) journalist, a snarky MFA poet back in the maid's room, and an Oh wow sociology grad student we called Sosh in the dining room. You had to pass in and out of his room to get to the kitchen, but Sosh said: "Hey now, good people, I sincerely enjoy interacting with you on a regular basis."

Anyway, aside from disturbing Sosh's studying on our way to make a cup of tea, there wasn't any interacting. Lorraine asked about house meetings, like the ones the Self-Actualizing Interpersonalists had, but we weren't the meeting type of commune, either. We had three bedrooms on the other side of the dining room: us, the journalist, and now Lorraine. We could go for days without laying eyes on anyone but Sosh.

The first week she moved in, Lorraine knocked on everybody's door and offered up a joint. Nights, a string of boyfriends came to see her. If the guy went home early she stood in our doorway, semi-clothed and reeking of sex, asking us in that bouncy Midwestern way if we'd gone on any auditions. "Meet any famous people today, guys?" She thrust out her bony pelvis while she looked at Jean-Paul with a Here I am in the next bedroom look. Once she actually stroked her own nipple, right through her camisole, and we both stared in fascination.

When I pointed out that she was trying to seduce him, Jean-Paul said: "No more than she's trying to seduce you." Well, yeah, I told him, I knew what she was doing with the shoulder-kneading— even Ethel Feeney would have known what that meant.

Sweet Lorraine professed awe at my married state: "I never thought I could be OK with, you know? One person? But Jean-Paul . . . ."

I tried not to bristle. By then Jean-Paul had the lead in a new translation of *The Lower Depths* at the Desperado Theatre Cooperative (no, really), and even if Lorraine hadn't been doing her best to get him into her bed, his dubious triumph on Avenue C already had me plenty jealous. I hadn't scored a single bit part since that crappy comedy, but Jean-Paul had landed two off-off leads, in plays I loved. He was a great actor, brooding but not too, fearless about blazing away with his dark eyes. And maybe he was on the short side, but that didn't stop avant-garde directors from casting him, or women from coming on to him. It sure didn't stop Lorraine.

Jean-Paul smoked dope with her late into the night, listening the way he listened to other actors. He specialized in rescues: he'd rescued me from my mother's fury, hadn't he? Lorraine told him she'd always wanted to go college, so every few days he gave her a new book, Castaneda or Wittgenstein or Stanislavsky, and she curled up with it for a good three minutes before she abandoned it for a High Times. I lay awake till two, three, four in the morning, listening to his good deep voice in the next room, explaining Wittgenstein, rescuing her.

"Why doesn't she just take a class at the New School?"

"She needs to build up some confidence. She's got some good ideas."

"Oh yeah? Such as?"

He grinned at me in his raffish avant-garde actorly way. My mother said Jean-Paul was naïve, but I didn't think he was, not for a minute. "Anyway," he said, "maybe I can give her some good ideas."

*

One night she stood in our doorway and made an alarming screeching sound. I followed her to the bathroom, where she sat herself down on the cold tile, gestured to her closing throat, and suggested that maybe she was losing her mind. I was terrified, but I played it as if she were just being melodramatic. "Want me to call Oscar?"

She drew a finger across the throat, meaning, I guessed, that she would rather slit it than speak to Oscar. So I sat there on the edge of the tub, panicking right along with her. I hadn't understood that she was on the brink. She was always so smiley at work, so touchy-feely.

"Oscar said professional standards were guidelines." She rolled her head in an alarming way. "Do you hear that buzzing? Oh God. Is the floor tipping?"

"Does this guy even have a license?"

And she launched in again. "License! Oh, man. I'm having some trouble swallowing." She sobbed and hiccupped for a while, then slowed down and became very formal. "When I was a little kid, I couldn't ever like sit still, so my mother would strap me to the kitchen chair with belts. And like the more I struggled, the tighter she tied. Sometimes she left me in the kitchen for hours." I wasn't entirely sure whether this was a factual history—she was pretty spacey by then—or some kind of control-and-punish metaphor, but I let her talk and talk, and when she finally fell asleep on the cold tile, it was almost midnight. I tucked a towel-pillow under her head and was covering her with another towel when Sosh showed up.

"Never mind," he said, blushing. "I can hold it."

In the morning she was in her own bed, but that afternoon she waltzed into the kitchen, naked, singing "Honky Tonk Women" so slowly she sounded like a dying turntable. I stood there transfixed: her hips curved as neatly as a nice cheap bottle of Mateus. By then Sosh, who'd been reading when Lorraine passed through—that must have been a vision—stood in the doorway. Even he could see what was going on this time.

"We've got to call her people," he whispered, but we were her people now—her ersatz people—and I hadn't guessed what it would cost her to leave her other people, or what it would cost us to nurse her through this. I walked her back to her room, feeling like a hospital orderly, and got her to confess that she'd taken a whole lot of pills since she got up off the bathroom floor.

"You mean your Valium?" She didn't appear to understand the question. "Reds?" She finally settled dreamily on ludes, but that was just to make the questions stop, and anyway she didn't have a clue how many. I walked her up and down to keep her from passing out. Jean-Paul was due home any minute, so I pulled one of her silky nightgowns over her head, and that was what she was wearing under Jean-Paul's camouflage jacket when the two of us coaxed her all the way to the E.R.

We waited up all night, praying they'd check her in. But she wanted to go home, so they pumped her stomach and released her to us, her ersatz people leading her from St. Luke's through the Upper West Side in a negligee and cowboy boots, Jean-Paul's jacket barely keeping her decent.

She liked to leave her door open, so sometimes I could see her staring out, grinning in an eerie way. It unnerved me that Lorraine and I both spent so much time alone, time I spent running lines with myself for the roles I fantasized playing when I was a grande dame of the theatre: Winnie, Mother Courage, Sabina. What was I thinking? I couldn't even get a walk-on. Most of the roles I had played, even back in college, were dumb new comedies that required me to take my shirt off. Jean-Paul was out discussing inflectionless readings with avant-garde directors and I was reading Backstage as a bedtime story.

My torpor grew in inverse proportion to my sense of my future as an actor. I could make them sit up if they let me play the whole scene, but lately their eyes glazed over before I even started to read. Once I'd seen Lorraine's slinky body naked, I found my own boobs maternal, though up till then I'd kind of believed they were the assets Jean-Paul joked about. I couldn't even afford classes anymore. The temp jobs were drying up.

The air on W. 100th Street started to smell rancid, fetid. Inside, it was Lorraine's smells that got to me: Kahlúa and dope and Marlboros, Shalimar and damp rayon panties. She'd quit typing and found a gig hostessing downtown: the way she went off to work now, in lowcut black, I figured it was a dicey lounge, maybe a strip joint. She stumbled into the living room with strange guys, mostly just business guys out tomcatting, but every once in a while a biker or a hardcore stoner. We all started locking up our possessions. Finally, when the last stoner stayed for three days and poked around the whole apartment, we convened an official ersatz commune meeting.

We all sat in Sosh's room on crates, bummed and silent. After a long while the journalist said: "We don't want to, uhm, interfere with your private life but we really don't like so many strangers coming in." He didn't even look at her. Lorraine was smoking a fat joint, blitzed out of her mind for a meeting she knew was called on her account, but after the journalist her head hung low.

"We just want to make sure you're all right," Sosh said in his gentle unironic way. "We're worried about you." Lorraine looked up—she made eye contact with me first, then Jean-Paul—and beamed a betrayed smile around the room before she rose.

In a while we heard the shower running and the sound of her singing "Gimme Shelter." I pictured her in there slitting her wrists, but she came out wearing lowcut black and smelling of Shalimar, and off she went off to work, same as always. We heard her coming in, alone, sometime before dawn.

I developed such an aversion to the sound of Lorraine's singing, the sight of her stroking herself, that I began scurrying away whenever she was home, but one morning she showed up in my doorway, wearing a man's unbuttoned dress shirt. I gave her my fake friendly Judy Garland smile. It was hard to believe we'd ever been friends, but she was still running her hands down her hips as if to say, Well, if you won't give me a hug I'll just have to do it myself.

"Guess what? I'm dating a record producer," she breathed. Did she think we were still two hippie chicks sharing boyfriend stories?

"That's great." Even I could hear the chill in my I-do-not-want-to-be-having-this-conversation voice, and Lorraine heard it for sure. Before I slipped past her, she got even.

"I just hope Jean-Paul doesn't get upset when he hears about it."

What else could she mean? It was what I'd been suspecting for months, but for the first time I gave her a hint of my fury: I slammed our door as hard as I could, and then I turned the lock we had installed against her stoners. It gave a cold click, but I could still smell her standing there, warm from her bed. Did they meet after curtain and get a room? Have hot and heavy quickies in the kitchen? Through the door I heard her say, in a voice from some bad trip: "It's not like he pays me."

THE SLUT. Jean-Paul and I had never once discussed fidelity. It seemed, I don't know, uncool: his folks were French. We were children of the sexual revolution. Love the one you're with! We'd always treated marriage as a big fat joke: a joke like living in an ersatz commune to cut down on the rent, to cut down on the strange loneliness of living with another person. I thought about it all the time, didn't I, what it would be like to give off available vibes to directors who saw me walk into the room with my cheap wedding band and stopped listening then and there. I could hardly breathe. Oh sweet Jesus. Had she been turning tricks in this apartment? Were all those skeevy men johns?

I did my deep-breathing warm-ups for as long as I could focus—about twelve seconds—and then I fell face-down on the bed. After a beat, I crawled up and grabbed a jacket. Let her come after me if she dared. In the elevator, I pounded the panel till the whole car jumped. Outside, I had no idea where I was going, but I turned south on scuzzy Broadway. Every panhandler and junkie and crazy I met set off my mother's voice: The city! Believe me, the filth and degradation will get old fast. And in the other ear, Lorraine: I hope Jean-Paul doesn't get. . . .

I tramped my filthy degraded city all afternoon long. By the time I turned west, I was nursing a blister and the winter sun was setting over the Hudson. My fury wasn't spent, exactly, but it had transformed itself into the same kind of detachment I could work myself into before a performance. On the elevator I recited the lines I would say to Lorraine, because even after all my hours of walking I still hadn't worked out what I would say to Jean-Paul.

But when I let myself in, the apartment had a weird empty vibe: no perfume or dope or incense, no light above Sosh's desk. I retreated to our room and lay on our bed, practicing how calmly we would work out who got stuck with the ersatz commune and who had to move out—we'd both signed the lease. In a terrifying flash I saw myself back in my old bedroom, my mother's holy cards tucked into every mirror. I must have drifted off finally.

I woke to the weight of Jean-Paul's hand on my back and the thick sweet smell of his breath floating toward me: Kahlúa. "Feeney, you awake?"

I didn't know whether I was awake, or where I was, or why Jean-Paul was giving me a blow-by-blow of some adventure he'd had with Sosh: a baseball bat, a doorman, a sprint from East Village to West. "Where've you been?"

He laughed into my ear. "Decking Lorraine's pimp."

The strangeness of that, or maybe the sweet puff of his laughter fluttering in my eardrum, had a curious effect: I fell back into a skittering sleep, and dreamed of Lorraine, that slut my mother had always warned me I might become. She paraded past me in tattered fishnet stockings, in red satin bustiers, in nothing but her corkscrew nipples. Sweet Lorraine: not just a slut but a whore, and not a metaphorical whore but a real live whore, the only whore I was likely to ever meet. She lived with me! She was my friend! Or once upon a time she had been my friend. I could feel her hand on my shoulder, where Jean-Paul's rested.

"Sosh said he'd get her money. . . . just riding shotgun. . . ." He still sounded euphoric.

Jean-Paul rode shotgun in a mobster's sedan. It was a lucid dream: I must have drifted off again, which made its own kind of sense. I'd been drifting off for the last six months, hadn't I, floating along on the little-enough money Jean-Paul made loading trucks, not sure how much he resented carrying me, or being married to me for that matter. I'd locked my dreamy self into a lonely bedroom in a lonely apartment in a dirty degraded city where your last girlfriend turned tricks.

In the morning I didn't even know if I'd dreamed the story or Jean-Paul had told it in voiceover, but in my sleep I'd learned it by heart. The pimp was only a kid from Brooklyn with a braid down his back. He'd sized up Jean-Paul and Sosh and laughed in their faces. When Sosh demanded Lorraine's money and the guy came at them, Jean-Paul summoned his stage fight training and landed a sucker punch. Then, having destroyed Lorraine's livelihood, they hightailed it out of there and ran all the way to the Lion's Head, where they drank themselves silly on her sweet drink.

That was the story. It could have happened, or parts of it could have happened. And I could have dreamed it, and Jean-Paul could have made it up. In the early light he drooled onto his pillow. I remembered one of his lines for sure: She'd show up at the Hilton and let some accountant from Cleveland handcuff her to the bed. I stared down at my husband—husband—and imagined asking him the true story. I'd watched her stroke her nipple. I knew I'd never ask.

He sensed me and stirred miserably in his own dreams. The Rescuer. The Defender. I whispered: "What's she going to do?"

He groaned like a man in the clutches of a head-splitting hangover, or maybe a serious case of guilt. "You mean," he said, "what are we gonna do." It was an uninflected reading.

We don't even know who told us to look in Brooklyn: we only knew it was as far away from the Upper West Side as we could imagine. We took a couple of long subway rides, checked out signs in brownstone windows. Give me a month, the landlord said.

I found I could worry about Lorraine again, now that we were leaving, and she gave me plenty to worry about: one morning I found her passed out on the kitchen floor. They let me ride in the ambulance with her, and after another stomach-pumping, she let me talk her into a week on the locked ward. I was her only visitor. I had so many questions. I don't mean the Jean-Paul question—the only way I was going to get out of the ersatz commune was to forget there even was a Jean-Paul question—but the kind of questions Ethel Feeney's daughter would never breathe: Handcuffs? What if they took too long? What if you couldn't get, you know. . . .

Lorraine came home from the hospital a whipped puppy. I could already see the blank wide-eyed look she would give me through her aviator glasses when I told her we were moving. Even Sosh was looking for a new place.

Face it, we were leaving her, just sprung from the psych ward, to fend for herself. This was serious bad karma. If Ethel Feeney had known, she either would have said we were well out of there, or she would have said we were committing a grievous mortal sin, and I didn't even know anymore which one she would pick.

On moving day, bouncing along the Brooklyn Bridge, Jean-Paul pointed out the Statue of Liberty as if he were a sightseer, not someone who'd spent his whole life in this city. "She'll be OK." He veered along the decrepit roadway in our rented truck, grinning obscenely at our liberation. What a tidy story he'd told me, complete with sucker punch. He made soothing sounds as I wept, his cheerful new patience as suspicious as the cheap new Brooklyn rent. I could see whatever happened between them looming over us as we tried to hang on: to acting, to the city, to a marriage made too young.

And I could see an afternoon when the sun was just going down over the Hudson and Lorraine, wearing a shrunken Sticky Fingers t-shirt and her pointy tooled cowboy boots, curled up in the bathroom one last time. The hairballs blew around her like tumbleweeds, and I sat on the closed toilet lid, helpless, looking down on her as she alternated full-body trembling and sweet giggling. Was I supposed to take care of her? I couldn't even take care of getting myself one good role, much less take care of Sweet Lorraine Straveski.

"I can't believe I could get so freaked out with you guys around." She started to choke. I wanted to get down and give her a good shoulder squeeze like the squeezes she'd given me, but I couldn't figure out how to get close to her on the floor. I stood up, sat back down, prayed we wouldn't have to go to the hospital again, seriously considered running away: from her, from Jean-Paul, from New York and all its sorrows. She looked up at me with those crazy green eyes.

"It's OK," she said, as if I were the one in trouble, as if I were just like her: an angry mother's daughter, lost in the city she thought would save her.

THE WOODCUTTER

Rachel Yoder

His name was Hunter Jim. Actually it was Jim Hunter, but once I got it in my head, that's what stuck. I bought a half cord of firewood from him, and he brought along this big guy in his navy blue pickup to unload it.

Hunter Jim didn't stay to help, just dropped off the big guy in overalls, then introduced me to a woman who had followed him to my house in her beat-up car. He referred to her as his *lady friend*, Jean or Marie or something, one of those meek, hippie types with long ashy hair and a macrobiotic diet, who looks like she might blow over if you say boo. She held her hands as though she were praying, except with her fingers pointed down.

"I need to see about some business dealings while I'm here in town. I'll be back in a while," he said, folding into the car, Jean/Marie at the wheel, and like that, they were gone.

The guy in overalls—Casey, he said his name was—I felt bad for him. He was out there all by himself unloading, and it was obvious Hunter Jim was taking advantage of his nature, shy and simple, with a thick tongue that stumbled through his sentences. I went out and asked did he want some water or something, and he said sure. After he drank, he threw me the pieces of juniper from the bed, and I stacked them in straight rows, one on top of each other, at the head of the driveway.

He didn't understand why I knew how to stack wood the way I did, and I told him I had done it for years back in Ohio with my dad, rode beside him on the tractor to the clearing at the edge of our property, helped him haul wood back to the house. We got the work done fast and he thanked me, then asked for another glass of water, which I got him, and then he waited there for a good forty-five minutes, sitting on the tailgate, swinging his big man legs until the woman and Hunter Jim came back.

"If you could just leave the payee line blank I'd be much obliged," Hunter Jim said as I wrote him a check, leaning close to watch. I could smell him, white soap. The skin on his cheeks was tanned and soft-looking. "It's easier to make it payable to one of my many creditors this way," he explained, folding the check and putting it in his shirt pocket.

Hunter Jim made me uneasy with his *much obliged* and *creditors* and the worked-over fisherman's cap and deck shoes he was wearing, even though we were in Arizona high desert, nowhere close to any place where you'd need his sort of coastal clothing. He was in his late forties or early fifties, with a moustache like a thick caterpillar that crawled when he talked, outdated eyeglasses with dark plastic rims and thick lenses. He reminded me of someone in a bad disguise.

"If you ever have a need of any kindling, you just give me a call. I've got plenty up at my place," he said, easing himself into the truck. I assured him I'd be fine on kindling, pointing at the ponderosa forest surrounding us.

"Pine doesn't start very well, and besides, it might get wet. I'd hardly depend on this stuff to get you through," he said as Casey slammed the passenger door. I glared at Hunter Jim, and he straight-stared back at me, the smile of his mouth pulling his face apart into expressions shaded and volatile. I looked at him openly and wouldn't stop.

I told him I owned this cabin. I knew how to build a fire. I'd be just fine. He looked at me through the open window, his face finally organizing itself into something familiar and human.

"Give me a call. Anytime," he said as he gunned the engine. The woman took off in her little beat-up car, then Casey and Hunter Jim. I was glad to see him go.

*

It was the first fall alone I'd ever had. I was twenty-four and far away from the religious upbringing I had been looking to leave behind. You might know this one: young and dumb with the story of myself. The last time I'd touched my parents had been years ago, when I left. I stood on the porch beneath a trellis wrapped thick with white moonflowers. The blooms blew in the breeze like clean laundry on the line. My mother's thin shoulders. My father's open palm.

It was about work. That's what I said. I had an unimportant job in a high-desert town. I thought I knew how to do it, head west toward nothing I knew, a big dry barren, full of threat of death or some ecstatic vision blowing up out of the dust.

But of course I was angry. I enumerated the amorphous wrongs: Raised Mennonite with outdated ways. Cursed female crossed with smart.

"At the very least, I wish I'd been dumb," I raged at my father. "Dumb and ugly."

"I am what I am," he said. "And you. You."

He'd been raised Amish and carried his childhood with him like a donor heart in a small white cooler that one day he might use to save his own life. As families do, his had aged into more moderate theologies, turned Mennonite. And this he had given to me. But I didn't want it and tried to give it back.

Before I left, I had only loved Ruth. This was my father's sister, a middle-aged Mennonite virgin who took her coffee black and tilled the garden each spring in a long skirt. She had tended house for a living at the residence of an old woman who was known for her proclivities toward verbal abuse, then worked for a time at the local day care, but finally settled on a job at the meat locker where she wore a thick navy coat regardless of the season. She spent her days hefting bloody sides of meat around the walk-in freezer and butchering with a big knife.

It was not normal for a Mennonite woman to live like this, and always the talk turned toward getting her married. My father knew so-and-so who is said to have a brother who's a good, godly man.

While doing missionary work, my uncle met a man in Kentucky who built his own house and lived off the land and wasn't picky. Men arrived at her house unannounced, sent by one of her brothers. She was obliged to smile and serve them coffee and cakes and talk about the harvest that season or the lesson of last Sunday's service.

But she never married. This I gripped across two thousand miles of highway, windows down, speeding through the flat grasslands, under skies painted with pink clouds, past a vast crater pitted from a long-ago collision. That Ruth existed meant I might exist, too.

I needed space. I wanted to be scared and strong. Instead I wound up living in a double-wide on a washed-out dirt road with an older man named Ezra. I tried not to think about this, how I wasn't on my own even though that's what I'd wanted, how my life had become a series of sad ironies. He wore a handlebar moustache and had a giant eye tattooed on the back of his neck. When I asked what the eye tattoo meant, he said it was personal and not to ask again.

I told myself I would only stay with him until I got on my feet, but I wound up living in the double-wide for three years. That last year with Ezra he fell asleep as soon as his head hit the pillow, and then I lay on my side staring at him for hours as he snored. Before he got in bed, I would lay there tucked in and watch him undress, watch him deliberately fold his pants and shirt, watch him look in the mirror and twirl the ends of his moustache between his fingers, watch him sit down on the edge of the bed with his back to me, watch him snap off the lamp, watch him slide his legs beneath the sheets, watch him arrange himself there and close his eyes. He'd do all this without looking at me. *Good night*, I'd say. *Good night*, he'd say, then turn on his side and be gone. This was the game we played as things fell apart, me staring at him and him pretending I wasn't there.

He collected books about dreams and reality, how one could provide insight about the other. He wanted to find a way to dream while waking and was convinced he could resolve the problems of his daily life while asleep. He believed the boundary between these worlds was fluid or perhaps didn't even exist at all. He spent weekends poring over his books in the makeshift study, a population of small clay men that he'd sculpted sitting on the windowsill and table beside him. As a hobby, he liked to photograph these men in tiny postapocalyptic settings he constructed. We had a number of these images framed on our trailer's walls.

Sober, he was one way. Drunk, the man was quite another, able to be manipulated into certain affections, but only after especially heavy drinking, a long afternoon and even longer night spent at The Birdcage downing two-for-ones and smoking rollies. He liked me best when I'd been drinking and had become simpleminded, hopping up and down and clapping my hands to Tom Petty on the jukebox, missing the dartboard entirely and driving steel-tipped spikes into the wooden wall. He laughed, self-satisfied. *My baby*, he said.

One night my high heel got stuck between the slats on the deck out back, and I had to slip my foot out and then pry the shoe from between the beer-soaked boards. When I pulled it free I knocked myself ass over teakettle and just sat there cursing and making little kitten noises and saying how I was all dirty and messed up and needed another drink. He pulled me up and wrapped his arm around my waist as I stood there lopsided with a shoe in my hand. I rested my head on his shoulder and sighed, then nuzzled my nose into his neck. We danced between the pool tables, and he kissed me on the lips, these little kisses, over and over again. When we went out, I always felt like we were performing for someone, but I didn't really care. I wanted him to love me even if it really was just cheap theater. That's how my whole life felt anyway, a big act.

We walked home from the bar since we'd been driving drunk too much. That night in the darkness, he became agitated with me for walking too fast or too slow. I hadn't listened. I wasn't nice enough. I hadn't waited for him while he took a piss in a bush. I didn't care. I slept on the couch that night and woke up feeling sick. He was in the kitchen brewing coffee with tobacco strewn all over the counter, rolling a crooked cigarette.

He moved away to Tucson, and I bought a cabin on Cherokee Lane with a couple thousand down. For the most part I was successful in avoiding happy hour and instead stayed home to paint a kitchen wall Christmas-ornament red and sew striped curtains for the screen porch. In the mornings, I smoked long brown cigarettes on the porch and stared out at the steaming pines, the blackbirds moving among them and up into the clear sky.

Soon enough the season grew colder and I started building fires with the juniper from Hunter Jim, blazing infernos that licked up the inside of the chimney pipe and heated the whole house like a sweat lodge. The house was so hot I wore tank tops inside, then opened the windows and kept loading on the firewood. At night, I closed the orange eyes of the stove and, lying in bed, listened to the metal tick and ping as it cooled. In the morning, I dug through the gray ashes in the bottom of the stove, uncovered the neon-orange coals, and started the fire all over again.

That same September, this guy named Chas, who lived in Colorado, was back in Prescott for an extended visit, working on a photo series, black and whites I knew had something to do with nudity. My friend Kate called me up one morning and asked did I want to pose for one. He'd asked her, but she didn't want to do it alone. He remembered my name and wondered would I be interested. Sure, I said. Of course.

Chas and I had met only once before, at his going-away party a year earlier. He was also older, a friend of Ezra's.

"It's a binge, my dear," he had said in a fake British accent. Chas tipped back a bottle of dark beer, and the veins in his neck raised. He wasn't a big man, but his body was all muscle, the human incarnation of a fist. He wore a finely trimmed, faintly red goatee. He seemed sanitized, as if he'd taken many showers that day.

I was drunk myself, in the living room staring at these huge photos he'd taken: Thumb Butte black against nuclear sunsets, a long panorama of this place called the Dells where smooth volcanic rocks bulbed up and out of the earth like mushrooms. Ezra was somewhere outside. I didn't know where, and I didn't care.

Chas was most notorious for being in lingering love with Beth Cantrell, wholesomely blonde, with perfect posture and a year-round tan from camping and rock-climbing and kayaking. She was eleven years younger than he was. They'd dated a number of years before, but now she stayed away from him for the most part since it was commonly held he was still a little obsessed. From the talk, I also gathered his general mental stability was questionable, as was his heterosexuality, and that most considered him a savant of some sort.

He drove me and Kate into the national forest, and we got undressed in a big drainage pipe that ran under the road. He had a gym bag full of tall patent boots and latex garments and dressed us up in them, then posed our bodies at unnatural angles and told us not to move as he stared through the camera, adjusting things. He took one shot and then the rain started and that was that.

On the way back to town, as water washed across the windshield, Chas looked at me and I looked at him and he said, "Movie?" and I said, "Movie at my cabin," and Kate, sitting between us, rolled her eyes. We dropped her off and then went to Cherokee Lane, watched a movie as a matter of formality, and crawled under my big down comforter out on the futon on the porch. It was still raining, and he started kissing me.

"I haven't been with a woman for three years," he said. This meant Beth had been his last. I liked that.

He bought bags of groceries at the health food store, spinach and tortillas and black beans and strawberries, food with whole grains and omega-3 and flaxseed, this tea called maté that smelled like freshly cut hay, which he drank through a metal straw from a gourd. He was very concerned with staying alive and wouldn't drink my coffee or cream.

"Poison," he said in the morning, boiling water for his tea. "I need to keep a clean system."

He left during the days to do whatever, and I went to work, and in the evenings he was there or he wasn't. I didn't keep tabs. It was come-and-go as we pleased, meet up whenever, no pressure. It was about sex and that was it. I only wanted to sink into someone.

"I love these thighs," he'd say, running his hands over the curves I would have rather not had. "Sexy." All I could think about though was Beth Cantrell and her flatness and straightness and how he actually loved her. I wouldn't have minded him falling in love with me, even though I knew that wasn't really what I wanted.

His birthday was in early October, and the week before, he propped himself on his elbows in my bed. He'd just done all these things to me.

"Do you think you'd have a threesome with me for my birthday?" he asked. "That's what I want."

I thought about it, and Chas looked at me sweetly, smiling his best underjawed smile. Thinking about being in bed with two other people made me feel as though I were full of punched-out windows. I wanted to be OK, wanted to be strong and unhurtable, but I lay there and could only breathe and stare at the ceiling as pairs of blackbirds flew in and out of me, their wings making the noise of skirts swishing together on a slow dance floor.

"I'll think about it," I said. The next day I told him no. Soon after that, I didn't want to sleep with him anymore. I didn't want him even to touch me. "Time to go," I said one morning, but he already knew. He packed his gym bags with the boots and latex and baby powder and masks. He gave me a hug. "It was fun," I said, even though right then, standing by the open door, the whole thing was poised to tip over into something else. I could feel it teetering inside of me.

"Cheerio, then," he said, patting my arm. He loaded his truck and drove up Cherokee Lane and over the hill.

There was this game I liked to play when I was a kid where I'd make the square-jawed neighbor girl pretend to be a man and then kidnap me and lock me in a tower, which was really the hall closet full of coats and flannel shirts that smelled of my father's sweet cigars and green hay perspiration. I made her hold my wrists behind my back, push me into the darkness, and tell me I could never leave. After she slammed the door and turned a key, a rush of dark, glittering heat moved up my legs and into my stomach. It felt like a thousand points of shorted electricity, a sky full of stars blinking into being and then dying in explosions. And that's what I had wanted, for Chas to take me away, to have me whole, to lock me up. I wanted the sky to fall into me and then split open. There were too many people in the world was the problem. For just one of them to want me all for himself—why was that so hard? Just one. That's it.

It started raining in earnest in late October, and rivulets of water slid down the slanted wood ceiling in the mudroom. I climbed up on the metal roof and fixed the holes with layers of thick black tar and wire mesh. I'd been diligent in collecting kindling from across the road in a cardboard box I kept on the porch, but once a constant drizzle set in and the kindling dwindled to nothing, I was shit out of luck. I tried using cardboard and scraps of lumber I had around the house, but eventually I didn't have what I needed to start a fire. I dug up Hunter Jim's brown business card and contemplated it. Easy, I thought, and free. I wouldn't have to pay a dime for what he'd give me, and I could get him to deliver it.

I called him and he answered the phone with, "Howdy." Just from the sound of my voice he recalled my name, first and last, and that I lived on Cherokee Lane, and yes, certainly, he had some kindling for me.

"When could you bring it by?" I asked.

"Oh, no," he said. "You'd need to come up here to collect it. I've got plenty at my house." I imagined it piled next to his woodshed, which would be flush with evenly cut logs. That's how my father kept things in Ohio, long rows of wood with pretty round ends that dwindled the further it wore into winter. Brown morning after brown morning, my father split wood out back. For the big logs, he drove a red metal wedge into the middle of the wood, then jimmied it out and sank the ax-head into the gash. After he loaded the hot orange mouth of the stove, he sat in an easy chair and read the Bible. As a child, once I learned about death, I cried thinking about how he'd be gone. Heaven didn't comfort me. I couldn't think beyond his body and its warmth, his thick-fingered hands.

The stack of juniper at the head of my driveway, the swaying pines with shaggy bark that smelled miraculously of vanilla, the cabin door I'd painted purple, the screen porch, the woodstove in my living room, the Sears Roebuck sewing machine heavy as an anvil on my kitchen table, the curtains I'd sewn and hung, the tulip bulbs I'd already buried in the flower beds, the mulch I'd covered them with—all of it was an attempt to return to goodness. But I was in the desert. I didn't believe in God anymore. I believed in myself, and this felt safe, like an armor. I could handle anything. I actually said this to people: I can handle anything. And Hunter Jim—what a joke, I thought. We made arrangements for me to stop by early the next week. I could get what I wanted by my own means and in my own way.

What I'm trying to get at is a sickness of the soul. I was ill that fall. The season was turning. I had no kindling, and the bar was warm. I went and I stayed. Ezra showed up, too. He'd ridden his motorcycle from Tucson, and I wanted him to come home with me but he wouldn't. He just sat on a stool, shoulders hunched, sipping whiskey from a short glass. I would have done anything for him, would have kissed the palms of his hands. He didn't know this, or maybe he did and that was the problem. He stared at himself in the mirror behind the rows of liquor bottles. I drank too much and laughed when I was near him. I assume I drove home later because that's where I wound up.

I don't know what time it was or how long I'd been home but someone came into my room at some point, and when I saw his silhouette I couldn't remember who I was or where I'd come from.

"Hey," he said. He kicked off his shoes at the foot of the bed. My brain was doing that thing, turning over like a dying engine.

"You," I said. I remember deciding the man was Josh, an ex of mine who did not even live in Arizona but had to go on antidepressants back when I dumped him. He was nice. I wanted it to be Josh in particular so I could just lie back down and not worry and go to sleep. I was so tired. He left the room and I blacked back into the bed and then he was there and slid beside me with his cool legs.

It was only after he began kissing me and I tasted his tobacco, I realized it was Ezra. It could have been anyone up to that point.

We started having sex, but once he really got going, it felt as if I wasn't even there anymore. I cried and told him to stop, please stop, and he rolled off.

The next morning we squinted at each other across the kitchen, him leaning on the counter sipping a cup of coffee, me standing next to the kitchen table in my robe with my arms crossed and all my hair piled on top of my head. Whenever Ezra and I had sex, I burned down there and swelled shut. I was actually allergic to him. I'd forgotten about this. In the driveway, as he left, he looked like a toy in his helmet and leather coat. He revved the motorcycle and peeled out. It was still early.

I was cold. I tried starting a fire with cereal boxes and balls of newspaper but the logs were too big. I got black soot all over my robe cuffs and burned my fingers with the matches. My head hurt, and I was searing between my legs, and my nose was stuffed up from too many cigarettes.

I went to the grocery store and bought a package of hot dogs and some buns, went home and ate three of them, ate two more, buried them in the trash, then pulled them out an hour later and ate the rest. I put on two sweaters and a pair of gloves. I watched as the day closed itself up like a box. I was waiting for something, a sign of kindness, relief. I smoked cigarettes on the porch, wrapped in a blanket, watching as the black bodies of the birds moved through the air.

Sitting out there, I thought about things, thought about quitting drinking, but then it was Halloween and there was a party at Beth Cantrell's house, and cheap red wine, and of course I had to. I saw Chas there, dressed in heels, black stockings, tiny shorts, and a shiny red corset. He was wearing eyeliner, which accentuated his high eyes. It was a binge.

"Chas," I said when he walked by. He turned his head but couldn't see me. He followed Beth out of the room. You could tell she didn't care about him from the way she walked, from her certainty he would follow her wherever she went. I pushed past a glitter fairy and a hairy man wearing a long blonde wig and drove home mostly sober, then lay in bed, lips stained purple from party wine, and stared at the ceiling, wondering when something would start to matter.

Hunter Jim looked the same as he had before, the deck shoes, the ratty jeans and plaid shirt rolled up at the sleeves, the caterpillar moustache, the thick dirty glasses, the fisherman's cap. I parked my car by his house, and when he came out, the way he smiled at me, I could tell he thought he was handsome. He liked the way his face looked when he shaved in the morning. I couldn't stand him.

"Well hello there, friend," he said. I searched behind him for the kindling pile, the neat lines of chopped wood, and saw neither. There was just a little shed back there with a padlock on the door, something wrapped in a blue tarp at the side. He lived next to the national forest in a rough-sided log cabin. I wondered if Jean/Marie was inside. It seemed she wasn't.

"Do you have four-wheel drive?" he asked, eying my car, a rusted wagon.

"Yeah," I said.

"It'd be better if I drove it up," he said, pointing toward the road. "It's rough going. You don't want to get stuck. Get out." His truck was in the drive. I wondered why we couldn't use that but didn't ask. I watched myself open the door and hand him the keys, watched our hands move next to one another and then away. I opened the passenger door and for exactly one second had a question in my mind, but it passed through before I could understand.

"I knew you'd come over," he said as he drove.

"I thought you'd have kindling at your house," I said. "That's the way you made it sound."

"Did I?" he asked. "Now why would I do that?" His question twirled and untwirled in the air as he drove us far into the woods.

The ruts in the road were worn deep from the rains. He finally turned on an old forest service road that cut steeply through the top of a wooded hill. When he pulled to a stop, the car was buried between the high earthen walls strewn with chunks of sandstone and clay and broken sticks. Hunter Jim pulled the emergency brake and smiled. A button on his shirt had come open, and I could see his chest and the hair.

"Oh," he said, following my eyes down to his shirt. "Believe me, I know."

I got out and started picking sticks off the ground and tossing them in the box I had in the back of the car. Hunter Jim meandered from stick to stick, as if sorting and selecting only the best ones. As he bent, I saw he was wearing a length of baling twine around his waist, threaded through the belt loops.

"I wanted to spend some time with you," he said, smiling again, and I smiled back politely. "You seem like you're a fascinating young woman." I laughed, politely again. Humor him. Be agreeable, kind. I had been taught from an early age to listen to men, to nod, to smile and answer them.

He started asking me questions, felt this was really the time to try and get to know me. Where I was originally from and all that.

"Ohio," I said.

"Whereabouts?" he asked.

"Oh, the eastern part," I said, trying to be unspecific.

"So you must have grown up on a farm," he said.

"Just a big garden," I said.

"And were you religious?" he asked.

"What?" I said. A fat little bird kicked up dirt under a bush. It seemed peculiar.

"Religious," he repeated.

"I was raised Mennonite, yeah," I said. He put his hands on his hips and leaned back, stretching.

"I knew it," he said, "but I was thinking Mormon, perhaps."

I didn't know what to say. I pressed a smile on my face. I wanted him to think that I didn't think anything was strange. This seemed important.

"You know, we met before I brought you that wood," he said. I squinted at him, and he nodded.

"Oh, right," I said. "Right." The box was half full. He was slowing down, collecting sticks neatly in his hands.

"I've been thinking a lot about you since I dropped off the wood," he said. I kept picking up sticks. He had stopped and was standing in the middle of the road, rubbing his hand back and forth against his stomach. My muscles pulled tight to my bones. "Your father," he said. He fidgeted with the knot of baling twine at the top of his pants. He fondled the frayed ends with his fingertips. "He was either a physician, a minister, or a politician. Am I right?"

Every grain of dust was coming into view. Rocks tumbled down the hill when my feet touched them, and I could smell car oil and creosote. A dark shimmer moved through me. I used to have this dream, of a jester chasing after me as I drove a jeep down a dirt road. The bells hanging from the points of his red and yellow hat jingled as he ran.

"He paints houses," I said. This was true. Hunter Jim was staring at me, leaning forward on his toes. I could see myself tossing him words like bits of raw meat and him plucking them from midair with his mouth. "He used to be a minister," I said. "And he's run in a couple of local races. Not a doctor, though."

"I knew it," Hunter Jim said. He went back on his heels and then took off his hat and felt his hair. He patted it down and whistled back at a bird, then laughed. "What a great day!" he said. "Don't you think it's beautiful out here?"

"That's plenty," I said. The box wasn't full, but I wanted to leave. He brought a handful of sticks to the car, and I moved away.

"Oh, no. Let's fill it," he said, looking in the box. "You want it good and full."

"OK," I said. I looked at his hands. They were pink and clean and without callus—the hands of a man who didn't know outdoor work. I missed my mother. She had a red birthmark on the pretty curve of her foot, and I hadn't seen it in years.

"You're so obedient," he commented.

The sky was flat with gray clouds. A bird sang. I was up there, far away from everyone, on a hidden road with Hunter Jim, who had my car keys squirreled in the warmth of his pocket. I had this feeling of having suddenly come to, as if I'd been gone for a very long time and was only now just opening my eyes behind the wheel of a soundless, speeding car on a dark highway.

This is it, I said to the girl bending to collect sticks from the dusty road. This is when it finally happens.

I was so calm, with red barns and castles and entire glittering cities, every place I'd ever seen or imagined or hoped to be, collapsing inside me.

I kept picking up sticks. They were crooked and had mint green fungus growing on them. He asked me something, did I like living in Prescott, something like that. I said yeah. He asked something else. I said yeah again. I stopped talking after that. It's that I couldn't.

"All good," he said when the box was full. I told myself to make him give me the keys, but instead got back in the passenger side without saying anything. This is when he drives you somewhere else, I told the girl in the car. She was so beautiful, so beautiful and stupid. I saw what Hunter Jim saw in her, and it was heartbreaking.

He drove, and we came to a drooping chain slung across the road.

"You're going to have to get out and get that," he said. I did. I got out and unhooked it, let him through, and got back in. I didn't know why I was the way I was. The windows were open as we drove. I looked at my hands. My cuticles were all torn up. We curved through the woods, down a hill, and then I saw his house. He pulled to the side of the road, turned off the engine, and handed me the keys.

"You can get more kindling any time you want," he said.

"OK," I said.

The driver's seat was still warm when I got in. I closed the door and stared at the road, feeling for the ignition. He stood beside the car, next to my open window. That's when he started clapping, slow, spreading his hands wide in between. The claps popped from his force.

"Bravo," he said. "Really, really well done." I got the car started, put it in gear, and undid the emergency brake. He laughed. "Ha!" he said, bucking his head up to the sky. "Ha!" I looked at him, and he had this smile on his face, not happy or hungry but something altogether different. He pushed his clapping hands toward the window. "Bravo," he said again. "Good job for making it through that."

The world outside was a photograph of itself, exactly the same but different. I let out the clutch and pushed on the gas. I could hear him clapping as I drove away.

I went to work and came home. I made fires. I listened to men and their guitars on the stereo long into the night. I thought about Ezra and what was so tied up inside of him he couldn't undo it. "Like a hard, black rock," he used to say of his heart, balling his hand into a fist. I thought about Chas and how, after a certain point, it was all I could do not to turn and try to hurt him when he touched me. One minute, we were sleeping together. The next, I couldn't stomach him, not even a little. I wondered, was this what normal people, walking around in the world, were these the things they felt and, if so, what did they do when they felt them? I mean, where did they put the feelings?

I had wanted to be alone and now I was, but it didn't feel like an accomplishment. It was the darkest part of the night, when even the wild, dirty pigs that liked to root up my tulip bulbs were somewhere with their dirty pig families rubbing noses against each other's hairy skin while sleeping. Inside my head, inside that cabin, I couldn't, so I walked.

I walked out the door to the bleached asphalt of Cherokee Lane and, farther, over the crooked roads in our pine-thick neighborhood, past the quiet-as-dead sleepers in their cabins, up and over and out onto the bigger streets, past the Safeway glowing cold with twenty-four-hour light, past the lifeless Mexican place that served cactus tacos, through town square where even the boot-scuffed doors of Whiskey Row were locked tight. I walked until I rubbed my heels raw inside my shoes and stopped in front of a low, ugly building where the Unitarians met on Sundays. It was a Thursday. I tried the door. It opened and I went in.

Dark shapes filled the dark sanctuary. I sat in a pew right in the middle of the room and watched the earliest light illuminate the windows like a candle. Modern items of worship—electric guitars, a retractable screen on which to project holy words, poorly painted ivy framing stenciled letters: "The way and the truth and the light"—slowly appeared at the front of the room. It was all so futile.

I closed my eyes to feel the heat of a faraway star on my cheek. When I was a small girl, twice a year in the empty Mennonite church at the end of the gravel lane, the men adjourned to one hallway, the women to another. I went with my mother, a young, dark beauty with slender ankles. In the clean hall, some of the women sat on a long backless bench with tubs of water at their feet, and the others knelt before them. The women on the benches lifted the hems of their skirts and raised one foot, then the other, above the basins. The women kneeling on the floor cupped their hands and spooned water over the feet, some bare and pale, others still in tan hosiery. No one spoke. Pairs of shoes were strewn about. It smelled of the dirt and creases of unknown bodies, of yeast and sweat and bathroom powder, balms made of beeswax, even of the summer garden, a whiff of a tomato plant, the ground they walked on, the freshly turned earth. It was an act of humility, my mother told me as she knelt and held a naked foot in her hands. It was an act of human grace.

A door creaked and I opened my eyes to find the room lit up like a greenhouse or newly painted nursery.

"Oh, hi," the woman said as if she'd been expecting me. She looked like she'd been crumpled into a tiny ball by a big hand and then flattened back out. She went to the back of the room where three coffee makers and stacks of cups sat on a long table and started making pot after pot. Soon a young, hunched couple with unwashed hair appeared and sat a few rows in front of me, touching shoulders but not saying a thing. A few more people milled at the back of the room where the coffee makers made dove noises. Men shaped like trash bags full of trash, skinny women with tight muscles wrapping their arms, insane boys with bright eyes, girls trying to make themselves disappear—one by one they filed in as if saints at the end of a hard pilgrimage.

Soon, a meeting commenced. They started talking about powerlessness—step one, they said, step one—and about getting fucked up, about God and surrender. They were talking about choices, how they'd made bad ones, talking about trying harder and then messing up again, apologizing, forgiveness. They were laughing and cussing, checking their palms when they didn't know the words. They were drinking coffee and Big Gulps, twitching, missing fingers, brains fried and scratching themselves, wrinkled, tired, homeless, thick men preaching humility in loud voices, cracking jokes, telling stories about diners and stashed bottles and empty wallets. They were broken down but not all the way. They were trying to wake up, five o'clock in the morning drinking coffee, so many cups of coffee, talking, saying how it was, how it is, how it will be.

PINKIE

Andrew Bales

PINKIE WAS A RODEO BULL—BRED TO BUCK, NOT REMEMBER—SO IT was with great intrigue that the past rushed back at him without solicitation. He wasn't aware of it as a memory at all, something plucked from a hunk of intertwined flesh in his noggin. It simply arrived, the way a letter from an old friend finds itself at your front door.

In Pueblo, life on Lincoln Bower's ranch was spotty fields and low metal buildings and a hazy view of mountains. Pinkie wandered the pasture and admired small changes in its vegetation. Noticed how his hooves depressed damp soil after a sprinkling of rain. But now these images flashed through Pinkie's mind. Some jarring and some tame, some long and others short. Still others that made not a wink of sense.

He recalled the two boys, how they arrived last summer in a semi hauling a silver trailer. The teens were mismatched, one tall and lean and the other an abbreviated version, as high as the first one's shoulder. They wore tight jeans and button-ups, hats large enough to conceal a small rodent. They walked towards Pinkie in a synchronized, lazy manner. As they came close, they ran their hands along his horns, over the bulging dome between his shoulders, down his worn back. Pinkie was in his prime, and the boys whistled lightly for it. Lincoln spoke to them, gestured to Pinkie. The boys spoke back. Their voices made a flat sound. A pleasant tone. Little puffs of laughter.

Later, Pinkie stood alone in that trailer as it zipped along the highway. The wind pushed through the grates and the bedding whipped up and swirled in tight loops. Vibrations from the chassis hummed at his hooves and worked through his muscular thighs and jiggled his haunches. He liked the sense of motion—the wind on his eyeballs and the trees moving by without any expense of effort. When the traffic died down, so did the commotion. The world became a blanket of wind, a washed out sound, and Pinkie could stare out for miles.

When the truck stopped on the side of the road, the boys came around back to retrieve him. Without a word they knew which of them would open the trailer's gate, knot the rope beneath Pinkie's flank, or walk him into a flat patch of grass. They were in love, Pinkie could tell. Not just a physical romp but the kind of love that came from time. In his mind, he could see the boys now: standing shoulder to shoulder, urinating at once into the ditch. Why did a stream of urine sound so *cold* as it splattered onto grass?

Yet after a few glorious weeks out on the road last summer, everything had changed. It was as if Pinkie had died in West Glacier, or vanished or otherwise up-and-transformed, because now he passed through his days in Pueblo like a hulking ghost. Lincoln would round the corner of a building and stare in his direction, then pivot and return to wherever he'd been before. All of this—the boys and Lincoln and the wind on his eyeballs—it all had something to do with the junior rider in West Glacier, he suspected, that Trevor Heptner.

Lincoln ran a small operation, but even a modest collection of bulls could figure towards a million dollars. The quality of his stock didn't come overnight, or that year, or even that decade. It was as if his entire life had been a progression towards a bull like Pinkie. Lincoln's studs were renowned. Most notable bulls had names like Colossal or Havoc or Big Pain or For the Win, but Lincoln preferred unassuming titles: Peach Pit, Ladybug, River Bend, Pop, Shoelace, Pinkie. And so, across the region, when a rider was flung into the air, it was possible you'd hear an entire stadium gasp and shout *Ladybug, Ladybug!* There was a certain beauty in it.

Lincoln desired these astonishing creatures—these *athletes*—and to produce a top specimen took time and care. It took the right bull and a healthy cow and a bit of luck. Lincoln was in the habit of collecting and preserving the seed of his best stock. It was a rather simple process. First, a cow would be tied in a stall. Her role was a bit of deception. Lincoln then walked in the stud, let him get a sniff of her from behind. It wasn't long before the bull would rise on his hindquarters. As the bull mounted and readied, Lincoln would grab hold of the protruding pink member and divert it from the cow and into a tube, a sort of prosthetic cow canal.

It saddened Lincoln to know that Pinkie must never rodeo again. That he'd felt himself too old to take Pinkie to Montana himself. That he'd had to hire those boys—a pair who'd found nothing but trouble for themselves up until that point in life and, apparently, had no other ambitions. In most cases, a public injury of the sort that occurred in West Glacier would launch a bull into an elite realm. Secure his status as an admirable and vicious beast. But Trevor Heptner had been so young, only sixteen, and so loved—the Heptner name was on specialty farm equipment across Montana—that it was out of a certain respect that professional riders wouldn't touch Pinkie, even if they secretly longed for the chance. Yes, the trauma of Trevor Heptner was too much to bear.

Still, Lincoln understood Pinkie's remarkable talent, knew that it was a kind of art. He'd once seen Pinkie chase a chapped cowboy in a tight circle as rodeo clowns danced at Pinkie's sides, trying to gain his attention and save the rider. But Pinkie ignored them, gave the rider just the right amount of room to survive. Kept the man dodging, spinning in a panic. Pinkie was in full control. He chased the rider up to the gate, where Pinkie lifted him out of the ring, *gently*, with his horns, up and over the rails. The veteran cowboy, back to safety, shook his head and began to weep from the joy of living. Pinkie had a gift that extended beyond his performances. Lincoln had witnessed something right away. He was there when Pinkie was born. It was during the deep of the night. Pinkie slid from his mother, who would die soon after from complications, and Lincoln swore that baby bull was smiling.

Pinkie recalled West Glacier. That afternoon when they arrived, the trailer slowed down, turned off the highway, swayed across an uneven field. This was no different than the procedure in Billings, in Sandpoint, in Helena. Pinkie remembered hills stretching out in the distance. Green grass and large pines and dirt roadways. A little girl in her father's arms waving at anything pulling into town. A rider from Idaho or Wyoming or Kansas or Texas. Another at a tailgate buckling up his chaps. Another taking a drink of water from an old milk jug, wiping the dew from his mustache. They were waiting for Pinkie. Waiting to try him on.

Metal bleachers were dropped in a circle on a dirt clearing. The ring was surrounded by pines. A few bare poles held bright halogens that, as things slipped into night, would flash on, making the whole affair feel sheltered from the rest of the world. The Porta-Potties and staggered rows of trucks and the buzz of the highway would be lost to the darkness, and all that would remain were those bleachers and dirt and the spectators and riders and the boys there watching, in the middle of it all, Pinkie.

It wasn't time yet. They'd have to wait till dusk came to West Glacier. The tall boy filled a bucket with water. The little one scattered hay beside that. As Pinkie chomped and slurped, they took two cigarettes from a single pack. The tall one made a flame and, one after the other, they lit them, and the smoke drifted up and away.

Lincoln never took a wife. He never moved from Pueblo. His parents passed away in a relatively timely manner and he buried them in a plot a few miles away. The family records and traces of genealogy went to his sister, who came to town to get a good price for her parents' property and never returned.

In the barn, Lincoln kept a binder on a shelf at eye level. The binder contained a record of the sample collection, but also notes about the bulls' temperaments. Some breeders didn't care about such things. They only documented the weight, the shape, or stats at the rodeo. Much of this was reasonable accounting. It was important never to forget, Lincoln knew, that the bull had a side to him that was built to hurt you. A bull was a meat machine, a bulk of muscles that could do great wonders, something you could never fully understand, no matter how hard you tried.

Lincoln took the log from the shelf. Each page contained twenty-odd lines, and each line contained one thought:

> *Pinkie, age 3 and 0 month 3 weeks— What a buck! Worth more than four quarters.*
> *Pinkie, age 3 and 1 month 1 week— Prefers yellow flowers.*
> *Pinkie, age 3 and 1 month 3 weeks— Ate two portions & rearing for more!*
> *Pinkie, age 3 and 2 months 1 week— Smiling as he eats fresh hay.*
> *Pinkie, age 3 and 2 months 2 weeks— Smiled again. Fresh hay again. Coy this time.*

It went on like this for dozens of pages. At the end, now at age 5 and 2 months, Lincoln stares at the final note—*Trevor Heptner. Trampled. Maimed. Pinkie devastated.*

That night in West Glacier arrives at Pinkie's brain. The white lights blasted on, bleaching the stands packed with sturdy men and women and their young. They clapped at Pinkie, waved their tiny hands.

The boys led Pinkie into the chute, where they waited over him, beside him. Pinkie's ribs were confined between cold metal bars. When it was time, Pinkie knew, the gate would make an awful clank, but before that he always felt a strange closeness creep in. A feeling of knowing the people around him for a moment. In Pueblo, Lincoln had always been nearby to steady him as a rider hopped onto his back, pulled a gloved hand along leather, and hooked his boots against Pinkie's sides. But in West Glacier, it was the boys with him. It was Trevor Heptner who came over the bars and down into the chute.

Pinkie felt the boy positioning himself on his back. His hands worked quickly. His fingers hard like little spurs gripped around the bull rope and pulled tight. His body was smaller than most, but warm, spread open, the legs bowed in a wide "U," a weight that held close before they were released into the cool night. Pinkie could hear him working hard to control his breathing, and the sound of the air through his nose wasn't that different from his own. The boy's breath smelled like sweet corn.

The announcer would always come over the fuzzy speaker with the rider's name, his hometown, how well he rode and what buckles it got him. Pinkie couldn't make out the words, but the names of the riders always stood out somehow. They stretched like the rumble of thunder. Then he heard it: Treeeeeeeevor Heppptneeeer! Pinkie's mouth and nose began to drip. The boy squeezed down tight and Pinkie shifted and rattled the bars to his sides. The crowd was wilder than he'd ever ever heard. When the gate finally clacked open, the ride lasted six seconds.

Pinkie flung his body forward and bucked his legs. He felt like a caterpillar in fast motion. Usually the riders tried to hang on, but Pinkie would feel a slipping sensation and finally a release. He'd see the look in the rider's eyes as he hit the dirt. The dilated pupils, the creeping smile as dust rose from his impact. This boy, Trevor Heptner held on tight, a light tick on his back.

Pinkie pounded his front legs into the ground. He bucked back. The feel of his own mass shifting gave him pleasure. The back and forth action dug dirt from the ground, shot it into the air, and Pinkie watched it move like smoke. He understood, just looking at it, how the air exerted an invisible force, that same something he felt moving across his back in the trailer. Pinkie felt limber and strong, and knowing that the boys watched him from the gate, witnessing his most elegant postures, kept him going.

Pinkie was so absorbed in the motion that he was surprised to find that the boy was already on the ground. That his hooves, which had felt light as air, had in fact been landing on Trevor's legs and arms and middle. He'd used the boy's elastic body to send him higher into the air. Yes, Pinkie had done well for himself. The men in overalls and silly paint waved their arms. Their faces had taken on a new kind of shock at his acrobatics. They dragged the boy across the dirt to the edge of the ring. Pinkie recalled now the sound that the crowd made, like all their excitement being sucked back into their bodies. An inhalation and then quiet.

After, the boys cracked their boots into Pinkie's side. They wouldn't look at him directly. Pinkie was taken to the trailer—no water to refresh him, no feed—and then, for the rest of the night, each cowboy passing by would bang his fist against the wall. Pinkie rested on the shavings and, after hours alone, finally dozed off and began to dream. He remembered this too—in his dream, Pinkie roamed various fields, chewed upon exotic plants and animals. Lincoln was there, had brought a lawn chair with him and set about watching Pinkie flex his muscles and even stand on his hind legs. Pinkie walked a loop with a cowboy swagger. He defecated wildly, until its height exceeded his own!

He woke that night from the excitement of the dream. The trailer was shaking, the boys driving him off into the darkness of the highway, and when they finally did stop how they got out and sat quietly on the roadside. They held their heads in their hands. They spoke softly at one another, and the shorter one leaned his head gently against the tall boy's shoulder. The tall boy, for his part, stroked the little one's hair.

They did not speak again. Not to Pinkie. Something had gone terribly wrong. The boys didn't stop to rodeo in Bozeman or Big Sky or Casper. When the truck did stop and the boys urinated on the side of the road, they did not check on Pinkie. Instead, their flannel shirts brushed quickly along the slits in the trailer, as if they were waving those shirts in his face, taunting him. Right then, Pinkie might have ripped the boys apart if they'd let him down from that trailer. If he'd thought it would have done any good.

Lincoln spotted Pinkie in a far corner of the pasture, a section he did not often wander into. Lincoln rounded the edge of a muddy patch and came to Pinkie's side. Lincoln placed his hand on Pinkie's flank. He walked Pinkie back to the barn, where he'd tied up the cow. The cow faced the wall. Her rump was boxy and her tail wagged once, sagged.

Under his arm, Lincoln carried a tube as long as his forearm. The tube was an industry tool, if simple. Hep, hep, Lincoln said, and Pinkie brought his face behind the cow. When Pinkie caught a whiff, he mounted. Even for Lincoln, that mass hoisted precariously in the air was striking.

Lincoln gripped the erect penis and guided it into the tube. The whole performance from Pinkie would take maybe ten seconds. The semen would be frozen and shipped around the country. Sometimes the world. Lincoln didn't mind this practice. In fact, he found some joy in connecting Pinkie with a bit of pleasure. Especially now. Lincoln imagined that Pinkie couldn't tell from his position, mounted on the cow's back, that his efforts had been diverted.

And from up there, as Pinkie rested his arms atop the cow's rump, he felt tall. Pinkie held the posture of a cowboy, a life on two legs. Pinkie looked down at Lincoln, who hunched forward with his attention elsewhere, downward, as if Lincoln waited down in the chute and it was Pinkie who would watch over Lincoln this time. Below, Pinkie felt a warm rush coming over his lower half. He felt the strain of the muscles in his thighs, a wonderful slickness and tingle. Yet Pinkie's mind wouldn't focus on it. His mind had gone away again. It was with the boys as much as it was with Trevor. It was with the grass outside as much as it was with those towns in Montana and the rodeo riders with the milk jugs full of water. Pinkie then thought back, far back, to something he could never have witnessed. He saw what must have been his birth, a cow who must have been his mother. This was as far back as Pinkie had ever gone. And there Pinkie was, slipping out onto the dirt and his mother licking him clean.

Lincoln, working below, caught what Pinkie produced and pulled the cylinder gently from the now retracting pink member. He looked at Pinkie, who dismounted and stared into his eyes, looked away, then turned his head to gaze elsewhere. The cylinder in his hands was worth an extraordinary amount of money and should be frozen right away. Yet Lincoln hesitated, looked at the tube, looked at Pinkie. He imagined the little Pinkies that might go romping around the world in his lifetime. It could be years or decades or even centuries before the last of his line arrived. Pueblo would be a different city by then, but the bull itself wouldn't have changed all that much. It was a wonderful thought.

EVEN HUCK,
EVEN EMMELINE GRANGERFORD

Lucy Biederman

1. A Day Like That

LIKE ME WHEN I WAS A CHILD, HUCK FINN HATES SUNDAYS. AND SUN-shine. One day, "Sunday-like, and hot and sunshiny," Huck explains,

> there was them kind of faint dronings of bugs and flies in the air that makes it seem so lonesome and like everybody's dead and gone; and if a breeze fans along and quivers the leaves it makes you feel mournful, because you feel like it's spirits whispering—spirits that's been dead ever so many years—and you always think they're talking about *you*. As a general thing it makes a body wish *he* was dead, too, and done with it all.

Why would God make a day like that? As actual—unyielding—as the adults' decisions I lived by, squinting in the heavy light, moving through the lonely air during an extra-special two-hour session of gym class, trying to understand the rules to some adaptation of softball: if I ever forget that feeling, I will have abandoned the very core of myself.

2. Huck/Dickinson I: Flies

When he pauses and looks around in that "mournful" way, Huck's cast of mind makes me think of Emily Dickinson's—attention to the world, *curiosity*, that spoils easily, turning into nevermind.

Dickinson's well-known 591 begins:

> I heard a Fly buzz – when I died –
> The Stillness in the Room
> Was like the Stillness in the Air –
> Between the Heaves of Storm –

Dickinson wrote those lines in 1863, before Huck was a glimmer in Twain's eye. Twain began writing *Adventures of Huckleberry Finn* in 1876, after *The Adventures of Tom Sawyer* was published. He worked on the novel on and off over the next several years, finishing it in 1884. It was published in the U.S. in 1885 (the year before Dickinson died). But there's no way Twain would have found his way to 591 while he was working on *Huck Finn*; the poem was not published until 1896, as part of *Poems, Third Series*, edited (heavily) by Mabel Loomis Todd and Thomas Wentworth Higginson, during the first, posthumous rush of public interest in Dickinson. Dickinson and Twain, although they wrote and lived in the same country at the same time, missed each other.

But on a plane where fiction meets history, I imagine Dickinson and Huck converge, their dark sensibilities humming in sync from time to time. *Huck Finn* takes place, scholars agree, in one of the two decades directly before the Civil War, either the 1840s or the 1850s. Maybe it takes place in 1858, the year Dickinson's writing life began in earnest, the year she began the practice of assembling her poems in bound volumes. She was twenty-seven years old. Huck was fourteen.

3. Huck/Dickinson II: Skies

"I never felt at Home – Below –" Dickinson writes in 437, as if she is already dead. Huck doesn't feel at Home Below, either; he searches—at first ping-ponging between living with his abusive father and with the do-gooder widow Miss Watson, later from the raft with Jim to the dangers on land—for a way and a place to be "comfortable."

And like Dickinson, Huck plays with death. He fakes his death at the beginning of *Huck Finn*, setting into motion his notorious voyage down the Mississippi. He shares Dickinson's intellectual and emotional interest in death, nudging at it, like Keats "half in love with" it. In that "Sunday-like" scene, Huck both wishes for death *and* wishes it away, fearful of it, attracted to it.

Dickinson performs the same push and pull with death, an uncomfortable, insufficient solution to a world that is neither comfortable nor sufficient. That first stanza of 437 continues:

> And in the Handsome skies
> I shall not feel at Home – I know –

If "Below" has been so sorry a home, why assume "the Handsome skies" will be an improvement?

Huck reports on Miss Watson's vision of Heaven: "She said all a body would have to do there was to go around all day long with a harp and sing, forever, and ever. So I didn't think much of it. But I never said so."

Even as I wondered why God made such sunny, still and silent Sundays, another part of me knew: people *liked* them. My horror was their reward. Heaven is for other people.

"I don't like Paradise," Dickinson writes in 437. "Because it's Sunday – all the time – ."

4. Legends

America has two legendary poets, Dickinson and Walt Whitman. Whitman "a kosmos, of Manhattan the son," Dickinson, the belle of Amherst.

It isn't that Dickinson *never* mentions a local town or city in all of her poems, but it's quite rare, and when she says "Amherst," she means it philosophically, wondering, in 241, of the inhabitants of Eden, "Do they know that this is 'Amherst'–." More often, Dickinson name-drops a foreign city or country, typically to connote the exotic (726: "I could bring You Odors from St

Domingo – / Colors from Vera Cruz – "), but even those occasions are few, particularly compared with the frequency with which she uses a broad term like place, or far, or world. In Dickinson's unique grammar, those words tend to be capitalized, as if standing in for where a proper noun would be, were the poem by a more conventional writer.

Whitman, meanwhile, sings "Boston, Philadelphia, Baltimore, Charleston, New Orleans, San Francisco," his poetics a rich catalogue of place names. But those cities could be in a different order, or they could be different cities altogether, say, "Cleveland, Sacramento, Albuquerque, Richmond, Baton Rouge, Nashville." In their greatness, Dickinson and Whitman, both, in different ways and combinations, are specific *and* general, regional *and* universal. They cover it all, together, describing and achieving the huge and the minuscule, across their different philosophies and prosodies.

It's probably not a coincidence that both our legendary American poets are from the East Coast, where the Puritans hit land. You can see the whole country from there. You can talk about it any and every way you like, from Boston to Place, World to New Orleans.

But I'm from the Midwest, and I want my own legend, a legendary poet from home.

5. *Prairie Style*

There's something in the Midwest that pulls against the registers of greatness, its lexicons and tones, its heights and depths of grief and joy, that Whitman and Dickinson draw and draw on. We don't do that where I grew up, I-90/94 looping into I-55 while the ground just sits there, nothing moving on a weekday afternoon; head pressed against the window, waiting. Cairo, pronounced K-Ro, a big little city in the part of Illinois that everyone says is basically Mississippi, down low, the secret South no one knows. "An arch at Ohio/Indiana, another—similar, more formidable—at the Mississippi. Eaton, Richmond, big Indianapolis, beautiful-sounding Terra Haute, don't forget Effingham, can't forget Effingham."

That's from C.S. Giscombe's essayistic 2008 book of poetry, *Prairie Style*. The book consists of chyrons of pithy but enigmatic statements about the Midwest, its landscapes, myths, and peoples. "One gets even in the midwest, one gets even in the midwest, one gets even in the midwest," Giscombe writes. Maybe he repeats the phrase for each of its meanings:

1. One settles the score in the Midwest;
2. even in the Midwest one can get what one is owed;
3. only one person settles the score (or gets what they are owed) in the Midwest.

"One gets even in the midwest." Said three times, it sounds like a tune with only one note but lots of rhythm. Or a highway that stays in a straight line as it goes on and on through various farms and towns.

I think *Prairie Style* is about *Huck Finn*, although Giscombe never mentions the novel or its author by name. The book takes place where *Huck Finn* does, down the Mississippi, in the Midwest. In the realm of jokes, bluffs, mistakes, accidents, tries, experiments, bugaboos.

6. Emmeline Grangerford

My favorite part of *Huck Finn* is when Huck swims to the Kentucky side of the Mississippi and there discovers the Grangerford family, with their country gentility and their poor dead daughter, Emmeline. Under an assumed name, Huck lives with the Grangerfords for a short while, awe-struck by the whiteness of Colonel Grangerford's linen suits, the abundance of food at family meals, the presence of books in the house. In one of the only detailed interior scenes in the novel—one of the few times Huck goes inside—Huck is captivated by the tackiness, grotesquery, beauty, and strangeness of the writing and life that Emmeline left behind.

I have two brothers, both younger, one by two years, one by nearly a decade. Every night, my much-younger brother would yell up the stairs to us—"Children! Dinner time!" Huck is like that, reporting of Emmeline, "This young girl kept a scrap-book . . . " He is impressed by the drawings she made "her own self when she was only fifteen years old," even though Huck, himself, is only fourteen. Like my little brother was, Huck is too far apart, too different, to deeply outside, to ever be inside childhood the way other children get to be.

But from his vantage point, he sees something no one else in the house sees: how stupid it all is. Some part of Huck is laughing, the way I know my brother was laughing at us, even as he admiringly describes Emmeline's superserious art: one drawing of a woman "leaning pensive on a tombstone on her right elbow, under a weeping willow," another of a "young lady . . . crying into a handkerchief . . . ," with "a dead bird laying on its back in her other hand with its heels up."

"Poor Emmeline," Huck says, "poor thing," not sounding at all like the hard-living teenage trickster I remember when I close the book. But when I open it again, I learn again that that *is* how he sounds.

7. *Poetical Domestication*

Although Emmeline is fiction, she isn't *pure* fiction, in that women and girls wrote and published a lot of poetry in the mid-nineteenth century. Even Dickinson, enduring emblem of the unpublished genius, published at least ten poems in newspapers during her lifetime, and corresponded with important, nationally known editors like Higginson and Samuel Bowles. When Dickinson herself was fourteen, she wrote to a friend that being "poetical" was "what young ladys aim to be now a days." Emmeline clearly had received the same message by that age.

But all that isn't anything Huck knows; he isn't that domesticated. Emmeline's life and writing excite Huck because of how little he has seen of such things. The town newspaper, which would have included poems by lady scribblers, wasn't delivered to his dad's weird cabin in the woods.

8. Before

Emmeline Grangerford's life was over before she became a woman. *Huck Finn* is over before Huck is a man: he has to go out West to do that. Out of the book, out from under Twain's and the reader's watchful eyes.

Huck will never grow up; he will never be a man. He is *boy-like*, as in unmanly, as in brave, as in playful, as in the blue-and-white *American Boys Handy Book*—first published in 1882, two years older than *Huck*—that my brother, the one closer to my age, and I loved, with its advice on how to tie knots and kill animals in your backyard. We never tried any of its tricks, but we read it all the time.

Huck will never be a man. He is *curious*, as in nonsexually sexual, snooping around Emmeline's stuff, a fellow poet, although he will never think of himself that way.

9. The Unwritten Land

Huck Finn begins with the line, "You don't know about me." The sentence doesn't end there. What Huck really is saying, or at least what he means, is that you don't know about him *if* you haven't read *Tom Sawyer*. But the way the novel ends, with Huck going out into the Oklahoma Territory, beyond our apprehension, we *don't* know about him, even after reading either book, *Tom Sawyer* or *Huck Finn*.

10. One Gets Even in the Midwest

"But I reckon I got to light out for the Territory ahead of the rest, because Aunt Sally she's goin to adopt me and sivilize me, and I can't stand it." In Huck's world, which is the American Midwest, you can't get what you want, and you're not in control.

But you can always choose what to say. And what to withhold.

Sing, poet: you don't know about me.

SELECTED EPISODES FROM WARTIME PHILIPPINES ON A SATURDAY NIGHT

Anna Cabe

WARTIME PHILIPPINES
Netflix Studios
BRUCE Productions
Philippine National Endowment Fund for Culture and the Arts

CASTING CALL

Calling all Filipino-Americans! Do you want to know about your grandparents' history? Do you want to know what it was like during the World War II Japanese Occupation? We are looking for participants in a reality documentary television series:

Must be of Filipino descent. At least 18 years of age. Knowledge of Filipino/Tagalog and other Filipino languages preferred but not required. Shooting in the Philippines will take 3 months.

If you are interested, please email castingwartimephilippines@ gmail.com with an audition tape answering these questions:

Why do you want to participate in Wartime Philippines?

What do you hope to learn from participating in Wartime Philippines?

Name: Francisco Dominguez
Sex: Male
Age: 24

Hometown: Chicago, IL
Position: Artist

Name: Leonidas Dominguez
Sex: Male
Age: 82
Hometown: Glencoe, IL
Position: Retired real-estate developer

Trailer #2: A Sneak Peek of the Barrio

Granddad tells us he came up with the idea himself. "It'll teach Kiko a few things," he growls into the microphone, accidentally revealing your embarrassing childhood nickname to the world and making sure none of us ever refer to you as "Francisco," the name which you go by as an adult would-be artist. We always refer to your Granddad, the impressively named Leonidas Dominguez, as "Granddad" or "Mr. Dominguez" in the break-room at work or in the comments of Internet recaps.

"Just so you know," you say, "I was the one who suggested it. I saw the casting call on *Buzzfeed* or something."

You tell us you were not sure if Granddad, vigorous as he was at his advanced age, would pass, but he does. The casting director is near-apoplectic with joy. "A real survivor!" she tells us joyfully. "We were hoping to have at least one." And after she mentions that, we are glad, too, since your Granddad adds a gloss of authenticity to the show we accidentally find on Netflix while browsing on a slow Saturday night.

You look surprised, though not really, when the woman looks at you conspiratorially and says, "You know, we weren't sure if we were going to take people who don't speak the language, but Bruce decided that the current generation needs to know what it's like. Anyway, it's the Internet!" As if slapping the "Internet" on anything makes anything strange and possibly unworkable OK, but we roll with it. A couple of decades of grown men screaming at the sight of double rainbows on the Internet prime us for this.

This is how it works: This is a real, transcontinental affair, an attempt to preserve and present rapidly forgotten Filipino history to the young, smartphone-obsessed American-born youth by asking a bunch of Fil-Ams to live exactly like it was back in the Philippines during World War II. Bruce, an eccentric naturalized Filipino-American multimillionaire who goes by one name, like Madonna or Cher, tried to take the idea to major American television networks, but it was deemed too "niche," even for PBS, despite the abundance of *1900 Houses* and *Frontier Houses*. Undeterred and possessing boatloads of cash and similarly starstruck Filipino legislators in his pockets, he was able to convince Netflix to "appeal to a previously untapped audience (Title Card: *Do you know there are over 3.4 million Filipinos in the USA? We sure didn't!*) dying for representation of themselves onscreen."

You'll live like Granddad and his family and neighbors did when he was a boy, suffering the same privations: limited food, air sirens (but no real bombs 'cause duh, liability), squads of trigger-happy soldiers (sans real guns).

You, Kiko, think you can handle it. We can tell when you first appear on our screens. You talk about those similar shows on PBS: genteel Brits living during the Victorian Era, Americans roughing it in "Oregon Territory" as pretend-pioneers. It doesn't look so bad to you, we realize. You say you like camping and hiking, and anyway, it's not like you had the money for luxuries until you moved into your Granddad's house, "bent but not broken," as you said by your stint in the Big City, trying to sell your spike-covered dildos and hairy televisions to elitist, uncomprehending art galleries. "They called me derivative," you say. "It's a *commentary*."

You tell us you can take care of Granddad. "I'll carry him on my back," you promise us, your skinny chest expanding into the manliness you want us to see.

From Agreement for Wartime Philippines Participants
[. . .] I understand that my participation comes with risks, including but not limited to illness, injury, and mental distress, for which I am releasing Producer from all claims and liabilities. Any and all disputes arising out of and in connection with this Agreement hereof shall be exclusively settled by binding arbitration [. . .]

Episode 1: Welcome to Villaguerra

After a grueling day-long journey by plane during which you record yourself on an approved camera, feverishly babbling that your feet's probably going to be in a coma forever, you arrive in Granddad's home island we immediately forget the name of. There, you are driven to a reconstructed barrio a couple of hours outside Manila called (unimaginatively for those of us who can understand any Spanish) Villaguerra. We discover this is not Granddad's native province. The narrator, a soothing British woman's voice, explains there are 81 provinces in the Philippines, spread over 7,641 islands, which we file away for Wednesday night trivia. See how much we're learning already?

"Who do these people think they are?" he demands. "Are Ilocanos like Kapampangans? Are Bicolanos like Cebuanos? And is that an Igorot?"

You tell us, red-faced, you wish your Granddad weren't so racist as we stare at a barely dressed man right out of *National Geographic* wander around the outskirts of the barrio. We nod in sympathy, recalling our own grandparents, creaky dinosaurs from a less progressive era we shuffle to another room when they say something about the "homos."

We know you wish you knew more about the Philippines. You realize you're not even sure what all those words Granddad said are (we sure as hell don't know either). "Hell, why didn't I even Wikipedia this shit before I came?" you pant. Your iPhone's been taken away, and even if you had it, we seriously doubt there are enough towers around for you to try that app, when we scan the rolling fields with scattered trees that surround your village. We see you dig your hands in your pockets and stare mournfully in the distance. The crueler of us, the Baby Boomers, laugh at your Millennial ADHD. Sucker!

You stare at your surroundings. Potholed streets, palm trees, and chickens, goats, dogs, and cats padding through the dust. The buildings, though, are more solid than you, we, expect—there are even concrete buildings.

You do not get a concrete house, and Granddad still has to puff himself up like a rooster. "This is nothing. When I was young, we only had two rooms and ten people in our house."

"But you have only five brothers and sisters," you say.

"You forget. Your Lola Monet lived with us. And my Lolo— Lola Monet was his sister." ("Lolo" and "Lola" appear on the screen with a translation—grandfather and grandmother.)

The house is sturdy enough, though, with a metal roof (which will later drive you crazy when it starts raining, which you rant about constantly to your one approved camera).

You feverishly wonder where the bathroom is, and then you discover you bathe in rainwater or river water and pee in an outhouse.

Your skin, our skin, used to running, filtered water, itches.

Your clothing isn't too bad, though. It's all 1940s wear, so no corsets or woven grass or whatever we thought you'd wear. Granddad, to your embarrassment, has to show you how to tie the tie on your one nice suit and at which angle you should wear the fedora to look fly, and then bitches at you about your shiny shoes, which rapidly become dusty in the unpaved streets.

"Some things never change," you tell us. We all nod in agreement.

Episode 2: Meet the Villagers

You get to know the people of the barrio slowly, with us. On-camera, you're encouraged to make comparisons between your old life and your new life. After all, this is *educational* not trash TV like those "hookers married to the rapper and that bakla on E!" as your unfortunately unenlightened Granddad puts it (some of us call him

"Racist/Homophobic/Transphobic Granddad" while others point out that dude, he was born in *1928* and grew up without a freaking flush toilet in some godforsaken country). You are encouraged to complain, a little, about the meager food, the outdoor toilets, the sweat, the dirt, the fear, those awful soldiers (but not too much). You are slightly discouraged from talking smack about your neighbors, even if they deserve it, like how your neighbors, the Malubays, stole a recently slaughtered chicken, a rare rare prize, from your tiny yard one night, the fuckers (Though a little smack never hurt any ratings—we definitely don't mind it).

The first days, the producers set up a party for all five households that comprise the official barrio. Since this is supposed to mimic the early days of the Occupation, there isn't any of the dishes you're accustomed to seeing at the raucous Filipino events you grew up with, certainly no lechon roasting slowly on a spit, the skin crackling and bubbling golden-brown. We know this because you mention that, afterwards, with greater and greater frequency, how much you miss lechon or any meat, period, though you dabbled with vegetarianism before moving into Granddad's house.

But there is chicken and noodles and rice and piles of unfamiliar greens and bottles of fermented fish sauce and soy sauce, rice liquor, and everyone is digging into the food with their hands, with gusto. This is the first time we notice there are no children, which later, we realize, makes sense, 'cause duh, liability.

One of them, whom we just learned is Mr. Delarosa, president of his Fil-Am organization in New Jersey, rises and snaps his fingers for attention. The novelty causes everyone to stop chattering.

Mr. Delarosa: "Nais naming sabibin, um, Kim nalulugod kami narito ng, no ang, pag-aaral aming kasayan yo."

Granddad: "What did you just say?"

Mr. Delarosa: "Ako nasiyahan narita, I mean, narito."

Granddad: "Your Tagalog is terrible. Just speak English!"

You: "Granddad!"

But we quickly come to agree with Granddad, since Mr. Delarosa and his wife, Kim, vice-president of their Fil-Am organization, continue to butcher Tagalog in their earnestness, so much so that even us, the non-Tagalog-speaking audience members, start muting every time they speak. Netflix helpfully adds subtitles in both English and Tagalog for all their dialogue. But this is later.

Meanwhile, you, Kiko, converse with the Malubays. At this point, the production company is allowing you to speak like the Millennials you are.

You: "So what do you do in the real world?"

Albert Malubay: "You know I auditioned for *The Real World* once. They picked another Asian that season."

Alicia Malubay: "It's OK, babe, you got that *Law and Order* gig after that."

You:"What do you do, Alicia?"

Alicia Malubay: "I'm a model. You know the Revlon campaign?"

You: ". . . No?"

Alicia Malubay: "I was the inspiration for that."

We pause this to Google. Albert Malubay's IMDB page does include a stint on *Law and Order* among this three credits, which showed that he was that episode's corpse. Alicia Malubay's public Facebook profile says "model," but besides some pouty selfies on Instagram, no evidence of a modeling career exists. Some of us also comb through Revlon results on Google search and not a one model looks anything like Alicia.

And this is when George Lim, The Professor, introduces himself.

George Lim: "How much does everyone know about World War II?"

You: "Um, the Nazis?"

George Lim: "That was in Europe."

You: "I know that. Pearl Harbor?"

George Lim: "Better. But to give you an overview of the Pacific Theatre, I was asked to prepare a few notes. . ."

George Lim turns out to be an actual professor, from UT Austin's history department. The resident expert, the one who gathers everyone into the one-room schoolhouse to give periodic history lessons about the Greater East Asia Co-Prosperity Sphere, Japan's cotton-candy name for the turd that was the mid-twentieth century Japanese Empire. They, George tells us, thought it'd go down better when they started swarming over every country they could get troops in.

It didn't. And sometimes, we wish George would shut his trap, but some of us, the ones who like to believe they're getting an education out of this, appreciate his forays into explaining what's happening. The rest of us prefer it when he gets knocked around by the soldiers for teaching the wrong things, the parts that have nothing to do with how rad Japan is.

The last one we meet is Billy Hernandez, who even then exudes more slime than a slug. He complains loudly about finding sand in his rice when the camera first pans to him. We learn later, quickly, that he was assigned to be the village's sagdalista, a word we had to pronounce a few times before we manage it. We immediately hate him because he's a snitch, a local who interprets for the soldiers, even though some of us try to remind ourselves he is actually an accountant from Fresno.

From here, this episode, we pick our favorites, who we root for, though this isn't *Survivor* and the only prize is *knowing how your grandparents lived*. We guess who'll choke (most of us bet on the Delarosas, their toothpaste-shiny teeth rapidly yellowing over the course of the series), who'll go axe-crazy (George, if the soldiers keep bothering him the way they do). We become addicted to watching everyone's every move. As for you?

There is camaraderie, but it's not right, you tell us. You band together because you all hate the soldiers. You gather in each others' little homes; you bitch about how hungry you are, how bone-tired, how you can't even remember your past life, the actual present, your real life.

But you realize that back in the twenty-first century, you would have hated all their fucking guts. We can see that, but we're thankfully separated from them via our laptop screens.

Episode 3: Meet the Soldiers
The soldiers introduce themselves to you and us when one hits you with his (fake?) gun and forces you to bow.

You're minding your own business when the news comes over the radio. The Americans (Your former occupiers, we learn with a twinge of guilt, because we weren't aware we ever owned you. Oops) have retreated, crushed like so many ants by the invading Japanese Army. You search through your meager stores of memory for what exactly that would entail (we do the same). You instinctively hurry back towards your new home.

Instead, you run smack into a whole squad of them as they march down the street, the newly terrified residents peeping at them through doors and windows. You, we, try to remember that they're probably just a bunch of under-employed actors they scooped from Tokyo, but they have guns.

You and we try to remind yourself, ourselves, they're probably high-quality toys. No harm.

Sneaking to an alley fails. They see you, and one glares in your direction. "Bow," he says in heavily accented English.

You stare dumbly, then he hits you with his gun. We see you reel, nearly tripping over a pothole, an errant chicken barely getting out of your way.

We don't know how painful it is, but you drop to your knees. Your forehead touches the ground, and when you stand back up when they're gone, you have dirt smudged on your face.

This is your first encounter with the soldiers, and you never learn any of their names. We never do either. Some of us look away from them when we see them on screen, having an inkling of what they threaten with their clubs and guns. We judge the ones who eagerly inch closer til their noses touch their laptop screens, even when we, too, peek through our fingers.

Episode 5: Rice, Rice, Rice
You are always hungry.

You tell us that you never actually thought that the production company would hurt you. It's a *simulation*, not the real thing. You never thought it would be *that* unpleasant.

But it is.

Your stomach is tearing itself apart for lack of food, you tell us. We try to imagine the hungriest we've ever been, our stomachs rumbling so loud we think people can hear across the room, and try (and fail) to quadruple that. There simply isn't enough of it, you say, and rice goes for way, way higher prices than you'd ever thought they would. You know for a fact that the soldiers confiscate any food trucked into town (we watch you when you ask the cameramen why the production crew even bothers; they say it's for verisimilitude).

Due to your Granddad's advanced age, he runs a little tailoring shop instead of farming or anything more strenuous. You did not know he was good at sewing—he grunts at you and mumbles that he had to learn a trade. Over voiceover, you recall for us all his immaculate clothes, as photos of him as a young man flash across the screen. Some of us giggle at how handsome this short, wrinkled turtle of a Filipino man once was.

You are his apprentice. Compared to others in the village, you're doing well. The shop is in front of the little house and you have the back-room for sleeping and cooking. But the pesos, even the centavos (Filipino currency, the text at the bottom of the screen inform us), go faster, faster than you'd ever thought. After you buy the rice (Granddad insists on this always), there is little left over, and that little won't pay for anything, maybe wilted vegetables at best. We grip our stomachs in sympathy and then realize we haven't ordered our Meat Lovers' pizza yet.

And those guys they got in there to play Japanese soldiers are bastards, each and everyone. No, not true, some are a grayer shade of terrible (for verisimilitude!), but mostly, all they do is go around and shout and glare and threaten with whips and guns and sticks and swords.

You didn't think the production company would allow an actual public punishment but now, you wonder aloud if they're dying for an excuse for an execution. When you say that, our fingers itch to hit the "Play next" button, and we have to ball our hands into a fist to stop them.

He won't say it either, but we notice your Granddad is getting slower. He's a barrel-chested man, short but powerful. He boasts to us that in his youth, when he first came to America, he worked all sorts of jobs: busboy, taxi driver, mover, while he studied for his master's in economics at the University of Chicago.

Your Granddad has never talked so much to you. We can tell. At night, you're bone-tired, and you can't help but listen as your usually stoic-unless-lecturing-you Granddad (How we wince in memory of our own grandparents!) starts to speak, slowly until he becomes frantic with need. We armchair psychologists wonder if being so close to the war-torn past has triggered something deeply repressed, that these simulated wartime conditions make him want to unburden himself, as if his brain no longer rationally understands he's not in danger of dying.

"I had wanted to be a professor before meeting your Lola," he says one night over a meager dinner of rice and tiny salted fish, whose minuscule bones you swallow, the ones you once complained about on camera but presently rationalize as extra calcium. "She was a nurse, you know, studying to be one."

You hadn't. Lola had died before you were born, and your Dad had often said Granddad had gotten harder and more dried out, like petrified wood, afterwards, though you could never imagine a Granddad like the one right now, wrinkles softened with remembrance. You tell us this, and we feel fluttery, honored that you're sharing this private moment with us. We vow to cherish this memory among our own.

"It was too much at the time. I wanted to marry her. So I left school after my master's. Got a job keeping books for an apartment building. Bought some real estate and rented them out. Made money. All for her, so she could finish, so we could have a family. Have your father and then you."

You didn't know the old man could be so romantic. We blink

away our tears and think of our partners, if we have them, and wonder: Would they ever do the same for me? Under these circumstances, poor in a strange land with a language that tangles in our throat? And try not to consider the answer.

Episode 7: *What's My Name?*

Your Granddad is stretching his aching, arthritic fingers (which you only realize because he surreptitiously takes modern-looking pills—he got a medical exemption from period doctoring, we figure) when he asks the unspoken question.

"You never call me Lolo. Why?"

You pause as you peer at the rice steaming on the finicky wood-burning stove. You have told us you've become an expert at this when at home, you barely even knew how to operate the automatic rice cooker. "I dunno," you say.

"It's more proper—to call me Lolo." Granddad frowns in thought.

You think about it. We speculate—American not Filipino? Um, he just looked like Granddad? You heard it from your peers and was like "Hey, that's what you call the old man that is not Dad?"

Before you can even answer, Granddad says, his eyes closed, "I haven't been always good to you, have I?" And we try to remember the last time our elders ever half-apologized for anything and pretend, for a moment, that Granddad is our grandparents, begging us to pardon them for their myriad crimes against us.

Episode 8: *The World Watches Your Shame*

You, we, don't believe the bastards, but they actually do it.

George Lim is hauled to the town square and lashed.

No, that barely describes it. George Lim is caught passing out "dissident pamphlets" and then is whipped within sight of the broken-down town hall and the looming cross of the church until he turns corpse-pale, faints.

It's not real, we tell ourselves uneasily. You, Kiko, are just minding your own business, haggling for a meager pile of tiny fish.

Your Granddad and nearly everyone else keeps correcting your pronunciation of what the fish is actually called, but your grasp of Tagalog is so poor that you don't even really bother to try. At any rate, you tell us you enjoy the haggling, as it makes you forget your grumbling stomach.

It's been three weeks, and you've lost more pounds than you thought would be possible in such a short amount of time. You crack a rambling, desperate joke about diets we can't laugh at, though the most game, the most shameless, of us try.

But that's all forgotten when you see George Lim brought to the town square, already pale and trembling, and Billy Hernandez shouts out the man's crime. You turn red when you see the sagdalista. We have discovered, via casual Googling, that it was historically true, native Filipinos betraying their countrymen, serving the conquerors. From a distance of the modern-day, we understand the impulse for self-preservation. That it's better to be a panting but breathing dogsbody for the men with guns than a breathless corpse buried in a secret spot in a field or worse, left out in public as a rotting example. From the closeness of the past, where we can practically taste the blood in the air, we see you telling us you hate the fucker's guts so much that you forget Billy Hernandez is merely an accountant from Fresno.

George is stripped of his shirt, tied to a post, and then the whipping begins.

We know, intellectually, they're not actually whipping him. They can't possibly be. That in real life, he'd be bleeding. At most, his skin is turning pink. They probably prepped him, told him to scream like he was dying. Maybe he did some Method shit, to get into the feeling of being whipped, that the production team told him to think of every oral history he's ever read, every interview he ever recorded.

But he's screaming, screaming so hard it feels like he's cutting the air to ribbons.

And then Granddad is at your side, with his brown, wrinkled face getting pale, slack.

You're startled. We're startled. He's not supposed to be there. That's why you go to the market as much as you can. You're younger, stronger. You're not weighed with memories laced with war. We know.

He's not supposed to be there.

He's staring at George Lim as he screams, his own mouth open. No sound is coming out.

You grab him then. Before he could collapse. Your own hands are rougher. From cooking and cleaning and cutting your fingers on scissors and needles, getting blood on the clothes, as your Granddad shouts at you, but they're as tough as they need to be for this moment.

"C'mom, Granddad," you whisper, hoping no one hears you, sees him (We do), but everyone's eyes are on George Lim. "You have to stand up. We can't leave. They might catch us." The soldiers want you all to see them, to see them punish George. You understand this for real now. We see this.

But, you're young enough and unburdened enough, and you know well enough—kind of—none of this is real. We, too, know it's not possibly real, even as we frantically hit the fast-forward button on this scene.

But not your Granddad, who we still see collapsing in your arms, in slow-motion, sped-up, then paused.

Episode 11: *The End Is Nigh?*

We see your stomach is tearing itself into pieces. Food supplies are getting low, and the local market has barely any food. We learn during individual interviews that production is currently corresponding with the end of the war, 1944.

You, all of you, the Malubays, the Delarosas, George Lim, Billy Hernandez, Granddad, you, Kiko, wish the show was over, wish the war was over, wish it all was over.

The air is thicker. Tension travels from body to body, like how a wire carries electricity. The soldiers are getting nervous, and they cover it up by screaming at everyone.

Again, we're not sure how much of this is real. The lines blur too much. Sometimes, you seem to forget your own name. That you're American. That you were born in the 1980s and that you grew up in abundance, the land of milk and honey.

You'd really go for milk and honey right now. We know. You're sick of rice more grit than grain, every tiny portion of tiny smelly fish, rotting wormy vegetables, shredded desiccated coconut. You tell us George Lim (who is whistling as he goes about his day, making your face turn red when you see him, because you know now it was all just an intellectual exercise for him) has been mentioning everyone would probably be slaughtering every dog and cat they could find at this point, and some of us hope (though not too fervently) that it's not the orange cat he's thinking of, the one we've gotten fond of who hangs around the empty, cracked fountain during the opening credits.

You really want a Meat Lovers' pizza, with extra-extra sausage, you tell us with increasing frequency.

Your Granddad, meanwhile, lies in his tiny bed not moving very much. You are now schlepping all the orders around. Your seams are crooked, even with the sewing machine (you show us your handiwork so we're sure to know), but you're amazed at your ability to make something useful, for once. Your art school projects, your Marcel Duchamp-lite, cracked, blood-splattered bowls with your initials slapped on them, seem pathetic in comparison. After breaking a precious bowl when you're clumsily cooking in the kitchen area, you wish you could rewind, grab a bowl from your senior year at Columbia College that you covered in paint (not even real blood), give it a good scrubbing with sand, and serve tinola in it.

Bowls are hard to find, after all.

Episode 13: Bombs Away

This is what you finally do for your grandfather: You know how to light a fire, what kind of kindling to start with, feathered strips of newspaper, dried leaves and grasses, exactly how much breath is required to keep it alive. What kinds of things will make it spread.

One night, when no one is awake, you go to the soldiers' quarters, the nicest house in town, the capitán del barrio's house. The capitán has mysteriously disappeared, you were told in the beginning, in an attempt to get you in the Occupation mindset, a silly piece of theatre that, you tell us, makes you furious remembering it.

You manage to find some gasoline. You get a match.

The result is exactly what you expect, and while you're not an action-movie badass, you flip your middle finger off in the direction of what you hope are cameras as flames nibble at the house behind you. For all you know that night, no one actually ever sees, but we see you and burst into spontaneous applause, full of a brief patriotism we usually only ever feel for our own country, jingoism graciously shared with you, this lazy Saturday night we're so glad we stayed in for.

From Agreement for **Wartime Philippines** *Participants*
[. . .] I knowingly and freely consent to participating in additional promotional events up to a year after production is completed. [. . .]

Reunion Show: Postwar Confessions
But you do get caught. You and your grandfather, and that is the worst part, he hardly blinked when he was woken up. He stood dully in a thin undershirt and shorts, when it's explained you both had to leave. Some producer, a man in a Lacoste polo, thought to put a denim jacket over Granddad's shaking shoulders.

And that is an image that still runs on a loop in your memory, our memory, your grandfather just listening to some men in suits, men in expensive polo shirts, tell them that you had fucked up. You're just lucky that the house had an actual fire alarm (They justify this as psychological conditioning, creating haves and have-nots) so the soldiers got out with not a singe on their eyebrows. Granddad wouldn't even look at you.

And here you are now, trying to organize your thoughts, because thanks to some clause in fine print on your contracts, you both are required to appear on a reunion show and answer the questions of the audience. Us. Because no surprise, after your stunt especially, the hits on Netflix went *way* up. We, all of us, then discovered that the whole series was an exercise in humiliation and punishment, but since it was *historical*, it's a legitimate act of rubbernecking. So, we're eager to to have a special, a follow-up to *those people who suffered exactly like their grandparents did* (or in Granddad's case, suffered exactly like he did when he was thirteen). Of course, we want to see the guy who tried to burn the bastard soldiers alive again.

You asked them to let Granddad off. They refused.

So you're both waiting in the wings. The other ex-villagers are standing off in the distance, in a huddle but still slightly spaced apart. They greeted you cordially but didn't take it beyond bland pleasantries. You can't really blame them; after you were kicked off the show, the next episode, which you barely forced yourself to watch, you tell us, they were told you were a rebel. That you'd been plotting to take down the soldiers with some other rebels (you can't just be a garden-variety half-starved resentful asshole who finally cut loose in a big way), and you and your Granddad had been carted off to a prison camp. Oh, and that they were going to be punished for your crime with rations cut in half, an earlier stricter curfew, etc. You can't really blame them. Did they really want to remember that much collective suffering? Did they really want to be this-close-to-touching the embodied memories of that time?

You tell us, haltingly, how alone your Granddad often seemed to be while you were growing up, and you have to ask yourself if that's where that came from. Him not wanting to wallow in the past. Preferring to tell the world, Look at me now, the terrified, starving little boy from the barrio who made good, who's the big American man. He didn't tell us this, your Granddad, but we, some of us anyway, saw it.

And here, now, is your Granddad. For once, though, instead of a sharp, tailored suit, he's wearing a sheer snowy shirt over black pants ("Barong tagalog" helpfully flashes across the screen). The shirt is white and so so bright, and yet, he looks like a funeral walking.

You stand next to your Granddad tentatively. Since the show, you have spoken, possibly, even less. You tell us this with downcast eyes. We armchair psychologists once more speculate that Granddad, having once shown the soft underbelly under his shell, never wants to come out again.

But you can stand by him, at least. Your shoulders aren't even touching, but you, we, hear your Granddad murmur something under his breath.

"What?" you ask, but before you can ask him to elaborate (like we're all begging you to do), Bruce is calling you out, and the spotlight is shining hard in your face. We're telling you to come out, Kiko Dominguez. Our applause already swallows the stage.

And this is what you've been trying to figure out, this whole time, before this moment. What are you going to say when we ask the inevitable question: Do you understand now?

Those words are bunched up in the back of your throat, when you take that first step into the blinding, devouring light, where our hungry eyes, our starving ears await.

THE SCARECROW

Wendy Chen

BEHIND THE BOARDING SCHOOL, THERE WAS A FIELD OF SUNFLOWERS. Big and bright and yellow, with dark, layered centers. Vast and unending, the field sprang up year after year as if by magic.

And in the field, there lived a creature. In their beds, the other girls spoke of him in whispers. Once, he wore a cloak of tattered blue rags. Another time, a mask of woven straw.

Not everyone who entered the field could see him, they said. He showed himself only to the chosen few.

Everyone knew who they were. The chosen ones. Afterward, in the classrooms and dormitories, they stood apart from the rest. Everyone was careful not to touch them.

X wanted to glimpse the creature for herself. One night, she snuck out of bed and slipped out of her dormitory. In her nightgown, she walked down to the field, pausing at the very edge of it.

The sunflowers stirred under the moonlight, all aglow.

Suddenly, X heard someone calling her name. Turning back, she saw her sister running toward her. Her shadow stretched long behind her, and her face was full of fear.

Frightened, X dove into the sunflowers. Before long, she was deep in its prickly yellow tangle. She could sense her sister had followed her.

Who was the one chasing, being chased? The two of them moved blindly through the field, searching with their hands.

As the hours passed, X's throat grew sticky and her arms red with scratches. Walking between the sunflowers, she noticed all of their heads were facing the same direction.

They were seeking her sister, she realized, not her. Now, they were the ones that frightened her. She was too scared to call out her sister's name, but she spun around, looking.

At last, she spotted her sister's head, bobbing between the flowers, in the distance. But before she could reach her, a tall shadow straightened up, splintering off from the darkness.

It was the scarecrow. He was the one leading her sister away by the hand.

X tried to follow, but she couldn't. The field folded into itself against her, and the night continued to darken until it began to moan in such an awful way.

The sunflowers tossed their heads: left, right.

So terrible was the sound, that she put her hands over her ears and ran with abandon. Somehow, she stumbled out. She paced along the edge, waiting for her sister to emerge. She did not.

Perhaps she had simply missed her in the darkness. X returned to her dormitory. Her sister's bed was empty.

In the morning, her sister was still missing. By evening, the field echoed with her name.

Everyone went out to search for her. Teachers swept their flashlights across the dusk and pushed aside thick, prickly stems.

Who would go into the field at night, they muttered. Only girls looking for trouble.

It was night again when they finally found her, lying in a patch of flattened sunflowers. She was naked, covered only with strands of golden straw.

Her eyes were open, filled with starlight.

X watched as her sister was wrapped in blankets and carried back to the dormitory. X curled at the foot of her bed, watching her sleep. It seemed worse, almost, to find her.

When her sister woke, she wouldn't speak. She turned her face away from the lights they shined on her.

The nurse who treated her shook her head. This was what

happened to girls who entered the field, she said. You would think they would know better, year after year.

The other girls exchanged knowing looks. It was the scarecrow, they knew, but didn't say. No one would believe them.

At the end of the week, their mother and father came to fetch them. At home, X kept a close eye on her sister. She was careful not to touch her.

Their mother and father did the same. Even their glances skirted around her.

It wasn't blame. Not exactly. But they knew she had been changed.

Her sister didn't seem to notice. Most days, she simply sat in front of the television, basking in its flowering light.

Sometimes, X caught her standing by the living room window. Who was she looking for? Or was she keeping watch? Her sister peered through the gap between the curtains.

X glanced through the window herself. But she never saw anything. Only the shadows of the trees, growing longer.

When guests came, her sister retreated by herself, up the stairs. No one ever heard her. Still their parents laughed shrilly, as if to cover up her sounds.

But in the night, X often heard her moving around in her room. Her sister paced back and forth the length of it, without ceasing.

Was she still finding her way through the sunflowers, through the darkness? Once, X heard her sister talking.

It had been so long since she last heard her sister speak. X pressed her ear against her wall. She even held her breath.

Her sister's voice was rising and falling. Between pauses, it was asking questions. And then there was another one—with a low rasp—responding.

X jerked back in fear. But when she listened closely again, all was silent.

The next morning, while her sister watched television, X searched her room. She opened her sister's closet doors. She swept a light underneath her bed.

There was nothing there. Only a few strands of yellow hair.

X rubbed them between her fingers. They were coarse and smelled of summers past.

Still doubtful, X left the room, taking with her what she found. She placed the hairs inside a nesting doll—the smallest one.

Her sister's glances turned cold, more distant, even, than before. X wondered if she knew what she had taken.

After a few nights, X heard the voice again—strange and alien. She leaped out of bed and ran to her sister's room. Her heart raced.

Stepping foot in her room was like entering the field. The sunflowers pressing in from all sides.

But the room was empty. There was no one. Not even her sister.

X looked around. The wind, cruel and icy, came through the open window. She crossed the room to close it.

Outside, in the yard, stood her sister with outstretched arms. The cold light of the stars soaked through her nightclothes.

Her head was thrown back, her neck exposed.

X drew back, feeling hunted. She closed the window and returned to bed.

After that, X avoided entering her sister's room. No matter what strange, pleading noises she heard, X only closed her eyes and tried to sleep.

Then, one evening in the living room, her sister began to moan in the voice of the sunflowers.

Their mother covered her with a blanket. X switched on the television. The sound of children singing filled the room.

But nothing they did could calm her. Her sister would not quiet.

She tossed her head: right, left.

Finally, their father put his hand over her sister's mouth. He wrapped his arms around her, coaxingly.

Still, X could hear her sister's voice, muffled behind the layers of their father's hands, arms, legs.

Her sister tore free of their father. She hunched over into herself: a bare wound.

Their mother was frightened. Their father was frightened. But X knew what was coming.

For what they had looked for, now they saw.

Her sister pulled at the hair that sprouted all over her body.

But it was not hair after all. It was straw.

WITH NUTS

Michael Czyzniejewski

WHEN YOU HIT A JOGGER WITH YOUR 4-RUNNER AND HE GETS UP AND runs away, turning to say, *Hey, I'm OK!* as he disappears into the night, it's logical to assume he's OK, right? You stay in your car, calm your kids down—because they're freaking out about the face that was just pressed against the windshield—and make your right turn, just like you planned. Soon you can think about it at the gas station while you pump gas, your kids still bawling inside the car, you unable to settle them because it's so damn cold out and the doors and windows are shut tight so they don't freeze. You can think about it on the drive home, when you're telling your kids not to mention anything about it to their mom because she's going to wig. You can drive around the neighborhood—in the opposite direction the jogger was headed—until your kids relax, stop and get them sundaes at McDonald's, partially as a bribe, but mostly to make them forget, because what makes anyone forget anything faster than ice cream? Later when you get home and tell your wife *Nothing!* when she asks if anything interesting happened while you were out, how the drive was, if there was anything to report. *Nada. What about you?* And you can even, when she tells you about running a yellow (but probably red) light as she passed a cop, lecture her that she ought to be more careful, that you (as in the household) can't afford a ticket right now. You wouldn't go so far as to ask her if she happened to be holding her phone when she blew through the light (or use the phrase "blew through"), especially when she nods and tells you you're right—especially because you were checking the score to the game—actually, checking the count on a hitter in the second inning of a game— when your front bumper air-lifted that jogger onto your hood. You wouldn't accuse your wife of such things, but instead, make her feel better about the whole incident, right? Then you'd start thinking about dinner, something the kids would eat even though they just devoured super-secret secret-keeping sundaes, with nuts, something like a big can of ravioli or grilled cheese with tomato soup, even PB&Js, heavy food, comfort food, forgetting food.

If I'm wrong about this, please let me know. I feel like I'm wrong about this and maybe I'm saying it all aloud because I, too, need to be told it's OK, that what I did wasn't so bad, that we won't even remember any of this tomorrow.

And, let me ask again: How are you?

Anyway, say you're heating the ravioli when your sister calls, the sister who lives a few blocks away. She's frantic, telling you to walk over, not drive, but *walk* over, that there's a guy on her front lawn and she thinks he might be dead and there're cops and an ambulance and a fire captain in a sedan and you want to tell her you're making the kids dinner but then she says no, you should need to get over RIGHT NOW, because the guy's going into some kind of fit, right there on her front lawn, but you're not really paying attention because you're busy, preoccupied—you deserve this pass. But as you're about to hang up, you absolutely swear you hear that word, *jogger*, and you drop the wooden spoon inside the pot of ravioli and tell your wife that you gotta run and you'll be back soon. *What about dinner?* someone says, your wife or daughter, their voices almost the same now, and you keep going, knowing they'll figure it out, just a pot on a low flame.

You think the whole three blocks to your sister's house how she said to not drive—*Walk, don't drive*—and it's not until you're there, bathed in blue and red, that you understand she said that because the streets are blocked—*not* because the dying guy might recognize your car, or some cop might see a dent in your bumper, a tiny piece of fabric from the jogger's sleek black stretchy pants hanging off a cracked piece of plastic. No one—save your kids—knows you hit that jogger, and your kids certainly haven't called your sister or the cops to indict you. *Not yet*, you think, as you make your way around the back of your sister's house, let yourself in, peek out her front window from behind the curtains, hoping you won't get a view of a dying jogger—the man you may have killed—flatlining in the daffodil bed. Behind the curtains you're shielded from anyone who might stop dying for a split-second to point you out, to gasp *That's him!* before he expires.

When your sister puts her hand on your shoulder and you jump, you should act cool, right? And you're supposed to say yes when she asks if you'll go outside with her to see the guy, right? Or do you instead fake being traumatized at the sight of a man dying, tell her it reminds you of when Dad died, even though your father died on a golf course sixteen years ago and you've never, ever thought of what that looked like? You could do that, but you know better. Your sister has her own death issues to think about, that shit in Roger's lungs moved on to his lymph nodes, which is why he's not at the window, too, the poor, frail bastard unable to stand, let alone walk across the house. You know that, so you just say that you had some bad tuna and then try to look gray—do you know how to look gray?—and tell your sister that you have to get home, even when she cries and cries and begs you to go outside with her. You tell her that the kids have to eat, make a crack about how Pam can't cook, maybe mention the warning ticket she got for running the yellow light, like you're trying to bond, connect, because you have nothing—zero, zip, nil—to say about Roger, who used to wrestle with you in high school and was a big fucker who now looks like Ichabod Crane on heroin. *What the fuck are you talking about?* your sister might ask you, growing more and more hysterical, so you just leave, tell her to say hi to Roger for you, but there's no way she heard you because you were on the back porch before his name ever came out of your mouth. Right? Right.

Because you have your own ass to look out for, you sneak

around the side of your sister's house, hop her chain-link, squat under the rose of Sharons in the dark, just to see what's going on. From there you can watch, without anyone seeing you, without your sister bugging you out. These paramedics, they're like the guys on TV, aren't they? The ones who miraculously save people, week after week, better at saving people than doctors are. They're out in the trenches, no fancy equipment, no diplomas on the wall, just them, their gurneys, and their wits. They'll pull out the shock paddles or the adrenaline shots or puncture the guy's lung with a ballpoint pen, drain the fluid, let the air do its thing. So, when you watch the ring of people around the guy on the ground all stand up, one of the ambulance drivers draping a sheet over the guy, do you panic? No, of course not. Your sister's out there, by herself, and she's losing her cool for the both of you, some dead guy on her front lawn, every city employee traipsing through Roger's beloved flowers. You even keep your composure when you think you hear Roger, from his window above you, mutter *Is that you out there, Justin?* in a voice so pathetic, he already sounds dead. Do you fall backward, onto your ass, into the neighbors' rose bushes, thorning the shit out of your neck and arms when you hear this? No. Shit no! Do you get up and hop that fence again, cut through your sister's yard, high-tail it down the alley—first toward your house, then double-back, past your sister's yard again—toward where you don't know, because you're not ready to go home yet, face your kids, face Pam, face your car's front bumper, which might be dented and have incontrovertible DNA evidence hiding in every crevice? That would be irresponsible. But you're not ready to go home yet, so that's what you do, head in the other direction.

I asked you how you are, didn't I? Did you answer me or did I get started talking again? Sorry. How are you?

Walking away from your sister's, away from your own house, do you ignore the cold and walk until you can't see the blue and red lights spinning on the treetops and roofs anymore, until you can't hear the squawking of walkie-talkies, until you get to a street where nobody knows anything about any joggers or ambulances or cops? Of course you do. Because you know, don't you, that this is no longer between you and the police or you and your squealy kids or you and that poor dead jogger crushing the daisies? No, it's not, because now it's between you and you. The kids are never going to find out a jogger died on your sister's lawn because Pam would never tell the kids about anything so horrifying. The kids don't read the papers and none of you watch the local news. Full of ice cream *and* ravioli with meat sauce, the kids have long forgotten the story, the man's face on your windshield. Nobody's coming after you but you. You might even convince yourself that you have to tell somebody what's happened. You'd tell them it was an accident, that you had your lights on, that you looked both ways, and the jogger, in this sleek, black jogger costume, ran in front of *you*? They, John Law, wouldn't send a man with no previous convictions (not even a run yellow light)—the father of two small children, the brother-in-law and best friend to a man dying from cancer—to jail, would they? They'd have to press charges, assign a lawyer, maybe even take that guy into custody, but they wouldn't even hold him overnight, would they? It was an accident. The jogger was wearing all black. He was jogging at night. Who would assume anyone would be out jogging in this type of weather, anyway? You laugh, but that first-time offender's not doing a second of time, is he? Fucking-A no. So, with no one on your trail, no one to point a finger at you, it's just between you and yourself. Why disrupt your whole life, have this involuntary manslaughter on your record, face the victim's family in a court of law, knowing you'll never actually go to jail, anyway? What's the point? Sooner or later you'll learn to live with it. Turning yourself in isn't going to bring this dead jogger back. Why ruin two families' lives instead of one, eh? It's punishment enough, that journey you'll take from the now to the then, that point at which you'll be able to live with yourself. It'll be a rough journey, bad as anything the legal system could throw at you—worse, even, because not turning yourself in would only add to the guilt, magnify it at least a thousand times, right? Maybe a million.

Who won the game, you're asking? Honestly, I can't say I know. Ironic, right? If I had my phone, I'd check, but I don't—it's most certainly in my sister's yard somewhere, buzzing away in the dark.

So, anyway, you keep walking until you hit a busy intersection, a street so busy that you have to stop—you wouldn't want to end up hit by a car, too, now would you? In more blocks than you care to count, you run into Main, see that diner across from the hospital and realize you never ate, the guilt only amplified by the twinge of hunger in your belly. You go inside, sit down like nothing's wrong (because nothing is, right?), like nobody in the diner knows anything (because they don't, right?). You seat yourself even though there's the sign that says PLEASE WAIT TO BE SEATED and when the waitress asks how you got there, who seated you, you say you didn't see the sign, so big and obvious in front of the host station that you maneuvered it like a sleeping dog. But it's late, a Sunday night, and nobody's there, right? Just you, the waitress, and presumably a cook, someone who's going to make the open-face beef sandwich with mashed potatoes and brown gravy that you're going to order. This diner has the best in town, doesn't it? Then you see chairs up on the tables in the next section over and feel bad, wonder if you're keeping this waitress and the alleged cook here late, then wonder what they have left, how old that beef will be, how long their gravy's been stewing. You order a piece of the lemon meringue from the glass case up front, some chicken noodle soup, hoping it's from a can. You ask for so many crackers it'll be more cracker than soup, but anything to fill the gap in your stomach, to make that rumbling go away, right?

As you wait on your soup and peck at your pie—you peel off the meringue because you just want the lemon part—you see someone come in, someone on crutches with a walking boot on his leg, someone who disappears behind the PLEASE WAIT TO BE SEATED sign. Because you're still decent, and you don't want anyone delaying your soup, you want to yell out that the diner's almost closed but decide not to. The guy's looking like he's as hungry as you just were, starving if he walked into a place like this, at this hour, all by himself, with a bad wheel. Unlike you, this man waits like he's told—decent people would, you know—and when the waitress comes out with your soup and a mountain of crackers, she rolls her eyes just a bit when she sees the man, tells him she'll be right with him. She places your soup in front of you, tips her tray so that eleven—eleven!—packets of crackers fall onto the table, twenty-two crackers to hide how old this soup is. You crumple and open every packet then eat the whole mess in four bites. Between the pie and the cracker soup, you should be full, that feeling in your gut gone, but it isn't, is it? No.

That's when you look up and see the crutches man in the booth in front of you, facing you, staring at you with deep, dead eyes. You don't know why this fucking guy is staring at you, do you, so you look away, toward hospital across the street, ambulances pulling in and out, then look back and see the guy still staring you down. You want to say *What?* to the guy, but you don't, because the guy stands up, sits down across from you. You see a cast on his arm to match the boot on his leg, then you see the sleek, black outfit, ripped— no, check that, *cut*—off all four limbs.

You recognize him, imagine half his face flat against your windshield.

You, the man says, still staring.

Then you start telling this story, ask him for the first time: *How are you?*

HOUSTON, WE'VE HAD A PROBLEM

Emily Greenberg

WE SEE JOSEPH GORDON-LEVITT WEAVING THROUGH NEW YORK CITY traffic on a battered, white fixed-gear bicycle. Gordon-Levitt is playing WILEE the bike messenger, WILEE the disaffected Columbia Law graduate, WILEE the underdog protagonist who face-plants a taxi windshield in PREMIUM RUSH. Or maybe we see Anne Hathaway riding around London in ONE DAY. Hathaway has just called EMMA's love interest and told him she's on her way and sorry about being so snappy this morning. We see Hathaway's back as she rides away from us. We see Hathaway getting smaller and smaller. Then we see Hathaway exit the blind alley, and we hear the screeching truck's tires an instant before we see it, we see it, we see it sweep her out of the frame. Or maybe we see a BICYCLIST peddling hard up hill on a poorly lit country road in a sleepy college town, but no, that's too vague. He is not just a bicyclist, he is a PROFESSOR OF POPULAR FILMS. He is not just a professor of popular films, he is a MIDDLE-AGED, PHYSICALLY AVERAGE ADULT MAN. He is BRUCE. He is MY BRUCE. He is a bicyclist and a professor of popular films and a middle-aged, physically average adult man I dated five years ago, after both our marriages ended in divorce, but have not spoken to since and who thus, USED TO BE MY BRUCE, though I will just call him BRUCE now for simplicity. Regardless, we see an eighteen-wheeler run BRUCE off the poorly lit country road in the sleepy college town. We see BRUCE somersault through the air in slow-mo. We hear the tires screeching and the driver cursing and BRUCE's bones crunch-colliding with the pavement. We see a bird's-eye view of BRUCE sprawled on the edge of the road. He is wearing faded Levi's rolled at the cuff, his signature red bow tie, and a tweed sport coat. No helmet.

This was no film. There were no stunt doubles, no cameras. Real blood trickled down BRUCE's pale, un-sculpted forearms. But when the hospital called ME after he was stable, when the hospital called ME and asked if I could see him, when the hospital called ME because his only living relative was an ELDERLY AUNT holed up in a nursing home halfway across the country, when the hospital called ME because, quite frankly, he must have forgotten to update his emergency contacts after our breakup, when the hospital called ME because, to be even more frank, he was apparently still not on speaking terms with his EX-WIFE and had no one else, not a single relative or friend or halfway dependable acquaintance except for ME—RACHEL, his estranged EX, an ANXIOUS MIDDLE-AGED WOMAN HAVING A BAD HAIR DAY—I couldn't help thinking it already sounded like a movie. And not a very good one.

The morning of the hospital visit, I lingered in the hallway and peered through the window to his room. I didn't know what to expect. How do you talk to someone you haven't seen for five years, especially after a horrible accident like that? What if he wasn't the same person? I was wearing a tan coat and black jeans and thought of MICHAEL visiting VITO in THE GODFATHER. BRUCE was sitting up in bed, a large bandage wrapped around his head, tubes snaking from his nose and arms to blinking machines and liquid-filled bags. Many university COLLEAGUES and STUDENTS had sent get-well tokens. Cards, balloons, flowers. Everything untouched.

I stepped into the doorway. When he saw ME, he smiled and quoted CASABLANCA.

BRUCE
Of all the gin joints in all the towns in
all the world, she walks into mine.

Same sense of humor, same spinning silver film-reel eyes. Same old BRUCE, just more wrinkles and gray hairs.

"I've been worried about you," I said, pulling up a chair. "How are you feeling?"

> BRUCE
>
> *(smiling)* Shaken, not stirred. After all,
> tomorrow is another day! I'm the king
> of the world!

I bit my lip. GOLDFINGER, GONE WITH THE WIND, TITANIC. We had watched them at his apartment all those years ago, the humid summer air drifting through the open window, our hands clasped around sweating bottles of pale ale. Something was wrong, and my face must have betrayed my suspicions.

> BRUCE
>
> *(frowning)* Why so serious?

I leaned forward but couldn't meet his eyes. I stared at my feet. "Bruce, do you know what day it is?"

> BRUCE
>
> I told you. I wake up every day, right
> here, right in Punxsutawney, and it's
> always February second, and there's
> nothing I can do about it.

He was staring at ME the same way PHIL stares at RITA in the diner scene from GROUNDHOG DAY. Calm, resigned, a little sad.

Later, the DOCTORS confessed they were stumped. There was no brain damage, and all the scans and tests showed BRUCE's mental faculties were completely intact. The DOCTORS had no idea what was causing this highly specialized aphasic condition, how to fix it, or how long it might last. They predicted BRUCE just needed time to recover. He would snap out of it eventually, but he would need help when he was released from the hospital. He had no car and had let his driver's license expire years ago. He was terrified to ride a bicycle again. SOMEONE would need to drive him to the SPEECH PATHOLOGIST. Given his inability to communicate with others, SOMEONE would need to help him at the grocery, the pharmacy, the convenience store. SOMEONE would need to be his translator.

That SOMEONE would be ME.

That SOMEONE would be ME because he had no one else, and I had nothing else. Nearing early retirement from my nine-to-five at the Parks Department, I was biding my time with no future plans. My CHILDREN were grown, my FRIENDS were boring, and my CATS hated my guts. Since BRUCE and I broke up, I had dated a little but nothing serious.

Three days later, I picked him up from the hospital and drove him home. On the drive, I turned on the radio so we wouldn't have to speak. BRUCE stared out the window, drummed his fingers against his knee. When we pulled into the driveway, he stopped drumming his fingers and sighed.

BRUCE

There's no place like home.

He lived a few miles from the university, a ramshackle apartment on a quiet street just like I remembered. Same sad hedges, same stupid lawn gnomes. He had lost his house key on the bicycle ride, so I used the spare. Still hidden under the same doormat after all this time.

Inside, little had changed. Sun-stained film posters plastered the walls, and dust-coated monographs lined the bookshelves. He still had the landline phone and the stacked print newspapers and the VHS player. Chinese takeout cartons in the garbage, chipped coffee mugs in the sink. No pictures of his SON. No pictures of the EX-WIFE he had recently divorced when we started dating.

Seeing the dishes in the sink, he shrugged.

BRUCE

(winking) I ate his liver with some fava beans and a nice Chianti.

I laughed. This was one quality I had always loved about BRUCE: before his SON's accident, he'd had an amazing, self-deprecating sense of humor.

He reached for the first chipped coffee mug, but I lifted it from the other end. Our fingers grazed.

"Why don't you go rest?" I said. "You've been through a lot. I can clean up."

He seemed genuinely touched as he put the dish down.

BRUCE

(grateful, squeezing my shoulder) I have always depended on the kindness of strangers.

Over the next few weeks, we fell into a routine. On the way to work, I would drop him at the SPEECH PATHOLOGIST. "Good morning, Vietnam!" he would say, slipping into the passenger seat, or "I love the smell of napalm in the morning." On my lunch break, I would pick him up again, and we would run errands. Determining our shopping list and route was always challenging since he could neither speak sensibly nor write nor read. "Houston, we have a problem," he would say, pointing to an empty milk carton or a squeezed-out toothpaste. Eventually, I pasted logos for the grocery, the pharmacy, and the convenience store on separate index cards, and he handed one of them to ME when he needed something.

In those early weeks, everyone was optimistic. His SPEECH

PATHOLOGIST said his range of movie quotes was expanding to include more obscure and recent films, Ingmar Bergman and GET OUT. STUDENTS visited and delighted in his condition. They turned it into a game, asking him increasingly bizarre questions to see which movies he'd quote. Even the university called to ask how he was feeling. On these occasions, he always passed ME the phone. "Houston, we have a problem," he would whisper, making it clear he didn't want COLLEAGUES to know the full extent of his condition. I always made something up about how he couldn't come to the phone right now, that we were late for an appointment, but yes, he would teach classes again in the fall. BRUCE would wink at ME when I said this, but eventually the routine was no longer funny. The phone rang less frequently. The STUDENTS stopped visiting.

One day, after I helped him put away groceries, he stopped ME by the door.

BRUCE
Houston, we have a problem.

It was early evening but already dark. The porch lights had turned on automatically. He had an elbow on the door frame and a hand behind his back. His hair was disheveled, but he was wearing a fresh, clean button-down. I asked him what the problem was.

BRUCE
Loneliness has followed me my whole life.

He smiled sheepishly at the melodramatic line like he didn't really mean it, not literally, but I saw the loneliness in his gray-blue eyes. The same look I saw each morning in the mirror. He brought forward the hand from behind his back to reveal an old VHS of TAXI DRIVER, one of the first films we watched together. I knew the lines by heart.

BOTH OF US
Everywhere. In bars, in cars, sidewalks,
stores, everywhere. There's no escape. I'm
god's lonely man.

He raised an eyebrow, and I understood his unspoken question. My answer was yes. I followed him to the den. He popped in the tape.

We began watching films together most evenings. Sometimes two or three. Occasionally, we shared a bottle of wine. One night, we were halfway through APOLLO 13. Houston has just told the astronauts to stir their oxygen tanks, and something's exploded. The alarms are sounding. A young Tom Hanks playing JIM LOVELL leaps into action. Houston asks for clarity, and the camera zooms in on Hanks staring intently off-screen, face shining with sweat.

JIM LOVELL
Houston, we have a problem.

Years ago, when I first saw the movie with BRUCE, he'd paused here. "My students are always surprised to learn that line's incorrect," he said, smiling. "The real astronaut said, 'Houston we've *had* a problem.'"

At the time, I didn't know why he bothered telling ME this. Only now do I more fully appreciate the difference between a present problem and a present problem with a past. Now all these years later, BRUCE pressed pause again. This time, he didn't comment on the line. There was no need. He threw the remote on the floor and then he leaned over and kissed ME.

As spring drifted into summer, we fell into old habits. We were HARRY&SALLY and ROSE&JACK and SCARLETT&RHETT and ILSA&RICK. We saw movies at the theater. Ate at nice restaurants outdoors. Strolled along the lake holding hands. He was not the best conversationalist, it was true, but I still enjoyed his company. It was just like those early years of our relationship, an uncomplicated love neither of us had expected after our divorces. Everything felt so right. Sometimes, I had to remind myself why we'd broken up in the first place. His SON. He had died in a terrible car accident after BRUCE and I had been dating a few years, and BRUCE was never the same afterwards. He never talked about his SON's death with ME, not even once. He grew cold and distant, watched his films for hours and hours without stopping to eat. Forgot birthdays and anniversaries and doctor's appointments. Talked about the characters like they were real people, friends of his. I begged him to talk to ME, begged him to see a therapist, but he only retreated deeper into his films. Eventually, he barely spoke to me at all. He's mourning, I told myself. This will pass, I told myself. But it didn't.

Eighteen months after the SON's accident, I reached a breaking point. There was nothing I could do to help BRUCE, and I couldn't live like this. BRUCE was in the living room, eyes glued to the screen, taking notes on PULP FICTION for the millionth time.

"Bruce," I said. "Bruce, I need to talk to you."

He didn't look up. I yanked the television cord from the outlet, and the image fizzled to black. "Bruce, I can't do this anymore."

He didn't say anything, just nodded like he'd known all along. He helped ME gather my things in a cardboard box and take them to my car. The toothbrush I kept in his bathroom, the paperback novels I'd lent him, the shirts I kept hanging in his closet. He didn't stop ME. He didn't defend his behavior. But just before I left, he grabbed my hand and held it to his chest. "Rachel," he said, speaking to me for the first time all day. "All this. It's not me."

His voice was hoarse and earnest, each word as deliberately chosen as the film posters lining his walls. Years later, long after I stopped speaking to BRUCE, after other relationships came and went, a part of ME still thought of those parting words and wondered what would have happened if I'd given him a second chance. Now I might have that opportunity.

As the school year approached, a pin burst this happy balloon. BRUCE was making little progress in his speech, and it was becoming harder to dodge calls from the university.

One Monday morning in July, we ran into BRUCE's COLLEAGUE

at the convenience store. "Bruce," the COLLEAGUE called before we could escape. "Bruce, how are you feeling?"

BRUCE smiled, but I could tell he was nervous. He swallowed hard. Repeated the same lines from that day in the hospital.

BRUCE

Shaken, not stirred. After all, tomorrow
is another day! I'm the king of the world!

The COLLEAGUE looked taken aback. She recovered and faked a smile. "Well, I'm certainly glad to hear that. We look forward to having you back."

The day only got worse. When I picked BRUCE up that afternoon, the SPEECH PATHOLOGIST sat us down in her office and said that BRUCE should stay home for two days. "I really think it will be best if everyone gets a little rest. Why don't we start back on Thursday?"

I looked at BRUCE, but he turned away. "What's the problem?" I asked the SPEECH PATHOLOGIST.

"Oh, have you not noticed?"

I shook my head. BRUCE avoided my eyes.

The SPEECH PATHOLOGIST explained that BRUCE's range of quotes had grown smaller over the last few weeks, that he was now only quoting IMDb's Top 100 Greatest Movies of All Time. "This is normal in a patient's recovery from a devastating injury like this," she explained, her voice sympathetic. "We like to think of recovery as a straight line, but often there are regressions."

On the ride home, BRUCE didn't say a word. When I asked if he wanted ME to stay over, he shook his head no. He was muttering the Houston line when he slammed the car door.

On Thursday, I returned to pick him up for his appointment. He was drunk, unshaven and still in his bathrobe, empty beer cans strewn everywhere like a scene from ANIMAL HOUSE.

"Bruce, what are you doing? You've got a session today. You need to go. You need to get better."

He inhaled deeply, licked his lips, hiccupped. When he reached across the door frame to clasp my hands, his eyes were soft and pleading, JACK TWIST in BROKEBACK MOUNTAIN.

BRUCE

Rachel, all this. It's not me. Inside, I
am . . . I am more.

Rachel, all this. It's not me. I drew my hands back like I'd touched something hot, those familiar words a film score running through my mind on repeat. *Rachel, all this. It's not me.* He was right of course. It wasn't him speaking. It was never him, I now realized, not when we broke up for the first time and not now. It was BRUCE WAYNE. It was BATMAN. It was Christian Bale and his perfectly chiseled jaw, loose wet hair strands arcing across his forehead.

"Bruce, deep down you may still be that same great kid you used to be," I said, repeating RACHEL's lines from the film. "But it's not who you are underneath. It's what you do that defines you."

His cheeks flushed red, and he slammed his fist against the door, shaking his head.

BRUCE

Houston, we have a problem. Houston,
we have a problem houston we have a
problem we have a main bus B
undervolt—

I held him by the wrist. His hand trembled. He stared at ME with those spinning silver film-reel eyes, and still he was the same old BRUCE, had always been the same old BRUCE. "Houston, we've *had* a problem," I corrected him. "We've *had* a main B bus undervolt."

RESURRECTION

Susan Neville

WHEN THE LEAVES TURNED YELLOW AND THE COLD OCTOBER RAINS began, children in the elementary school were given egg babies to care for. They spent recess making cribs out of shoeboxes, and some of the children made cunning little onesies out of cloth cut from the legs and arms of old clothes purchased from the five cent box at yard sales.

Those who were interested in design (and there were several) put shoeboxes together to make a sort of house, often with back yards, and playground equipment made from spoons and straws smuggled in from the lunch room. The most elaborate of these were displayed on the craft table to show the grandparents who showed up on Parents Day.

Some of the children wrapped construction paper around the shoeboxes and drew on windows and doors and made dividers for the inside of the box. When the teacher said the box was supposed to be a crib, these children scoffed because the box was way too big for one baby and besides, the baby would never grow any larger. They made a smaller space inside one corner of the box for the baby and picked grass and then crunched leaves for the baby to sleep on. Then they made paper dolls or brought in little plastic or rag people the size of grown-ups' thumbs, usually toys from fast food meals or discards from larger sets of army men or Playmobil or Fisher Price. They put the little people in the boxes with the babies and said they were the mothers or fathers or brothers or sisters or cousins. There were no boyfriends or girlfriends or step anything because the children decided that adults would only be known by their blood relation to the baby.

During the day, the children would take the little people out of the box, leaving the babies alone in their mangers. They made the little people hop from desk to desk looking for something to do while the children were supposedly filling out work sheets, preparing for their futures. Sometimes a child would sneak a mother or a sister inside a desk with a plastic soldier or miniature man and they'd do what older people do in the dark. The man would leave after and maybe go into another desk and the mother or sister he left behind would come out with a dusty penny or piece of hard candy and then go back into the box with the baby and fall into a sleep so hard you had to shake them to wake them back up. It could have been a girl soldier with a father or brother of course, but that's not a scenario any of the children had seen. Usually the fathers and brothers died in cars or basements or wars and the mothers and sisters were left with the babies, though lately a lot of them had been dying too. Everyone, it seemed, waited for the grandparents and great-grandparents who, at least a few of them, could sometimes be counted on, if only to grieve.

The children were supposed to take the babies home with them each night. They had to walk home with the babies without dropping them on the street. Some of the babies didn't make it, and a child had to watch its baby's skull crack, the yellow brains ooze out. It was not a contest, but the children felt the one who kept its baby safe the longest would win nonetheless. One child lost so many babies at night and even during the day at recess that his desk was covered with death and birth certificates, because of course you couldn't have one child doing nothing in a classroom while the other children were caring for their babies. So the child's baby was given a funeral and a certificate of dying before being composted, and then the child was given a new one. Clumsy child, though. The new baby was usually gone before the day was out and a replacement brought from the refrigerator.

The compost heap was in the back of the playground near the wildflower garden, right next to the exhibit of native prairie grass. In early fall, explosions of stinging yellow jackets flew out of the ground by the compost, and the children adopted a zigzag pattern of running to get away from them. The teacher kept an Epipen in her pocket, cocked and loaded, because she didn't want to move the graveyard away from the gardens. She'd read on Facebook that both compost and bees were good for flowers and she was a young enough teacher that she hoped to save the world. She added table scraps from the lunchroom and coffee grounds from the teacher's break room, and along with the dead babies, she was making some rich loam where before there had been nothing. Little wasps. Now fall was here and the workers were all dying off, leaving one fat satiated queen and these babies raising their own fragile babies and so on.

The babies had been the teacher's idea from the beginning. She learned it at college, so it wasn't an original idea in the larger world, just one new to this community. It had started years ago as a way to remind children, when the hormones started in a few years, what it meant to care for a baby. It's fragile! You can't get rid of it! Of course none of them remembered that lesson any more than they remembered their multiplication tables. She knew this because she'd been in school with some of their parents and now here they were, the offspring.

The fragile shells in the shoe boxes were porcelain and brown and spotted and some of them shades of aqua, but inside all of them was the same goo. Perhaps that was the real lesson.

Wouldn't it be easier if we boiled them, one of the children always asked her, as though he'd been the first one to ever think of it.

You could, she told the child, but then the baby would be dead, wouldn't it?

Oh yes, the children said, but we'd be off the hook. We could throw them to each other on the playground, have them sit next to us on the buses without worrying that if they fell on the floor and rolled away, they'd die. They might crack, of course, but inside they'd be all soft and sweet, like a puffball, ready to be born.

Not entirely, the teacher said, because the smell of rot would not be pleasant.

I would eat mine before it rotted, one of the children always said and then the ones with active imaginations would turn to the child who said that and hiss *cannibal.*

One of the children said she realized you couldn't put the goo back inside when it came out, but she wanted to start a hospital for the slightly injured and the teacher said sure, why not. They decided to put the hospital underneath the stage in the cafetorium.

The child who ran the hospital had a mother who was an LPN, so she had been around hospitals. She chose as her assistant a boy whose older brother had left the house in an ambulance, his body covered by canvas, even his face, so the boy knew about emergency vehicles. It was his job to run sick or cracked babies down to the cafetorium in the watch box that the teacher's Christmas present watch had come in.

When a baby's child thought she'd heard her baby crying like she was sick or hurt but didn't have any outward signs of cracks or pain, the doctor who ran the hospital would simply keep it for a day or two in a dark place and let the child come in to rock it at recess. The doctor knew that sometimes it was the child that needed the quiet dark space for just a while and not necessarily the baby who was ill. The doctor would get the child to talk about what was wrong with the baby and sometimes the stories of what the little people had done to the baby were so horrific that the doctor would think of closing down the hospital so she wouldn't hear the stories anymore. She was such a good doctor that sometimes a child would bring a little person who had stopped moving into the hospital, hoping for a miracle. He's dead isn't he? a child would ask and the doctor would nod her head gravely and say she was afraid there was nothing she could do. They would cry together then and when the child was done crying he would go back to the classroom where another child would help him write an obituary. The teacher was pleased at how the children worked together and all the life skills they were learning.

Once or twice the doctor herself, or her assistant, would accidentally drop a baby and the teacher would sneak a replacement down to the hospital, and the baby's child would usually never know the difference. There was in fact only one hyper-observant child who had held her baby up to the light once and was able to identify the tiniest bit of gray transparency in one spot on the baby, and so wasn't fooled.

All of this went on through October. The first week in November the skies turned the leaden gray they would remain until April and the little people in the boxes went into a kind of funk. More and more of them began disappearing together into a shoebox owned by a child who was spending a few weeks with his father. The teacher always kept his desk just like it was when he left so there would be some consistency in the child's life when he returned. But when the owner was away, no one was taking care of the shoebox and it became a place with an unsavory reputation. The children told their teacher about it, and she asked the principal if a social worker might be persuaded to come to her classroom, but he reminded her that there were only two in the entire county and their plates were full. The only child temperamentally suited to take on a social worker's role was the doctor, so as was usually the case, the children did without one.

So the little people kept going into the abandoned shoebox and some of them stumbled back to their own shoeboxes and some were covered with canvas and sent by watch box down to the hospital. When they didn't return, no one knows what happened to them except for the doctor and perhaps the teacher. They were too toxic to put in the compost heap. A couple of them were in the back of the hospital with IVs and breathing tubes made from the same lunchroom straws they used to make playground equipment. It was rumored that the rest were thrown in the trash.

No matter. The doctor's main concern was the babies of course, keeping them alive. But some of the babies seemed to be showing signs of abrasions and if you looked at them long, the baby's child said, you could see them jerk like they were having seizures and inside, their poor little hearts were beating irregularly and you could sometimes see the heartbeat through the fragile skin.

By the end of the first week in November, the doctor was overwhelmed and sad. She had permission to stay late after school and she sat underneath the stage listening to the AYS kids doing their homework and eating their snacks. It was all a distant sound, and it sounded a little bit like music to her as she sat in the semi-dark surrounded by babies. There were ten in the neonatal unit this week, lying there so still. She took the vital signs of each one, and there were, as far as she could tell, no vital signs, or only very faint ones. What would she tell her classmates? Her teacher couldn't keep supplying babies. Soon it would be the holidays and she would have other things to think about. And what purpose did it serve to keep replacing them? They would grow up to be the little people who hopped from desk to desk or spent the day sprawled out on the floor of the absent boy's shoebox.

The doctor's mother had sent her to school that day with a safety pin holding up the hem of the pants she was wearing. Her mother, the LPN, was not doing particularly well and the doctor was feeling a kind of despair she wasn't used to feeling. Most days she woke up feeling that she was a real doctor and she believed despite everything that someday she would be one or a teacher like her teacher. But some days, like today, she didn't know how she could make that happen.

She looked around her at the babies lying in the soft flannel nests she'd made from one of her mother's old nightgowns. She could still smell her mother's scent on those nightgowns. Maybe she was meant for something different in this life or maybe she wasn't meant for anything at all. It was in this mood that she took the safety pin from her hem and picked up one of the babies. She placed some tape over the places she would pierce and then she carefully pressed the pin into the skull of the baby and then into the baby's bottom. She put the baby's fontanel into her mouth and she blew everything the baby had inside it, every last bit of potential, into a bowl. She did it with all ten of them and took the bowl of goo back to the compost heap and said a prayer.

She was careful to wash the babies after that and she put them for a few seconds into the microwave in the teacher's lounge to kill any lingering bacteria and then she brought them back to the infirmary where they would spend the weekend being cured.

On Monday morning she came in early and the teacher let her go down to the cafetorium with some poster paints and glitter. The doctor had some of her mother's clear nail polish in the pocket of her white lab coat, an old shirt that had belonged to her mother. It took her about an hour to paint each one of the babies, each a glorious rich gem or Easter color with dots of glitter and glue. She covered them with nail polish to make them stronger. They were empty inside but they were so very beautiful now. She carried them back to the classroom and distributed the marvels to their parents. Don't cry, she told them. See how light they are? Their spirits have gone to heaven with the others. They're angels now, and nothing will hurt them, she lied. They're watching over you and loving you, she lied. What you're holding is just the beautiful reminder of where the life used to be. There's no more suffering for them, so please don't cry. See how they sparkle? Even if you crush them, they'll be beautiful.

THE LANGUAGE OF THE STARS

Amber Sparks

Celestial Time

THE FUTURE, IT TURNS OUT, LOOKS A LOT LIKE THE '90S. DO YOU remember those old television programs, the ones highlighting D-list celebrities, fashion mistakes? Cataloging fads like fades? Neons and novelty songs and 2-D video games?

This is a future bereft of all such bright trappings. Think instead clumsy car phones, gray pleated pants, office parks, and ladder climbing. Think overtime and pagers. Think shared custody. Think children's breakfast cereal, eaten alone, in the dark.

But I still have you, Emmaline. I still love you, I still summon you, I call you up, the vision of the way you were. The way the summer sun could make a story of your copper skin and hair. The way your freckles faded in the winter and your eyes looked tired and kinder. The way you laughed, more generous than you really were, and far too loud.

Do you still laugh, Emmaline? Do you ever miss the sun?

Aberration

We have no idea what we look like to the robots. We know exactly what the robots ought to look like; or at least, we know what they looked like when we built them. They looked like us. They still *appear* to look like us.

But now, like so many things, we assume they have no fixed form. We assume they have evolved beyond shape. We suspect they sometimes step inside our skins; that sometimes, unbodied, they open our lives like envelopes, peer inside, fold in new dreams.

We have no idea if the robots have developed a language of their own. They are so inscrutable, so distant and cold. What language do the stars speak?

Spectral Features

Each day, we settle into narrow cubicles, open paper calendars, mark important dates in red ink. We glance at framed school pictures of the children we don't see for more than a few moments each night, once they are sound asleep. We hold endless meetings in conference rooms, lengthy and serious phone conversations over big black plastic receivers. We put people on indefinite hold.

Our work, of course, does not exist; rather, it is a nagging suggestion, a vapor trail, a troubled miasma that surrounds us and sticks with a strange insistence. It worries us always.

Our future was more hopeful once. Not this aimless purposefulness, these itineraries full of meetings about meetings. The robots gave us leisure, at first. Blue water, white sand, clean city sidewalks. Time to linger, to putter. To frequent coffee shops and concerts and bars, to linger longer in restaurants. To catch up with old friends. Time, at last, with children, with spouses, with aging parents and grandparents.

We think it was that last thing that did us in. No one wants to spend that much time with the people they love. We gave up the ghost, and though I think the robots were baffled, they gave us ghost lives in return. Phantom productivity. Days full of so much serious nothing. The robots, so mathematically pure, provide addition only, or subtraction only. There is nothing in between.

It is rumored that there is another sort of space, a separate place for those with different dreams. Mind-altering substances, strange sex, darker fantasies. This may be why our offices feel so strangely deserted. Sometimes it seems I can go weeks without encountering another human, though the HR bot is warm and chatty. She asks about you, Emmaline, every now and then.

Abluvion

They don't understand, the robots, how our memories eroded. They don't understand how memories are runoff, washed away in the end like everything else. We cannot know exactly what the robots intended—the robots, like angels, are ineffable—but I believe they also meant for us to keep the past. Powerful processors, they could never have understood how fast the human memory fades. Not in eons, or even generations, but in decades, years, days. If they feel pity, the robots must surely pity us for this.

Or perhaps they envy us? There is pain in memory, after all. I've heard of a rare disease humans had once, where no memory could be shed, not even the slightest errand, nose twitch, conversation. How terrible that must have been, never to lose the most acute embarrassment and suffering, always to keep thumbing through minutiae to find the things that actually mattered. So perhaps I am wrong, and it is the robots draining our memory banks. Perhaps they are sparing us suffering, the burden of the chronicler theirs alone.

Interstellar Abundances

Oh, Emmaline, Emmaline, I would have jumped off a mountain for you, back on Earth. I would have drowned myself, shot myself, baked myself in a pie for you. I would have kept myself to myself if you'd loved me. I wouldn't have texted you so much, not after ten.

The robots have said that I alone am stubborn. You still carry your past with you, they have told me, kind and terrible in their patience. Why, they ask, must you remake your old worlds, cling so tightly to your old same sadness? Even in our sky ships, you dream of things we don't understand: castles, passion, love. Dragons?

It's all for you, Emmaline. I have not given up my passion for you. I bind you, like the knights of old, my honor in a silk scarf I stole from your desk. It is tied to my sleeve. It is made of scent and stars. It has grown, it's true, a little bit musty. Like most things.

I remember that night when you stood under all those stars, when there were still selfies, and you smiling into your phone. You thought you were alone, beautiful and relaxed for once in solitude. I watched, and I watched, and I watched. I memorized your ankles.

O, how we did not understand, then, how we would lose ourselves so quickly, even in all these floating images and films. How could we perceive a life without connectedness? But now we barely remember connection at all. It seems a hazy thing, any picture of us together, any comment I may have left on your page. The robots must have taken them all, I suppose, though I don't remember when. Maybe they made us sad.

Now it's whispered you are somewhere on a sister ship, vice president of something or other. PR? Sales? It doesn't matter. We're not selling anything but time. And I love you still, in a way the beige days can't change. I should have thrown myself off that mountain. I should have known you'd take whatever you could get when it came to power. O, Collaborator, O, Emmaline. I'd go on, but I have a conference call with Johnson in ten.

Of Stars

I have been so lonely, O gods. I have been like the stars, white hot with endless longing. Where is my companion? Wishing, now, I could fall to Earth. I spend days with my cheek against the cold plastic laminate of my desk, building a place in my head where a human could actually live. It is a castle, a pink sandstone thing hung with tapestries and fireplaces. It is grand, enormous, warmed by the sun—the Earth's bright sun.

Someone once said—a poet?—that all light is starlight. Does that mean it's all dead on arrival, more echo than embrace? Is light just another way to be alone? I draw the kinds of light in my day planner, crumpling crisp white pages when the light isn't diffuse enough. I use my expensive pens for crosshatching, trying to spread the light across the cubicles and cafeteria.

Johnson says all this dreaming is hurting my chances of promotion.

Supernova Remains

My father used to hit my mother, hard and often. My mother would counter, strong, with stories for us, stories for herself, knights and champions and magic doorways. They centered, always, around the castle. Or the Castle? They always seemed to be stories about rescue, and all of us were too small to help. When she finally left, rescuing herself at last, my sisters and I kept our ears open for her tales to reach us, sure they were the bread crumbs she'd dropped for us to see the path forward.

When we didn't, we were sure it was we who had failed. And my father too—he who drove her away—he wilted, he shriveled, and he husked without her. It is this the robots cannot understand. That human love is mostly failure. That failure may be very sad, but it is yours, and you hold onto it if you can.

Emmaline, I know I lost my heart to you, and this is not a metaphor. I know I lost my blood, my bones, my skin cells, my DNA—everything has peeled away from me and stuck to some spectral outline of you, some constellation lost to history long ago. The robots tell us nothing is really lost. All turns, reverses, becomes, dissolves, reforms, and streams out among the stars. They tell us they have seen it, over and over, the cycle long but eventual. Everything returns in the beginning and the end.

Celestial Coordinates

To be clear, this was never the robots' fault.

Johnson and Bradley said yes to endless cocktails, but only if they came with secretaries. My sisters liked the way the work meant no more stories and selfies. My brothers liked the way their wives disappeared into cubes down the hall, liked the way they no longer had to be interesting or thin or emotionally available. People liked the way their children were cared for, and they liked that the robots taught them quickly to learn, and grow, and come to self-sufficiency. The kids weren't sitting in front of screens all damn day, and wasn't that nicer? The robots didn't understand how small and *analog* human ambition could be, how easy to feed. Of course we dream of filing cabinets and paper trails, the vast most of us. Bigger dreams are hard, are messy with feeling. Connection causes pain.

The robots, I wonder if they ever read Kafka? I don't think there are books here, outside of *What Color is Your Parachute?* At least, none that I've seen.

Relativity, Special

My mother built herself walls of story and so I will rebuild her story castle, right here in this cubicle. Surely, I can't be the only one left lost, the only one dreaming himself out. Surely others will refuse the endless meetings, the swivel chairs, the florescent lights, the traffic jams, the built-in ashtrays, the stacks and stacks of paper. Surely someone on this ship wants to feel something more than the smallest feelings. Where, after all, are the humans who built the robots? Who went to the moon? Who built the pyramids, the skyscrapers, the aqueducts, the highways, the internet? Who trekked across the hard wide world to find a home?

Long ago, I decided I would live (many didn't), and that I would live for love. But living so long has begun to cloud that intention. The furniture falls apart in these rooms. The shabbiness shows through. If I don't act soon, the walls will shift and sink, the dreams will dissolve, and I will be left with nothing but stray pixels and this cold hard ship, empty, I suspect, of everyone but them and me.

Emmaline, I am building this castle for us. I plan to scale these walls and escape to you.

Zenith

Time doesn't pass, nor weather—everything is cold, hard space. Space was not prepared to receive us and does not receive us now. To the robots, it is immaterial: we needed to leave the planet, the oceans were swallowing us whole, and so we went. We were given no choice. We are lucky they felt some responsibility for their makers, as clumsy and backward as we are to them.

But for us, who built Elysian Fields for our dead, who tore down our forests and burnt the sky to please the living, who made the robots to make us whole—we might have made another choice. We might have burned along with the world, drowned along with the dead. Are we living now? Landscapes are malleable, organic; a human can make a mark. But we are making nothing.

I shall construct this castle in honor of that memory of earth, the conquest—Earth, the colony. I shall build my walls of red stone and wet sand, of glass and clay and rope and wood—all the things we have thrown away for good. I shall build my walls around that ossuary, the bodies of our saints, our human bones. These relics can be called up at anytime. They smell of sky, of grave, of deep wet earth, loamy and brown. I will dig the stars from the sky; I will bury them like seeds and we will grow a new and living home.

Of Stars, Coda

I was ten years old. My grandfather had eyes the color of moons, the result of his blindness. He was a seer, one of those working on the prototypes. He thought we were ready to be relieved. He was happy I would never need to work again. He talked about it, often, the way we would have leisure time at last. I laugh to think of it now, leaving for my Tuesday afternoon brainstorming session.

Sometimes I think we already died, years or eons ago. Sometimes I think we are living on only in dreams, as brains in jars, or maybe just ones and zeros. I don't like to think past this thought.

Post Script

Emmaline, the HR bot says the person matching your name and description is no longer a person, but a pile of ashes. Emmaline, they won't give me details, won't tell me where and when in time I can ride to rescue you. They tell me lies; they say 'old age'; I say Emmaline was young and so am I.

They say, and I swear to you, there is a look of pity in the HR bot's eyes, they say, sir. Sir, we are sorry, but the '90s has been a very long decade.

TIN

Maggie Su

THE NIGHT A STRANGER CRAWLED THROUGH MINDY LEE'S DOGGY door, shimmied his hips against the plastic flap and pulled himself through, Mindy was asleep, dumb and dreamless.

Her mutt, Lucy, was also asleep by her place on the rug in front of the dishwasher.

Mindy had found Lucy three years ago during a morning run. The dog was lapping up gutter water and peeing on doorsteps, but even in the dim light, Mindy saw the sadness in the girl's eyes. She chased her five blocks before catching her, hooking her fingers around her neck in the parking lot of a bank. Mindy had retired after thirty years teaching English at a community college, and Lucy was just the project she'd been looking for.

The whole walk back to the house, Lucy whined and tried to break free of Mindy's grip.

"Poor baby. God knows what you've been through," Mindy whispered.

After four blocks, the whine turned into a howl, and Mindy put in her earbuds and blasted Adele to drown it out.

The dog woke to the thud of the man hitting the carpet and padded softly into the foyer to investigate. The man was a foreign object: blond, slender, and damp with rain. Lucy moved closer to him, and when he held out his hand, she licked it. He scratched her lips with his fingers then held those lips together as he pulled her head up and slit her throat with a knife he'd stowed between his belt and his pants, just a kitchen knife sharpened and resharpened.

*

That morning, Mindy had driven across the city to the Indiana Women's Prison. It was her first day volunteering; she'd been accepted to teach an introductory poetry workshop to the inmates. Her syllabus was full of angry women: Anne Sexton, Sylvia Plath, and a few contemporary poets she'd heard of but hadn't yet read. Confessional poetry for inmates—what could be more fitting?

Mindy wasn't nervous when she stood up in front of the group; she'd spent hours on her syllabus and introductory remarks. Had even made a "Getting to Know You" PowerPoint with star-shaped fade-out transitions.

"I'd have liked to have kids," Mindy said. She clicked to change the slide and up popped Lucy sitting on a playground swing, her tongue lolling out. "But I have a dog instead."

A couple of students chuckled, but a few shook their heads as if to say, "That's too bad." Was it possible that these women pitied her?

"Freewriting is a process of excavation," she continued. "For the next five minutes, I want you to turn off your brain, that self-conscious voice in your head. Let your real selves breathe for once."

The room fell silent and Mindy wandered among the desks as they wrote. She imagined they were writing about their crimes, creating dark fantasies of freedom, blood, guilt. But the first student she called on, a woman named Wendy with long curly hair, read a love poem.

"In the meadow, I see you," she said. Her reading voice was loud and dramatic; it boomed through the classroom. "You flit around me, deep in the azaleas."

Mindy nodded earnestly and gave Wendy a thumbs up when she finished. She thought it was a fluke, but all the inmates read similar pieces. A lover's bed-sheets, a mother smelling her child's hair, the sand between the speaker's toes. Her students weren't concerned with their inner darkness, they wrote cliché little couplets just like her most promising community college students would have.

These people, Mindy thought after the last inmate had filed out, as she shuffled their papers together and erased the chalkboard and turned off the lights in the classroom. They really believe they've been saved.

Lucy's blood slid to the left; Mindy's house had been quietly falling apart as the cheap foundation settled unevenly into the ground. The man stepped over the dog's body.

In the kitchen, he brushed his bloody hands over the clean white countertops, the hanging green and orange dish towels, the decorative mug that read, "Funny Catchphrase Goes Here." He lifted the kitchen sink faucet slowly, let out just a drizzle of water, and scrubbed at his fingers like every particle could be obliterated.

Mindy's fridge was almost bare. Just a magnet from a 5K fun run for the local animal shelter, a cut-out *New Yorker* cartoon, and a photograph of Mindy atop Mount Hood with her arms flexed. The photo was taken from the ground, a self-timer, you could tell by the way the boulder protruded out of the corner. In her fridge was bread, lunch meat, tomato, lettuce. A whole bag of lemons, unopened. The blond man bent down and sniffed a lemon deeply.

When Mindy felt the rough pad of a tongue on her toes, she figured Lucy had somehow nosed her way around the door and decided to wake her gently. She pulled her feet away, giggled, and turned over.

"Lucy, stop it," she said, but the licking continued.

When she finally opened her eyes and saw the shadow crouched at the foot of her bed, she didn't scream.

"Hello?" said the shadow. It had a British accent.

Mindy turned on the light, but she wasn't prepared for the shadow to become a man. She wasn't prepared for his five o'clock stubble or his damp blond hair curling slightly at the ears or the raindrops glistening on the shoulders of his peacoat.

She slept with the windows open and the autumn air had snuck through and chilled the room. Mindy crossed her arms, shielding her chest.

She remembered an article, some online opinion column she'd found while scrolling past her friends' photos of grandkids. The author said it calmed rapists when you feigned an interest in their lives, asked them questions about their hobbies, their passions. One commenter even advocated digging into their childhoods, really getting to know the motivations behind their actions. They were human after all.

"Where are you from?" Mindy asked. The man couldn't have been more than thirty; he was just a kid and kids could be reasoned with. Wasn't that what she was good at? The blond man wasn't one of her students though; she would've remembered him, he was very handsome.

"Sheffield," he said.

Deliberate and slow, the man rose from his squatted position. He sat down on her floral quilt. His coat dripped.

"It rains a lot there," she said.

"Yes," he said.

Mindy looked down at her pink pinstriped nightgown, the bow tied at the back of her neck like a present. She had bought it on a whim in the junior's section of Macy's. It was a stupid purchase, but she hadn't known anyone else would see it.

"Why are you here?" she asked.

"I love you," he said, ruffling his fingers through his hair like he was Hugh Grant in a romantic comedy and this was all a big misunderstanding.

He looked appealing and Mindy wanted to run, but her body gave her away. Her kneecaps tensed and jumped beneath the quilt. The blond man straddled her quickly. His knees were on either side of her hips; his arms braced his face just above hers. Their bodies didn't touch.

Mindy stared into his eyes, the large pupils ringed with blue.

The blond man unbuttoned his peacoat and the lapels hung against her sides. She expected his teeth to be yellow, but they were white.

"Where's Lucy?" Mindy asked the man above her.

"I killed her," he said.

"Tell me a story," he said. "It's bedtime."

He lowered his full weight on her now. His body matched hers, his head resting on the bare skin just above her breasts.

Mindy wondered if Lucy had struggled, if she growled or bit. If she had, Mindy had slept right through it.

"What have I done?" she asked. Her throat caught on "to deserve this" because it sounded like bad scripted reality television. No one deserved anything, she knew. "What have I done" felt like the phrase she'd been searching for.

"Tell me a story," the man said again.

"Once upon a time," Mindy began. She closed her eyes. She was tired of looking at the blond man, his face had already become too familiar. "A tin man lived in a tin house."

The man sighed, his warm breath kissed her forehead.

"Every time he tapped the walls they vibrated. He sent messages out this way. A boy on the outside helped him. He was human," she said.

With her eyes closed, Mindy could hear the insects outside of her bedroom window, the bus passing by on its way into the city. Mindy always hated living so close to a busy road, but she'd never considered the people on that bus. How their bodies might sway with each stop as they read their newspapers or listened to music or rested their eyes on the early commute.

"The tin man would tap out: more bread please, more milk please, more deodorant please, and the boy would tap back: yes, sir, yes, sir, which type, sir?"

"But then one day, he tapped out, I love you, and the boy left. He ran through the hills, crying, and climbed into the mountains without shoes."

His weight had started to become uncomfortable. She felt the air getting thinner, her body flattening.

"The man cried too, he dried his eyes with pieces of tin," she said.

"Did he leave?" the blond man asked.

"No, but he wanted to. He stood at the door for hours, willing himself to open it and walk through, but he couldn't."

Mindy paused. The man crossed his arms and leaned on her throat until her bones creaked. Mindy looked past the man, straight up at the ceiling, praying for words, an ending.

"He couldn't exist in the world of air. He was not made up of those things, do you understand? But the boy did not return to him. There was no more milk."

The man was silent for a long time, his breathing even, his eyes closed. Mindy wondered if he'd fallen asleep.

THE OPHELIA PROJECT

Valerie Vogrin

The Folk Artist Takes a Stab at It,
Having Tired of Roosters, Fish, and the Angel Gabriel
THE ARTIST HAS SCULPTED A WEATHERVANE IN THE FIGURE OF OPHELIA
wrapped in a sheet. Her feet are bare. She is festooned in garlands
of flowers. We are meant to admire the artist's hammerwork. She
is holding a crow beneath one arm. Her other arm sticks straight
out, pointing whichever way the wind blows.

> *Ophelia*
> Artist unidentified
> Possibly Massachusetts or New York
> c. 1800
> Molded copper
> 36 x 43-½ x 4 inches
> gift of Mr. and Mrs. Francis S. Andrews, 1982

Nan, age seven, sits on the floor in front of the weathervane.
She is sucking her fingers. They taste of the pebbles surrounding
the gingko tree outside the museum where she played while her
mother finished her cigarette.

There is something terrible about that crow, Nan thinks, and the
girl. *Why would you make a sculpture of someone you didn't like?*

Nan recently learned that people—she and her mother and
everyone here—are made mostly of water, which is soft, except when
it freezes. She does not think she would like to be made of metal.

Every morning the meteorologist on TV makes note of the wind, as if it's an essential fact. South-by-southwest at thirty-two miles per hour, northerly winds about five miles per hour. Her mother loves The Weather Channel. Grown-ups are weird.

Nan tries to sound out the name on the placard, but she can't remember what to do about the digraph.

Nan's mother is leaning against a pillar. Sometimes her mother will tell her how words are pronounced and sometimes she just sighs and says something snarky about the state of elementary education. Nan wipes her shriveled fingers on the back of her skirt. "Only babies put everything in their mouths," her mother says.

The placard states that the weathervane is made of copper, but it looks green to her. *Weather vane, weather vane, the weather is vain.*

A door slams. A group of school kids wearing dark green uniforms stomps in. The air shifts and so do Ophelia and the crow.

Nan remembers that "ph" sometimes sounds like "f." The name forms in her mouth. *Ophelia. Ophelia.*

Family Feud

Fifty people were asked, "What is the first thing you think of when you hear 'Shakespeare's Ophelia'?"

Your job is to accurately come up with the most popular answers.

Survey says:

(7) flowers

(6) water

(3) hair

(2) drowning

(2) nunnery

Other answers include: eye, floating, escape, wandering, flotsam, small feet, song, go take a swim you dirty hooker, hands outstretched with petals, honor, desperate, ankle, a cold stream, Hamlet is a jerk to her, Kate Winslet, Levon Helm, he's just not that into you, Natalie Merchant, John Everett Millais, pawns, death, bad swimmer, vaginal mist, rejection, wrong dude, wandering, willows, suicide, a tree by a river, lily pads, lungs, mad, honor, misdirection.

Bright-Eyed and Eco-Friendly

A Garnet Hill catalog exclusive, "The Ophelia." Sleep soundly in petal-soft pure Pima organic cotton. Our lightweight, flowing, tiered, floor-length nightdress exudes fashionable melancholy with its empire waist, lace hemline, a modest neckline embroidered with leaves, and flattering bell sleeves. Sleeves may be worn loose or tied in back. Imported. Machine washable. Choose from white, hydrangea, or lilac dust. Petite sizes available.

Ophelia reads the tea leaves

They gather like something exploded in the bottom of her cup. Fecund, sodden, scant. She closes her eyes, relaxes her gaze. She makes out a wing, no, two wings and large green eyes.

What does it mean, we might ask. *What do you see?*

"They say the owl was a baker's daughter," she replies, and who are we to say otherwise?

Do you have any other words of wisdom?

"For to the noble mind / Rich gifts wax poor when givers prove unkind."

We wonder if she's pulling our leg.

A Feminist Response to Ophelia's burial:

"Why is it, I want to know, that a playtext crowded with male bodies presented in all stages of post mortem recuperation, from ghost-walking Hamlet to fresh-bleeding Polonius to moldering Yorick to Priam of deathless memory; a playtext whose core issue exhaustively and excessively examines the imperatives of male reaction to the death of men ('remember'; 'revenge'); a playtext that valorizes killing and heroic death (but nicely condemns murder): why is it that this playtext, when it finally arrives at the grave, lays out a woman's body for speculation?"

Dr. Carol Chillington Rutter asks, "How do we look at it? What do we see?"

Ophelia Serving Many Masters, or Ophelia's Fourteen Questions:
Do you doubt that?
No more but so?
Good my lord, /How does your honour for this many a day?
My lord?
What means, my lordship?
Could beauty, my lord, have better commerce than with honesty?
What is, my lord?
What means this, my lord?
Will he tell us what this show meant?
Where is the beauteous Majesty of Denmark?
How should I your true-love know / from another one?
Say you?

And will he not come again?
And will he not come again?

The various lords are jackals. The queen as well.

Future Ophelias
Ophelia at the beach. She is re-reading *The Bell Jar*. She loves the book but is distracted by a man walking by, humming. She reads, "I saw the world divided into people who had slept with somebody and people who hadn't, and this seemed the only really significant difference between one person and another," and then there he is again. About a half-inch of his penis is sticking out the bottom of his swim trunks. He walks by and by and by, as if he is lost, his diagonal shadow moving over her. She can't decide if he knows his dick is winking at her.

Ophelia holding the Ophelia doll (by American Girl). The doll is wearing a pink-and-white-striped lacrosse jersey with lime-green trim, a sporty skort, striped knee socks, and shoes with cleats. (Not pictured are Ophelia-the-doll's game-time gear, including a protective face mask with a stretchy strap, a lacrosse stick she can really hold, a bouncy orange ball, removable mouth-guard stickers, and two fabric hairbands.) The doll is wet in Ophelia's wet arms.

Ophelia undrowning. It's like watching a time-lapse video in reverse of a candle, wax and wick reconstituting themselves until the flame flickers on the match. Air bubbles are exhaled, water drawn out and out and out through the woman's nostrils and mouth, until she stands, walks backward, pauses, clothing and hair dry. There's a director, directing the illusion. Even from a few feet away, the photographer who was hired to film the performance can't figure out how they're doing it. Each time the woman lies back down in the water, she looks dead, for real, heavy in a bad way.

Ophelia, the rock opera. Lyrics and music by Pete Townsend. Hamlet, a bit part, is played by Sir Elton John.

Ophelia at Coney Island. Ophelia riding The Cyclone: one minute and fifty seconds of centrifugal force and gravity having their way with her. Ophelia winning a giant pink rabbit at the Whac-a-Mole game.

Ophelia celebrating the Day of the Dead. Down a cobbled street, she is pushing a wheelbarrow containing a facsimile female skeleton. Ophelia's shoulders are draped in *Claudea elegans*, a red algae shawl. She has a swing in her step despite the weight of the barrow. A bit of seaweed is stuck to her cheek.

Ophelia Rearranging the Silverware Drawer

Ophelia is troubled by the sight of cutlery slung loose in the drawer. She stacks them in sets, each according to its kin—soup spoons, porridge spoons, forks, knives—but they commingle in the dark, urged together by the opening and closing of the drawer.

She orders a bamboo silverware organizer online from The Container Store, but it doesn't fit her drawer.

Perhaps you saw this one coming. There is only one solution—to discard all but the knives.

BIOGRAPHIES

Andrew Bales's stories have appeared with *Electric Literature, Gargoyle, Tin House, Passages North, Juked*, and other publications. Andrew has been a Tennessee Williams Scholar at the Sewanee Writers' Conference, received the Mississippi Review Prize in fiction, and holds a PhD in fiction writing from the University of Cincinnati.

Charles Baxter is the author of the novels *The Feast of Love* (nominated for the National Book Award), *First Light, Saul and Patsy, Shadow Play, The Soul Thief*, and *The Sun Collective*, and the story collections *Believers, Gryphon, Harmony of the World, A Relative Stranger, There's Something I Want You to Do*, and *Through the Safety Net*. His stories have been included in The Best American Short Stories. Baxter lives in Minneapolis and teaches at the University of Minnesota and in the MFA Program for Writers at Warren Wilson College.

Lucy Biederman is a novelist, essayist, scholar, and poet. Her novella *The Walmart Book of the Dead* won the 2017 Vine Leaves Press Vignette Award and was a finalist for the Foreword Book of the Year. Her stories, essays, poems, and visual art have appeared in *North American Review, Poetry, AGNI*, and *Ploughshares*. An excerpt from her novel-in-progress about the Salem witch trials recently appeared in *Early American Literature*. She teaches creative writing at Heidelberg University in Tiffin, Ohio.

Jason Lee Brown is the editor-in-chief of *River Styx* literary magazine, director of the River Styx Reading Series, and co-series editor of *New Stories from The Midwest*. He also co-edited, with

Shanie Latham, the poetry anthology *The Book of Donuts*. He is the author of three books, including the forthcoming story collection, *Midwest Everyman*.

Anna Cabe is a Pinay-American writer from Memphis, Tennessee, who now lives in Chicago, Illinois. Her writing has appeared in *The Masters Review, Slate, Vice, Bitch Media, The Toast, StoryQuarterly, Slice, Joyland, Fairy Tale Review, Unbroken Circle: Stories of Cultural Diversity in the South, Not My President: The Anthology of Dissent, Forward: 21st Century Flash Fiction*, and elsewhere. She earned an MFA in fiction from Indiana University and has been supported by institutions like the Fulbright Program in the Philippines and the Millay Colony for the Arts. She is currently assistant fiction editor for *Split Lip Magazine*. You can find Anna at annacabe.com.

Bonnie Jo Campbell is the author of the novels *Q Road* and *Once Upon a River*, a national bestseller. Her critically-acclaimed short fiction collections include *American Salvage*, which was a finalist for both the National Book Award and the National Book Critic's Circle Award; *Women and Other Animals*, which won the AWP prize for short fiction; and *Mothers, Tell Your Daughters* (Autumn 2015). Her stories have been awarded a Pushcart Prize and the Eudora Welty Prize. She was a 2011 Guggenheim Fellow and recipient of the Mark Twain Award from the Society for the Study of Midwestern Literature.

Wendy Chen (wendychenart.com) is the author of *Unearthings* (Tavern Books), editor of *Figure 1*, and managing editor of *Tupelo Quarterly*. She is the recipient of the Academy of American Poets Most Promising Young Poet Prize and earned her MFA in poetry from Syracuse University. Her poetry, translations, and prose have appeared in *Crazyhorse, A Public Space, Mid-American Review,* and elsewhere.

Michael Czyzniejewski is the author of three story collections, most recently *I Will Love You for the Rest of My Life: Breakup Stories*

(Curbside Splendor, 2015). He teaches at Missouri State University, where he serves as Editor-in-Chief of *Moon City Review* and Literary Editor of Moon City Press.

Emily Greenberg's writing has appeared or is forthcoming in *The Iowa Review, Michigan Quarterly Review, Witness, Santa Monica Review, Chicago Quarterly Review*, and elsewhere. Winner of the 2020 Witness Literary Award in Fiction, she holds an MFA from Ohio State and has taught writing at Ohio State and Columbus College of Art & Design. "Houston, We've Had a Problem" was recently awarded a Pushcart Prize Special Mention.

Justyn Harkin is a writer from Chicago.

Christie Hodgen is the author of four books of fiction. The most recent, *Boy Meets Girl*, won the 2020 AWP Award for the Novel and will be published by New Issues Press in 2022. Hodgen's short fiction has appeared in dozens of literary journals and anthologies. Her awards include two Pushcart Prizes, a grant from the National Endowment for the Arts, and a John Simon Guggenheim Memorial Fellowship. She is a professor of English and editor of *New Letters* at the University of Missouri-Kansas City.

Shanie Latham is a proofreader and publication designer for *River Styx, Boulevard,* and *Story* magazines. She co-edits the *New Stories from The Midwest* series with Jason Lee Brown, with whom she also co-edited a poetry anthology, *The Book of Donuts*.

Michael Martone has retired from teaching after forty years. He has authored or edited many books of fiction and nonfiction, among them *The Complete Writings of Art Smith, The Bird Boy of Fort Wayne, Edited by Michael Martone*; *The Moon Over Wapakoneta: Fictions and Science Fictions from Indiana and Beyond*; *The Blue Guide to Indiana*; *Four for a Quarter*; and *Michael Martone*. He lives in Tuscaloosa.

Susan Neville is the author of seven books of creative nonfiction and four story collections, including *The Town of Whispering Dolls*, winner of the 2019 Catherine Doctor Prize for Innovative Fiction; *In the House of Blue Lights*, winner of the Richard Sullivan Prize; and *Invention of Flight*, winner of the Flannery O'Connor Award. Her stories have appeared in the Pushcart Prize anthology and a long essay about the Klan in Indiana, "Into the Fire," appeared in 2020 as an ebook from *Ploughshares*. She lives in Indianapolis.

Noley Reid is the author of three books: the novels *Pretend We Are Lovely* and *In the Breeze of Passing Things* and the short story collection *So There!* Her fourth book, a collection of stories called *Origami Dogs*, is forthcoming from Autumn House Press. Her fiction and nonfiction have appeared in *The Southern Review, The Rumpus, Meridian, Pithead Chapel, Split Lip Magazine, The Lily, Bustle, Arts & Letters*, and *Los Angeles Review of Books*. She lives in Indiana with her two best boys.

Yelizaveta P. Renfro is the author of a collection of essays, *Xylotheque*, and a collection of short stories, *A Catalogue of Everything in the World*. Her fiction and nonfiction have appeared in *Glimmer Train, North American Review, Creative Nonfiction, Orion, Colorado Review, Alaska Quarterly Review, Witness, Reader's Digest*, and elsewhere. A past resident of California, Virginia, Nebraska, and Connecticut, she currently lives in Indiana.

Valerie Sayers, professor of English at the University of Notre Dame, is the author of *The Age of Infidelity and Other Stories* (2020) as well as six novels including *The Powers*. Her novels have appeared on notable books of the year lists at the *New York Times Book Review, Washington Post*, and *Chicago Tribune*, and her stories have won two Pushcart Prizes. She is a recipient of an NEA fellowship for fiction.

Amber Sparks is the author of three short story collections: *The Unfinished World and Other Stories*, *May We Shed These Human Bodies*, and most recently *And I Do Not Forgive You*. Her short fiction and essays have appeared in numerous publications on and off the web, including *American Short Fiction, Paris Review, Tin House, New York Magazine, Granta*, and elsewhere. She lives in Washington, DC, with her husband, daughter, and two cats.

Maggie Su is a fiction PhD candidate at University of Cincinnati and assistant editor at Acre Books. Her work has appeared in *Four Way Review, TriQuarterly Review, Puerto del Sol, Juked, Mid-American Review, Joyland, The Offing, SmokeLong Quarterly*, and elsewhere.

Laura van den Berg is the author of the novel *Find Me*, longlisted for the 2016 International Dylan Thomas Prize, and two story collections: *What the World Will Look Like When All the Water Leaves Us* and *The Isle of Youth*, both finalists for the Frank O'Connor International Short Story Award. Her honors include the Bard Fiction Prize, the Rosenthal Family Foundation Award from the American Academy of Arts and Letters, the Jeannette Haien Ballard Writer's Prize, a Pushcart Prize, and an O. Henry Award, and her fiction has been anthologized in *The Best American Short Stories*. She is a Briggs-Copeland Lecturer in Fiction at Harvard.

Valerie Vogrin's collection *Things We'll Need for the Coming Difficulties* was awarded the Spokane Prize for Short Fiction (Willow Springs Press, 2020). She is the author of the novel *Shebang*, and her short stories have appeared in journals such as *Ploughshares, AGNI, Hobart*, and *Los Angeles Review*, and in *The Best Small Fictions 2015*. She teaches creative writing at Southern Illinois University Edwardsville. She lives with her husband, dog, and cat on a tiny unnamed lake in Moro, Illinois.

Alexander Weinstein is the author of the short story collections, *Universal Love* and *Children of the New World*, which was chosen as a New York Times "100 Notable Books of the Year" and a best book of the year by NPR, Google, and *Electric Literature*. His short stories have appeared in *Best American Science Fiction & Fantasy* and *Best American Experimental Writing*. He is director of The Martha's Vineyard Institute of Creative Writing and a Professor of Creative Writing at Siena Heights University.

Rachel Yoder is the author of *Nightbitch* (Doubleday 2021), her debut novel that explores motherhood, rage, ambition, and art-making, and she is currently adapting the story for film. She earned an MFA in fiction from the University of Arizona and an MFA in creative nonfiction from the University of Iowa, where she was an Iowa Arts Fellow. Raised in a Mennonite community in the Appalachian foothills of eastern Ohio, she now lives in Iowa City with her husband and son.